The Time
of Cherries

MONTSERRAT ROIG

THE TIME
OF CHERRIES

Translated by Julia Sanches

With an Introduction by Colm Tóibín

THE MODERN LIBRARY

NEW YORK

The Modern Library
An imprint of Random House
A division of Penguin Random House LLC
1745 Broadway, New York, NY 10019
modernlibrary.com
randomhousebooks.com
penguinrandomhouse.com

2026 Modern Library Trade Paperback Edition

Originally published in Catalan as EL TEMPS DE LES CIRERES
by Editions 62. This English translation originally published in
the United Kingdom by Daunt Books, London, in 2024.

LIBRARY OF CONGRESS CATALOGING-IN-PUBLICATION DATA
Names: Roig, Montserrat, 1946–1991, author | Sanches, Julia, translator |
Tóibín, Colm, writer of introduction.
Title: The time of cherries / Montserrat Roig ; translated by Julia Sanches ;
with an introduction by Colm Tóibín.
Other titles: Temps de les cireres. English.
Description: First edition. | New York, NY : The Modern Library, 2026.
Identifiers: LCCN 2025047596 (print) | LCCN 2025047597 (ebook) |
ISBN 9780593978801 trade paperback acid-free paper | ISBN 9780593978818 ebook
Subjects: LCGFT: Fiction | Novels
Classification: LCC PC3942.28.O38 T4413 2026 (print) | LCC PC3942.28.O38 (ebook)
LC record available at https://lccn.loc.gov/2025047596
LC ebook record available at https://lccn.loc.gov/2025047597

Printed in the United States of America

2nd Printing

BOOK TEAM: Production editor: Cassie Gitkin •
Managing editor: Rebecca Berlant • Production manager: Katie Zilberman •
Proofreaders: Rachael Clements, Lori Newhouse, Russell Powers, Jinah Yoon

The authorized representative in the EU for product safety and compliance
is Penguin Random House Ireland, Morrison Chambers, 32 Nassau Street,
Dublin D02 YH68, Ireland. https://eu-contact.penguin.ie

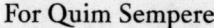

For Quim Sempere

INTRODUCTION

Montserrat Roig's classic novel *The Time of Cherries* captures a sort of still point in the history of Barcelona—a moment that came before great change. In the novel, no one has any idea that within eighteen months, Francisco Franco, the old dictator, will be dead. Roig's novel was first published in Catalan in 1976, the year after Franco expired.

The Time of Cherries became an essential book in post-Franco Catalonia. It appeared at a time when there were few images of the culture whose youth had cast off Franco long before 1975. The novel is infused not only with a cast of vividly made characters but also with a precise and sharp vision of middle-class Barcelona before democracy was restored. The story follows Natàlia, now aged forty, dealing with unfinished business: her conservative brother and her fearful and neurotic sister-in-law, her father, her old friends, but more than anything, a stifling political atmosphere that she abruptly ran away from. Not long after its publication, the novel became available in a cheap paperback and was on sale in the newspaper kiosks that dotted downtown Barcelona.

When I first encountered Roig's work, I was struck by the freshness of her tone—and the fact that the new generation was being depicted in a fearless and dramatic way. There was, for example, a sexual frankness in the novel that came as a relief in a time when many films had been banned for their sexual content. When Roig portrays characters from the older generation, many of them emotionally and spiritually maimed by the long years of the dictatorship, she is careful to make the gap between them and the new generation complex and ambiguous rather than simple or easy to predict.

The middle class in Barcelona remained, for the most part, undisturbed by the First and Second World Wars, and even by the Spanish Civil War. They held on to their spacious apartments in the Eixample, the area of the city that was developed in the late nineteenth and early twentieth centuries by Modernista architects, including Gaudí. They remained innately conservative; they kept their heads down and looked after business during the dictatorship. This made things ripe for a revolt by the generation who came of age in the 1960s.

Montserrat Roig was born into a middle-class family in Barcelona in 1946. Her father was a lawyer and writer deeply embedded in the world of Catalan politics and culture. Her mother, also born into this middle-class milieu, was a feminist writer and suffragist. While growing up, her parents' apartment was a gathering place for writers and those involved in progressive politics.

In her late teens, Roig published articles on current affairs in the magazine *Triunfo*. Before going to university, she began to train as an actor. During these years, she got to know the feminist writer and left-wing activist Maria Aurèlia Capmany, almost thirty years her senior, who introduced her to the writings of Simone de Beauvoir. Capmany, even when I met her in the last years of her life at the time when I was writing my book *Homage to Barcelona*, was what might be called "an indominable spirit"— witty and sharp, loud when she needed to be, radical. Like Montserrat Roig herself, Capmany became one of Barcelona's leading cultural figures in the 1980s. When I knew Capmany, she was an energetic and visionary head of culture in the Barcelona City Council. Readers of *The Time of Cherries* will see much of her in the figure of Harmonia.

Roig uses the trope of the returned daughter, in this case one who has bathed in the freedoms of England, as she herself had done in the early 1970s, before returning to Barcelona as both insider and outsider. It is unclear what has changed. The novel explores the strange way that time passing makes some aspects of family dynamics subtly different and allows other aspects to stay the same.

The dates in *The Time of Cherries* are important. Natàlia's exile begins with the execution of the communist Julián Grimau by the Franco government in 1963 and ends with the execution of Salvador Puig Antich in 1974. Natàlia was born in March 1938, the month the Coliseum Theatre was bombed in the war. Both her father and her brother Lluís were born in important years in the history of Catalan nationalism.

According to her biographer Betsabé Garcia, Montserrat Roig spent three years planning *The Time of Cherries* and then wrote the actual book in twenty-six days, thus placing it among those masterpieces of twentieth-century literature created at speed, such as Kerouac's *On the Road,* Faulkner's *As I Lay Dying,* and Burgess's *A Clockwork Orange.*

Although she wrote about her own world, Roig insisted that her novel was not autobiographical: "I have learned to laugh when it is called autobiographical. If only they knew how it lied!" She also noted that in her imagination there were three obsessions: death, sex, and growing old. All of these themes are explored in *The Time of Cherries,* while Roig explored changing elements of the world in which she was brought up. She worried that if she set her novels in a working-class milieu, "they would not be convincing." Rather, she would dramatize "the world that I know," bourgeois Barcelona, aware that Balzac and Proust had written about a similar class.

While her novel dealt with the interior life of her protagonist, Natàlia, it also re-created a Barcelona, some of which was about to disappear. In 1974, the airport bus did indeed go as far as Plaça Espanya. Rich people did indeed shop for domestic goods at Vinçon. Men bought their hats in Can Prats. Catalans did indeed look to Switzerland as their ideal state. "Switzerland was the dream," Roig writes. Men drank a cognac called Torres 10, had dinner in a restaurant called Set Portes, and owned paintings by Ramón Casas and Isidre Nonell, two nineteenth-century Catalan painters. People traveled to Perpignan just over the border in France to watch banned films. Intellectuals gathered at L'Ateneu. Middle-class kids who had been brought up in the Eixample loved the seedy beauty of downtown Barcelona. "What she missed was a certain aroma, a street, the laughter of friends strolling down La Rambla in waves, the shadows around Santa Maria de Mar, the chilly mornings, the leaves of the plane trees when they fell in autumn."

Anyone who knew Barcelona in these years will recognize the "bar on Carrer de Banys Nous where grizzled card sharks and students drank wine and ate olives around barrels that doubled as tables" as El Portalón, and "the old textile-warehouse lobby" near Santa Maria del Mar that was now a "large, drafty hall" where "a pair of thick velvet curtains separated two open-plan rooms" is Zeleste, the nightclub for progressive young Catalans of that time.

The time of cherries is not far away from a time of fear. When the novel came out, so many citizens of Barcelona had experienced baton charges and vicious police attacks. But no one had written about them. There was no free press. Roig's account of police attacks on students, among them Natàlia and her friends, who were protesting against the Franco regime, has a sense of urgency that came from her own experience of such attacks as a young activist. Such attacks were ongoing even as the book was being written and when it was published.

Roig herself had taken part in one of the most famous sit-in demonstrations that took place in Catalonia in the years before the end of the dictatorship. In 1975, when she wrote *The Time of Cherries,* the memory of La Caputxinada in 1966 still felt fresh. This was when more than four hundred intellectuals and students (including Roig) demonstrated against the regime in a Capuchin convent in the outskirts of Barcelona and were surrounded by police for two days.

While other novelists wrote about what it was like to navigate these repressive years in Barcelona, no one had written about a protagonist having a back street abortion in the city. Once again, Roig's novel broke a silence.

There is also a powerful ghost hovering over the book, that of Salvador Puig Antich, the anarchist who was executed in March 1974 using the *garrote vil,* a system whereby the victim is slowly strangled. At the time, it was unclear whether this execution was the regime flexing its muscles or emitting one of its last gasps.

His execution causes one of the family arguments in *The Time of Cherries.* When Lluís, Natàlia's architect brother, refers to Puig Antich as a thief, he gets interrupted by his son: "He wasn't a thief, Dad." Lluís then refers to Puig Antich as a moron. And then, more weakly: "In any event, those zealots are going to make a mess of things and ruin our chances of joining the Common Market." Lluís is a good example of a kind of pragmatism that reigned in these years among the Catalan middle class.

For others, the execution was chilling. One of the characters considers Harmonia's response to Puig Antich's death: "None of us wants to admit just how powerless we are. It's been years and we're getting old. Nothing has changed." The change came later: No one in this novel could have imagined that in the future there would be a street named after Maria Aurèlia Capmany and a square in the suburbs honoring Puig Antich and another one named after the author herself, a tribute to her contribution to the reimagining of Barcelona in a time of change.

—

COLM TÓIBÍN is the author of eleven novels, including *The Master* and *Brooklyn,* three collections of stories, and a number of nonfiction books, including *Homage to Barcelona.* In 2021 he was awarded the David Cohen Prize for Literature. He is the Irene and Sidney B. Silverman Professor of Humanities at Columbia University.

PART ONE
POOLS

Lost time. Lost time. Lost time.
Saying the same words over and over
for greater depth may perhaps be like
undressing to reach the other side.
Pools.

JOAN VINYOLI, "Pools"

Natàlia decided that she would go to her aunt Patrícia's flat instead, on Gran Via and Bruc, when she returned to Barcelona. Her brother Lluís, who'd been married to Sílvia Claret for eighteen years, lived on Carrer Calvet, near Via Augusta, in the upper part of the city. She wouldn't have stayed with him anyway. Not because of Sílvia, with whom she at least shared a love of cooking, but because of Lluís. Natàlia had forgotten a lot in the twelve years she'd been away, yet she hadn't managed to wipe from her memory the sarcastic smile on her brother's face the day he rushed her to the clinic in his car. Natàlia had been at risk of sepsis—By all means, screw around, but think things through first, use your head, he'd told her as she writhed from the pain in her lower belly.

The airport seemed much larger and brighter, and far busier than Natàlia had imagined. It was bustling, with people of all stripes wandering about and air-traffic-control lights signaling the frequent arrival and departure of planes. As she waited for the *tapis roulant* to deliver her suitcase and two purses—*scant baggage*—Natàlia discreetly observed the people around her. The man who had lectured her about the impressive performance of Puig cologne—"we export it all over Europe, our little Catalan cologne has traveled the globe"—thankfully stood at the opposite end. Two Irish nuns huddled close together, looking askance. The woman with flaming red lipstick, like a model in the 1950s, gazed contentedly at the display windows facing the terminal—*I wonder if she's looking for someone*—and the man reading the *New Statesman* while smoking a pipe, who looked like a British Council teacher, checked his watch against the airport clock. The baggage finally arrived. Ant-like, the passengers filed tidily and somewhat drowsily toward the exit. Natàlia Miralpeix hesitated: She could take the Ibèria bus, which would drop her at Plaça Espanya, or she could take a taxi. She had changed her last few pounds, hardly anything, really—*poor Jimmy and his capital*—at Heathrow. Thankfully, the pound was stronger now and the exchange had worked in her favor.

She hailed a taxi, then turned around to take one last look at the airport. She recognized Miró's whimsical, childlike strokes and smiled. *I'm home.* She climbed into the car. "Gran Via and Bruc, please." The cabbie's eyes were leaden in the rearview mirror. He glanced at her every so often—*I wonder how I must seem to him. Is it that weird for a woman pushing forty to be traveling alone? Maybe it's the jeans* . . . Jimmy, who dressed more shabbily than she did, had talked her into buying a pair at Portobello Market. If there's one thing you've got going for you, it's your arse, he'd said. You've got a bullfighter's arse, and these jeans are a nice, snug fit—the snugger the better. The sky over Barcelona was the same heavy, solid gray of past springs. It was as if a single mass of clouds were slowly descending on the city, skimming the edges of the trees. A narcotic, headachy sky. What we need is a good storm, the cabbie said, addressing Natàlia with his eyes. All she could see of the man was a short, thick neck with rolls of skin down to the top of his spine and, in the mirror, a small rectangle of face, from his forehead to the bridge of his nose. Outside, the landscape was cut through with car cemeteries, shades of brown and gray, broken engines, shopping trolleys, dusty leaves, crumbling street gutters, dead trees, and the Ermita de Bellvitge, itself surrounded on all sides by concrete blocks. Natàlia gazed out at cypress trees smothered in dust and thought of the yellow-tinted days when she had visited the chapel with her father. Other cars zipped past, centimeters from the taxi. *They warned me: there's more money now, you'll see.* Natàlia rolled up the window.

Two days had gone by since Puig Antich was killed, and Natàlia told herself she wasn't naïve enough to expect things to feel different. She thought of Jimmy's new friend, Jenny, and the desolate look in her eyes. *I went over to say goodbye. The evening before, I'd cooked them my special roast chicken. See, you take the chicken, ask them to gut it for you, then slip in a couple of cubes of Maggi or something of the sort, and a halved lemon.* She had explained all this to Jenny because roast chicken was a favorite of Jimmy's. You're an excellent cook, Natàlia, he used to tell her when they lived together in Bath. *I got tipsy on sangria—too much ginger, maybe?—and knew for sure I'd have indigestion later. I can't eat much rice because it makes me feel bloated. Besides, British chickens are fattier than ours. Before the sangria, I had three glasses of sherry and then some of that dreadful red wine they sell at the pub, the kind that comes in those massive bottles. But Jimmy wanted sangria.* It's *our* goodbye, isn't it? Even if Jenny is here ... Even though Jenny was there, Natàlia had made her special lemon-stuffed roast chicken—tubby Mrs. Jenkins, the sweetheart, had let her use her oven. "My dear, I completely understand . . ." she had said, with a smile. The English will always understand everything and happily loan you their oven for a farewell dinner. Jimmy had been charming and even kissed her a couple of times, partly as a joke and partly in earnest. Jenny set the table and warmed the dishes up beforehand so they wouldn't have to eat their chicken with cold rice. The whole affair had been *very nice, indeed,* and Natàlia saw for herself that Jimmy had in fact changed. He finally had the setup he had always dreamed of—in Liverpool, where he'd grown up—although he said he would always remember their time in Bath "as some of the most wonderful days of my life, I promise." And he was so earnest and focused when he said *I promise* that Natàlia couldn't help but laugh. This was what he, Jimmy, said to her, Natàlia, as they enjoyed a cream tea in the Pump Room, a dining hall with a neoclassical ceiling and large picture windows that looked out on to the old Roman baths. As Jimmy smeared butter and jam on his scone, Natàlia told him that Jenny was absolutely lovely. It would have been pointless to add that she was a perfect fit for this new chapter in his life—that was clear enough. Jenny was a Hogarth through and through—rosy cheeks, resolute chin, cat-like eyes, brown hair, and a nose that tended to go reddish in cold weather. Her delicate, fair skin seemed always on the verge of cracking. When she first met her, Natàlia thought Jenny was fortunate to be petite and brunette, and to have bright, cheerful eyes and, most of all, a button nose that turned red the second it hit the cold. English films were easy to identify, not only because of the sweeping meadows and red-brick houses but also because of the actresses' noses. A nose like Samantha Eggar's in *The Collector*, the film that had made Natàlia fall in love with Hampstead, was hard to forget. Must you really go? Jimmy asked, adding a dollop of clotted cream to his scone. Natàlia said yes, and yes again as they strolled along the River Avon—it was the swans that brought tears to her eyes, though she still couldn't say why—yes, she must, Natàlia thought, she must go home to Barcelona. If I don't leave now, I never will, I've been gone nearly twelve years. Why go back? he asked. I don't know, she said.

The day after their farewell dinner, Natàlia stopped by Jenny's house. She had left the oven dish and needed to return it to Mrs. Jenkins. That's when Jenny told her she'd heard something on the radio about a Spanish anarchist being executed— Puchantik, I think he was called. Natàlia let the dish fall against her skirt—she'd bought a black corduroy one that morning and sworn to herself it was the last—then sat on the arm of one of the easy chairs next to Jenny's chimney. At first Jimmy told her he wasn't going to live with Jenny, but the house had a little garden, and it was tempting, since every now and then a gull would alight there, having lost its way from the sea; besides, he was moving to Liverpool in four weeks, and yes, maybe he would marry Jenny after all. Jenny and Jimmy were the same age, both twenty-five, it was only natural. Natàlia sat in silence for a while. Jenny was a little alarmed, and she opened her cat-like eyes very wide—Oh, my dear! Did you know him?—and who can say what Jenny must have thought, seeing Natàlia like that.

The problem was that Natàlia didn't know how to explain any of it to Jenny. She could've said, It's like Proust's madeleine, see, him dying right as I'm about to go back . . . The problem was that Natàlia had left the same year as the miners' strike in Asturias—she and Emilio had sung "Asturias, patria querida" and "Astúries, llibertat!" up and down La Rambla de Barcelona until they were both hoarse—and as Grimau's arrest. Grimau, who was executed a year later and said he hoped to be one of the last victims of fascism . . . And now they'd gone and killed Puig Antich. Do you know they caught him not far from your flat? In our neighborhood, of all places, quiet, peaceful Eixample, Natàlia read in one of the letters she got from Blanca Cortades, the only person back in Barcelona who wrote to her with any regularity during her twelve years of voluntary exile in Paris and London. Natàlia didn't think of her time in Rome with Sergio as exile but instead as a period of bliss; besides, Sergio's aunt, Aunt Sofía from Cuernavaca, had left him a decent inheritance, so she didn't even have to work. The days Natàlia spent with Sergio in Trastevere were green; she'd never forget their walks through the Renaissance palaces strung with laundry, the cats slinking through the ruins, the weeds spilling from the windows of the Cinquecento, and the faded ochre of the houses . . . As she was saying, Blanca had told her in detail about Puig Antich and the young anarchists, though she never believed they would actually kill him. There were rumors he would be pardoned at the last minute and that all kinds of people had written letters on his behalf, from the abbot of Montserrat to the Pope. And so it continued, as the Council of Ministers met week after week, and Franco's government still would not issue an *enterado*. They're going to let it go, Blanca thought. It would be a disaster to kill him, if, as everyone claims, we're just about to enter the Common Market. Though Blanca's father, a well-known journalist, was of the belief that while the left was sure Puig Antich wouldn't be killed, the right—not the far right but the civilized right—was scared, quite scared there would be an execution. As you can see, Blanca continued, my father still believes the left in this country is exceedingly naïve. The mood here, wrote Blanca, is either restive or calm, but everyone is clinging to the possibility of a pardon. They can't possibly kill him, she wrote again in her last letter.

The Sunday after the execution, the week she left England, Natàlia went to Reading. It was a beautiful day. The air was clear and the meadows a brilliant shade of green. Couples strolled along the banks of the Thames while swans glided regally along. Children and dogs chased each other through the tall grass, tumbling around until you couldn't tell them apart. Natàlia took photos of everything: the meadows that sloped down to the river, the children and the boats, the swans and the dogs, the bridge, the red-brick houses, the Reading Jail. A Victorian prison with a small tower at each of its corners and a large castle-like gate, Reading Jail stood beside one of the oldest factories in the county. Oscar Wilde, serving a two-year sentence there, had drifted around that fortress in search of "that little tent of blue which prisoners call the sky": "But grim to see is the gallows-tree, with its alder-bitten root, and, green or dry, a man must die before it bears its fruit!" Natàlia wished she could write down how she felt in that moment and tried to find the best angle to capture the light on that beautiful day, all the while thinking of Puig Antich, who would no longer bear fruit. Jimmy was the one who'd spoken to her most passionately about Oscar Wilde, the writer who had found "life just as he was losing it":

And as one sees most fearful things
In the crystal of a dream,
We saw the greasy hempen rope
Hooked to the blackened beam,
And heard the prayer the hangman's snare
Strangled into a scream.

And all the woe that moved him so
That he gave that bitter cry,
And the wild regrets, and the bloody sweats,
None knew so well as I:
For he who lives more lives than one
More deaths than one must die.

That Sunday it was impressively warm. Natàlia set down her secondhand Leica on the grass and lay back. She glanced at the vast dome of blue sky, then at the quails circling the weeping willows. She had bought a copy of the *Sunday Times,* like she did every week. Next to the pictures of Wilson—petting his dog as always, and smoking a pipe as always—and of pallid, mystifying Jeremy Thorpe—aged fifteen, parading around Eton in a top hat with his parents—was news of the deaths of Puig Antich and the Pole, Heinz Ches. "Two police killers garroted in Spain," the first civilians executed in eleven years. When Natàlia left Catalonia, Puig Antich was thirteen years old.

Say, Natàlia, Jenny had asked her that night—they'd met again at the house of their friend Henry, from Gibraltar—what's a garrote? Jimmy, ever the know-it-all, answered: A garrote consists of an iron collar, a seat, and an iron post. They strap the victim to the seat, which is attached to the post, and place a collar around their neck. The executioner then tightens the collar with a screw until the spinal cord snaps. I looked it up today in the *Britannica,* he added. And the neck goes *crack,* said Henry, eyeing Jenny to see how she would react. Oh shut up, you're vile! she said.

Natàlia went to Reading because she wanted to say goodbye to Jimmy's uncle, Mr. Philip Hill, before leaving England. It was still early when she arrived at his house, and the low-hanging fog wouldn't clear until later that day. He was mowing the lawn of his little garden and ceremoniously took off his little rubber gloves to shake Natàlia's hand. They had never shaken hands before. I hope this isn't goodbye forever, said Uncle Philip, a plump man with a lymphatic face. His skin was the color of baby peaches and his eyes a clear, watery hue. Certainly not, Natàlia answered and then felt at a loss as to what to say next. Uncle Philip had given her so much, far more than anyone else: he had taught her a profession, photography, giving her the tools she needed to make a living. No one, not even Sergio, who loved her, or Jimmy, who introduced her to a world of senses, nor Emilio, who opened her eyes, had given her anything as valuable as sweet old Uncle Philip, who knew nothing about her past or her country. Now Natàlia felt she could be truly independent, that she could pick her setting and the objects in it. What other choice did she have, she asked herself, at the age of thirty-six? Either sex work or marriage. Needless to say, Uncle Philip had never heard of Puig Antich—and why should he, when his future was set and he paid all his taxes, which would help Queen Elizabeth II to live a long and healthy life? All the same, Natàlia explained in broad strokes that her home country might be a bit unsettled. Hadn't he read the *Sunday Times?* They'd executed an anarchist. Don't you think it's barbaric, the way they killed him? It's always barbaric if you think about it, no matter the method. But poor Uncle Philip only knew Spain by reputation, he didn't like hot countries—Me, I prefer the cold, he was always saying. It wasn't easy for Natàlia to make him see that Barcelona was nowhere near Torremolinos. Uncle Philip had specialized in marine photography and spent half his life on those cod-fishing vessels that sail around the coasts of northern England and Norway. The day Jimmy introduced her to him, Natàlia had expressed amazement at the idea of his working with photography—she'd recently watched Antonioni's *Blow-Up*—and said she herself would love to learn. Uncle Philip had looked at her with his ocean-water eyes and gone, Let's get cracking, then. I'm bored, I've got hardly any work. I can teach you how to frame a shot and give an image value, which may sound easy but isn't.

Early Monday morning, she was still in Bath. By noon, she was in a taxi on her way to Aunt Patrícia's. Plaça d'Espanya, with the Mona de Pasqua in the middle, seemed even dirtier and uglier than usual. Maybe it was the day itself that was wrong. In the middle of the square was a mishmash of cars and buses—there were still trams when she left the city—and the cabbie started grumbling. On either side of the avenue were huge posters of Mao, Lenin, and Che: *Why did they revolt? A history of revolutions . . . the answer (in collectible installments)*. All around them, the din of car horns grew louder while a police officer with a pepper-red neck dashed from one side of the street to the other. *All that whistling makes him sound like a goldfinch with a bad cold*. The cabbie was used to it and calmly told Natàlia about a time when there were hardly any cars on the street—you know how much we make for a run these days? Peanuts. They could at least give us a discount on petrol. The man was from Murcia, via Albacete, and Natàlia, who hadn't spoken much Catalan in a while, enjoyed the sound of him speaking her language with a southern accent. "Listen, I don't know how long you've been away . . . twelve years? Goodness! You'll find that things have changed here. I was cannon fodder, you know . . . Go on, how old do you think I am? Fifty? Well, I'm forty-two, and all I want is for my children to have an easier time of it than I did. They used to come to our village and steal the potatoes. They'd ask: Whose side are you on? Whoever wins . . ." The cab driver's gray eyes no longer seemed steely, but more like an overcast sky.

Natàlia sent her aunt Patrícia a telegram that said: "Arriving Monday. Don't worry, only staying until I find a flat." She didn't have the courage to admit to her aunt that she was broke. Mind you, Patrícia was her godmother and had always claimed that Natàlia was her favorite, despite her temper as a little girl and her habit of constantly winding her up. Patrícia often said Natàlia was a cross between her own sister Paquita—who died a floozy, though she was lovely in her day, God was she lovely, and rich too, and yet they found her bundled in newspapers, having squandered her late husband's fortune on lovers; she had a soft spot for bullfighters and flamenco dancers and, it was said, a special understanding with her brother-in-law, a young man from the Dominican Republic—a cross, then, between Paquita and Kati, crazy old Kati, who committed suicide in 1939, God rest her soul. While Natàlia was wandering God's green earth—why didn't she write?—Patrícia lost her husband, the poet Esteve Miràngels—Aunt Sixta liked to say his surname didn't suit him, his eyes were too busy roving to look at angels—and Judit died of a stroke in 1958. She had been brain-dead for years before a hemorrhage finished her off. Left on his own, Natàlia's father moved in with her brother Lluís and his wife Sílvia. In her twelve years living abroad, she saw her brother and sister-in-law no more than twice. The first time was in Paris, where Lluís took Sílvia on a flying visit, the second in London, for Easter. Natàlia and Sílvia had gone all over London, exploring the shops and markets. Sílvia had talked Natàlia's ears off as usual, then been "bored to death" at the Tate. What can I say? I haven't the faintest idea about art. So they wound up talking about food. Lluís once secretly went to London to see an American woman he had met at the Picasso Museum in Barcelona, but neither Natàlia nor Sílvia knew about that trip. Natàlia only heard news about her family on these brief visits and from the occasional letter

Sílvia or Patrícia sent her in Spanish. Natàlia never wrote to her father and Joan Miralpeix never forgave his daughter for not coming home, not even for Judit's burial.

And even though she hadn't given it much thought in the past twelve years, by the time the taxi dropped Natàlia in front of Aunt Patrícia's building, on Gran Via, between Bruc and Girona, her stomach was in knots. Nothing had changed. There was the same marble staircase, the banister that curved left, the bronze modernist figure holding a globe, the hall, the chrome ceiling, the bright golden doorknobs, the polished windows, a cast-iron piece for scraping mud off boots—back when tarmacked streets were only a distant dream for the gentlemen of Barcelona—the long, narrow hall runner with frayed edges . . . Everything was in its place, the burnished details, the quiet of the staircase, the scent, the marble still gleaming despite some of the steps being chipped. A child with long hair and a feather headdress dashed out of a corridor. He wore a blue-striped school smock with a dark waistband. *I wonder if this is Constància's son.* Constància was twelve years old when Natàlia had left.

The doorknobs of the first flat on the second floor were a burnished gold color, as were the peephole and the Sacred Heart. Everything had been polished repeatedly with Netol. Natàlia smiled. Patrícia, ever so clean. She pressed the new doorbell, which let out a sentimental ring-ring. She heard a chain being released and a latch drawn, then the rustle of someone looking through the peephole—Who is it? Before Natàlia could answer, the door had opened and someone was squeezing her in their arms—Why didn't you say what time you were getting in?

Encarna, the Miralpeix family housemaid, had moved in with Patrícia when Joan Miralpeix left the flat on Carrer Bruc to live with his son Lluís and his young wife Sílvia Claret. A native of Granada, Encarna had big eyes, a large behind, and a generous bosom. Her hair was black, her lips the color of blood. In the Miralpeix household, Encarna ruled the roost—especially since Judit's stroke—and kept everyone in line. The moment she heard Patrícia cry out, she started muttering under her breath— I guess the girl's back—yet went on washing up the lunch things as though she hadn't heard a peep. *What had Natàlia been thinking, living abroad all those years, alone and half lost, when she could have been right here in Barcelona, closing her mother's eyes? God forgive her.* Still, Encarna couldn't resist the urge to nose around the hallway, so she rinsed her bleach-aged hands and dried them on her apron. She caught a glimpse of Natàlia through the half-open kitchen door. *Hasn't changed one bit.* Natàlia was tall and a little disheveled, as always, with her hair up in a bun, trousers that hugged her curves, suede boots, and a cashmere cowl-neck sweater. She dresses like a gypsy, Encarna mumbled to herself. She lingered in the kitchen a while longer before stepping into the hall— solemn, her chest puffed out, wearing a mock expression of anger. Encarna, Patrícia shouted, look who's back! Encarna looked at Natàlia and thought: *Her figure may still be young, but her face is chapped and wrinkled, especially below her eyes*—which were pale, like those of all the Miralpeixes—*and in the corners of her mouth. She's got old.* But Encarna and Natàlia were already embracing, and it was a short, firm embrace. Encarna often experienced hot flushes, particularly when upset. Her large bosom juddered like a car driving down a cobbled street. *I raised the brat myself,* Encarna thought, drawing away to hide the tears welling in her eyes.

Patrícia went on to update Natàlia on all the news. Encarna's getting married, would you believe it? Encarna straightened up and stood like a queen newly introduced to a town—and I will be left all on my lonesome, Patrícia continued, which is why I'm so happy you're back. To think I had finally got used to her cheek and constant griping, now she goes and gets herself wed. At the age of fifty-two, no less! Encarna made as if to leave—*Why should she care what I do with my life? It's none of her business*—but stayed right where she was, eyes fixed on the middle distance, which was a lace curtain with yellowed edges drawn over the door to the conservatory. He's a shopkeeper from Santa Coloma, Patrícia continued. A widower, no children, a flat of his own. They met ten years ago at a relative's house. At my sister Rosalia's, Encarna clarified. After her husband fell from a scaffold and was crippled, Rosalia opened a bar not far from Jaume's shop. Patrícia and Encarna took turns fleshing out the engagement story, their voices growing fainter and fainter until all Natàlia could hear was a distant murmur. She was looking at the conservatory, which was drenched in the gray noon light of a foggy, humid day. Her eyes searched for the lemon tree and the bougainvillea. Where's the lemon tree? She took a step forward and stopped at the window. Where's the lemon tree? she asked again. What happened, Aunt Patrícia? Something looks different. Oh, dear, of course it does! I sold the garden. You sold the garden? Natàlia asked. She was outside now, level with the conservatory, where a spiral staircase of enameled iron used to lead straight to a garden on the ground floor, all of it now occupied by a flat. What had once been a garden was now a large terrace of faded pink tiles—

a solid, uniform color broken up by damp patches and skylights. Around the terrace, in place of the classic black wrought-iron fence, was a brick wall with white plaster paint and occasional rough patches. Natàlia walked from one end to the other, brushing past the laundry hung out to dry, while Encarna watched with an exasperated look. I sold it to the neighbors. They wanted to expand their offices. Can you hear the typewriters? Patrícia asked. The inner courtyard had been covered in small pebbles that crunched underfoot. When she was a child, Natàlia would stash them in her pockets so she could later drop them on any pedestrians who ventured beneath the balcony of her flat. The two lemon trees had been there, near the adjoining courtyard, where a boy stuck out his tongue at her, and the oleanders had been on the left. Remember to wash your hands if you touch the flowers—they're poisonous, her mother always told them. Then one day, when Natàlia genuinely wanted to die, she swallowed one of the oleander flowers whole. A pink, cloying thing. Although she didn't die, she did find out grown-ups lied through their teeth. Aunt Patrícia claimed she had enough work keeping up the flat alone and so had let the garden become overrun with brambles and weeds. This garden is full of bad memories, she would say and then refuse to hear otherwise. Joan Miralpeix had sent over a gardener every now and then, calling in a favor from Joan Claret, who was chummy with a handful of city councillors. Esteve Miràngels was grateful for the attention, declaring the garden helped him write his sonnets. In the middle of the garden was an oval tiled pond with inlaid shells. A set of carved stone swans sat around the edge. Water spouted from their beaks toward a cherub at the center, his clothes wet and clinging to his thighs. The cherub didn't have a mouth. They smashed his mouth, Aunt Patrícia told little Natàlia one day when she caught her staring at the cherub with the smashed mouth. Why? she asked. To keep him from talking, Patrícia answered in a sad voice. And she refused to hear otherwise about that too. On the right side of the garden, a pair of acacias had yearly announced the arrival of spring. The garden spanned nearly a quarter of a city block and never felt overcrowded. Natàlia had whiled away several evenings in the conservatory, listening to the frogs trilling. There weren't only frogs in the pond either, but also lily pads and red-colored fish. One All Saints' Day, while everyone else was eating chestnuts at home, Natàlia and Lluís scooped every last fish out of the fountain to see how long it took them to die. Some of their tails were still twitching when Encarna found them. You children are rotten! And Lluís said, No, you're rotten! You're a witch and you won't ever get married. Lluís used to hang from the copper-colored ivy that crept up the white walls and tear out the moss growing around the base of the swans. Your mother lets the two of you get away with murder, Encarna said, then turned around and left, muttering under her breath. There was no ivy now, only a couple of bare branches and some skylights edged in tar where there had once stood a pond. All that was left of the garden were a couple of potted hortensias and geraniums. They're easier to water, Encarna and Patrícia explained. Look, Patrícia said, pointing at a ridged, slate-gray lump limping across the terrace. A prehistoric creature, the last vestiges of the old garden, trundled impassively forward. That thing always turned my stomach, Encarna said, scowling down at the turtle.

Patrícia's flat hadn't changed. Though she wished she could have updated the kitchen, laid down ceramic tiles, and put in new cupboards. Esteve left me nothing but problems, she said. I can't raise the rent either—the tenants have been with us for years! I was lucky to get an offer for the downstairs. The sale went through when Esteve was still alive, and he left me a lifetime annuity. The enclosed balcony was still the same; on one wall, the painting Francisco Ventura had given them—the watercolors that Francisco, of the Mundetas, God rest his soul, painted in the style of Modest Urgell—the two rocking chairs, one with a hole in the seat—what do I have to do to get it fixed?—the brazier table, the sewing box . . . The dining room, à la Chippendale, the chandelier with its glimmering prisms, the busy display cabinet—I managed to get almost everything back from the pawn shop, you know—the Sèvres crystal, the Limoges dinner service, the collection of little boxes—I kept the one that used to belong to Judit, with the orange blossoms worn by all the family's brides—the silverware, wine glasses that chimed when you flicked them . . . the giant varnished mahogany table with the silver fruit bowl, the satin Empire-style chairs, their great-grandfather's clock, the credenza with the framed mirror . . . The dark-green velvet drapes . . . Natàlia got goosebumps when she touched them . . . The satin on the chairs was threadbare, two had at least one broken leg, the drapes had warped, Great-Grandfather's clock no longer ticked, the mahogany table wobbled, one of the glass panes in the display cabinet was cracked, and there were tiles missing from the floor and prisms from the chandelier. Time had passed. In the hall, Natàlia recognized the Elizabethan wall sconces and the paintings depicting the Massacre of the Innocents, clipped from a copy of *Ilustración Española*. On the table with modernist feet sat a figurine of an elderly woman washing a teenager's hair. The woman's sleeves were rolled up and her hands buried in the boy's soapy curls. The image so terrified Natàlia as a small child that she used to cover her eyes whenever she passed it. She couldn't bear to see the figurine, nor the furious look on the woman's face with her crazed eyes and pursed lips, nor the boy's expression as he tried to escape her grasp—arms thrown up, eyes blinded by soap, groping for something to hold on to. When she was little, Natàlia thought this was exactly what life was like for grown-ups.

Patrícia Miralpeix had fixed up the room that looked out to the lightwell. She'd emptied the rococo dresser of the altar linen and of the starched rugs steeped in thyme. Stay as long as you like, I appreciate the company. Aunt Patrícia shut the door behind her. You must be tired. I'll let you freshen up, she said. Natàlia smiled. She was still smiling when she gazed at the mirror above the dresser. *You left all this behind because you thought it was fusty. And here you are, right back where you started . . .*

It felt deliberate, the fact that neither Patrícia nor Natàlia mentioned their family. Patrícia knew what had happened at the Miralpeixes' when Natàlia argued with her father and left, and she'd made a conscious choice not to reopen old wounds. *Lluís and Sílvia will fill her in over lunch tomorrow.* Patrícia and Natàlia dined together that night: spinach, soft-boiled eggs, brown bread, and peaches in syrup. The toc-toc of the mahogany table when it wobbled set Natàlia's teeth on edge, and she had to steady it three times. Natàlia turned in early. Won't you watch a bit of TV? Patrícia asked. They're showing some theatre later. The noise in the lightwell went on a while longer. Hushed voices, oil heated for a late-night meal, the sizzle of meat in the frying pan, eggs being beaten, conversations punctuated by a child's crying—and then, like a full stop, the dishwasher rumbling. A brief period of silence. Then the noise started up again. Muffled voices on TV, tears, laughter, shrieking. The volume was mostly low, yet every so often it grew loud again, and you could hear a man and woman speaking. A leaky tap dripped and water flushed from a toilet tank. Finally, at midnight, Natàlia fell asleep.

Natàlia's first thought the next day was to look for work. The sooner the better. She would go and see Harmonia. She needed to find a flat, a small one, all for herself. Over breakfast, Natàlia gave Patrícia and Encarna their presents. Encarna pretended not to care and went on setting milk and buttered toast on the table. Aunt Patrícia often had diarrhea, so all she ate that morning was grated apple. She loved the Indian-style white shirt Natàlia gave her, with its three-quarter sleeves, embroidered neckline, and slits on either side. Do you think it suits me? Patrícia asked, holding the shirt in front of her with both hands. She admired herself in the mirror above the credenza. Such a fine piece of clothing, she said. Encarna did the same with her gift— a long, thin scarf covered in big, garish birds with trailing tail feathers. First Encarna tried it around her neck, but she had a rather squat neck and it looked as if her head were being swallowed by her shoulders. Instead she wore it like a turban, the bright colors accentuating the black of her hair.

Natàlia observed Patrícia over breakfast, chattering nonstop. This colitis won't give me a moment's rest, her aunt said. And trust me, I've been to every doctor in town. Natàlia couldn't put her finger on it, yet there was something different about Patrícia. Maybe it was her hair, which she wore curlier than before, and "styled at the salon." Aunt Patrícia's hair was a mahogany color, though every so often a white strand would coil out, only to immediately blend back in with her dyed locks. Patrícia had soft hands—*They don't look like an old woman's*—and nails the color of wood. She caught Natàlia eyeing her nails and said, Do you like them? I had them done to match my hair. Aunt Patrícia talked and laughed a lot. *She used to be so sad and untidy,* and Natàlia was bored senseless when she visited—the woman always looked so downtrodden. She would wander around like a shadow and never make a peep, cloistered in her small world of sorrow and tears. But look at her now: dyed hair, painted nails, talking nineteen to the dozen. After breakfast she got up and opened one of the credenza drawers, from which she retrieved a leather tobacco pouch. She pulled out a cigarette. Want one? she asked, smirking at the surprised look on Natàlia's face. Light or dark? I prefer dark myself. Natàlia finished smoking, then told Patrícia she was going to telephone Lluís and Sílvia about lunch. Just wait until you see their flat, Patrícia said. It sure is something, Encarna observed while clearing the table. I guess I'll see Dad when I'm there, Natàlia said.

Natàlia failed to notice the look that Patrícia gave Encarna.

The day Natàlia met Harmonia she learned that some women didn't whine like Patrícia, or spend their whole lives in hiding like Judit. Judit had a stroke when Natàlia was twenty years old. From then on, Natàlia did all she could to avoid her mother's expressive, emerald eyes. In any case, Natàlia and her mother had never had a meaningful conversation. Judit was peculiar and Natàlia held on to her "childlike innocence," as people called it, well past her childhood. Nor were Judit's maternal instincts especially strong: she showered all her love on Pere, her son with Down syndrome, perhaps out of a secret guilt, and at the expense of Natàlia and Lluís. By the time Pere died, Natàlia no longer sought out her mother's company. After her stroke, Judit spent all day in an armchair—they'd cut a hole in it to fit a bedpan—in the conservatory, staring into the courtyard with her dead eyes. So when the principal told them they would be taking a drawing class with a celebrated painter called Harmonia Carreras, Natàlia was intrigued. She knew a thing or two about Harmonia's story: her father had been shot by Francoists when she was a young girl, after which she fled to France. From there she sailed to Mexico, where she lived for a decade, studying mural painting with a disciple of Diego Rivera. Later she returned to Catalonia, where her ragged figures with horror-struck eyes catapulted her to fame. She always snuck a flower into a corner of her paintings. Her style was a mix of Cubism and the art of contemporary Mexican Indigenous painters. At first Harmonia annoyed Natàlia. Harmonia was known to be difficult and tended to sulk when people disagreed with her. She was short and slim, raw-boned, and with a parchment-like complexion that turned purple in the cold. Although she wasn't yet forty when she and Natàlia first met, her gray hair already matched her gray eyes. She dressed as the mood struck her—one day she might have on three or four Guatemalan necklaces and a poncho from Peru, the next she would be wearing a sari. She lived alone, even though it was common knowledge, or so people said, that she had a lover: a young man and amateur filmmaker who won a prize at a festival—also, people said, thanks to her. Wagging tongues alleged she was a lesbian who had found an outlet for her "deviance" in the education of teenagers. She was an atheist, something she made no effort to hide. This, added to the fact that Harmonia, a woman, regularly raised her voice in meetings—they seemed to have trouble hearing her otherwise—was inexcusable in the eyes of the more established artists. "Let her paint," they said, "and wear whatever she wants. But we won't have her telling us what to do!" They were united by their gender and by their shared fear of a woman who unnerved them because she did something uncommon: She spoke her mind. As a matter of fact, Harmonia never shouted in class, instead addressing her students in a calm voice. She only took a tone when something or someone stood in the way of her imposing her opinion. She had the virtue of being loyal to her friends, her country, and her art—and the fault of wanting always to be right, even when she knew she was wrong. Her two greatest passions were Mexico and Catalonia, and she hated the "arrogant smallmindedness" of the *mesetarios*—of the Spain that "scorns all that it ignores," to put it as she did, citing Antonio Machado. It was this arrogance and small-mindedness that had subjugated the two countries she loved more than anything, plunging them into a permanent state of confusion and an unending search for their shipwrecked roots.

And so Harmonia, whose outlook had been shaped by a life in exile, had an outsized impact on Natàlia and her restless, volatile spirit. Harmonia introduced her to the work of Catalan poets, some of whom Natàlia already knew by name, given that her father occasionally cited them. Harmonia initiated her in the oeuvre of Salvador Espriu and Bartomeu Rosselló-Pòrcel, Pere Quart and Joan Salvat-Papasseit, Ausiàs March, Josep Carner, and Guerau de Liost. One evening, Harmonia announced: Riba is dead. Who's Riba? Natàlia asked. Harmonia was furious. Carles Riba was a Catalan poet and translator. Are you postwar kids really so ignorant? Then, as if mumbling to herself, she said: This exile never ends. For a long time, until the room was swaddled in darkness, Harmonia read to Natàlia from *Bierville Elegies:*

> ... *over the exile who through dark woods suddenly*
> *perceives you, oh life-like, oh ghost-like! and knows*
> *by your strength the strength that saves him from fortune's blows,*
> *rich in what he has given, and in his ruin wholly pure.*

Natàlia had such fond memories of those late nights with Harmonia, of their unfinished conversations, incomplete puzzles with pieces in desperate need of recovery. The poetry Harmonia read or encouraged Natàlia to read seemed somehow related to her father's world and to the music Judit played on the piano. But no one ever talked about poetry or the arts in the Miralpeix household. When Natàlia listened to the frogs singing in Patrícia's garden, she was transported to faraway cities and reminded of the poetry of Màrius Torres, who died of tuberculosis in Puig d'Olena after the war: "If only we could forget the crumbling city, distant, freer, there is another perhaps." The crumbling city was often on Natàlia's mind, especially as she searched for somewhere further away and freer. Harmonia thought Màrius Torres was a second-rate poet, but Natàlia didn't care. When Sílvia and Lluís had their first child, she insisted they name him Màrius after the poet who died without ever forgetting the city that was crumbling.

Harmonia lectured her students on Catalan Romanesque art and urged them to visit Taüll. She spoke to them about the Gothic artist Ferrer Bassa, the modernists Ramon Casas and Isidre Nonell, about Picasso. Look at their eyes, she said, Picasso doesn't seek, he finds. She was especially fond of his blue period, of the *demoiselles* of Avignon and the nude woman in a red armchair. But more than recite names or list paintings, Harmonia had instilled in her students a passion for observation. So many people die without ever looking around them; their hearts are cold. When you are out in the world, you must learn to truly see. Natàlia understood this when she left home: as her past faded behind her, she began to look, and things took on new meaning, becoming a part of her. Maybe, without realizing, she had spent the past twelve years "looking"—now she was coming home, ready to see. Who could say . . . But one thing was for sure. Natàlia had been drawn to photography because Harmonia, her difficult and contrary teacher, taught her to observe a world that had previously slipped through her fingers.

After two years as Natàlia's teacher, Harmonia found out her pupil was seeing Emilio, an Andalusian student "from a very good family—don't be fooled, no matter how hard he claims to be a communist." The relationship between the two women cooled after Natàlia's arrest. Throughout the years, they wrote to each other a handful of times, and Harmonia made it clear in her letters that she led a "perfectly rational existence," surrounded by art and books, scraping by "in this state of internal exile we have all been doomed to live in," as she put it. Natàlia knew her former teacher had changed lovers at least two or three times; in her letters she was always citing the new men in her life—"Joan says," she wrote, or "Narcís says." Her lovers were always right.

Harmonia was already waiting—Natàlia had telephoned that

morning. You're staying for lunch, she declared the moment Natàlia walked through the door, though by the time Natàlia explained she had plans to see her brother, Harmonia's mind was already somewhere else. Harmonia still lived in the same small, top-floor flat near Avinguda Diagonal; she was renting a studio upstairs, where "every night I gaze out at our city's impassive rooftops." Her tiny flat was as messy as always. One wall was covered in shelves bearing necklaces, masks, and Aztec-style vessels. In the middle hung a solar calendar with an Alexandre de Riquer poster beside it. An enormous tapestry took up another wall and three bookcases stood by the window. There were books all over the floor too, amid stacks of magazines and newspapers. Beneath the window was a dresser and on top of the dresser a portrait of Harmonia's father: a man with white whiskers and a passing resemblance to Francesc Macià. Harmonia greeted Natàlia in a floor-length, wide-sleeved robe patterned with orchids. I bought it at the Encants market, she said. Manuel says that from afar I look just like Greta Garbo. Harmonia now smoked with an ivory cigarette holder, held in her right hand. For a while she had only smoked with her left, until one day she decided she was done copying men. Who's Manuel? Natàlia asked. A poet, she said, a real poet. Like Josep Carner. We live together. And you? What's your plan? Will you be going back? No, I'm staying. Harmonia stared at her blankly. *I can feel her examining me.* Natàlia took a drag on one of the Gitanes she had bought at Heathrow. *She's thinking the usual, that I'm back but won't do anything worthwhile.* Harmonia Carreras hadn't aged, perhaps because she'd always looked older, though she had filled out a little. I'm traveling down to Valencia next week for an exhibition; I'm quite happy about it. Later I can show you some of the pieces I still have upstairs. Alfaro, the sculptor, was worried they wouldn't fit the theme. Natàlia stood up to take a closer look at the necklaces. You've got new ones. It's been years, darling. I've visited Mexico twice since you left. Do you paint much these days? Natàlia asked. Yes, though it's mostly ceramics at the moment. Harmonia had always done a thousand different things, and she was good at nearly all of them. In her view, most women were pushovers who didn't give a damn about leading meaningful lives. Women who are treated unfairly, she often said, only have themselves to blame. The people listening, most of them teenage girls and boys, would nod excitedly, if only because everything Harmonia did was exciting. Harmonia isn't a woman, she's a man, the men would declare.

I take photos now, Natàlia said. Is that right? Harmonia asked with a tinge of irony. Yes, I've been doing it for three years or so, ever since I moved to England. I took lessons from a professional photographer. I've had a couple of commissions, mostly from the University of Reading. Natàlia talked fast and without pause, much like she used to back in art school whenever she felt the need to prove to Harmonia, at whatever cost, that she too "had a mind of her own." I need to start earning a living. I was hoping you could help. I can't move back in with my family. You know how things ended between my dad and me . . . Harmonia fixed her with a gray gimlet eye that seemed to say, You'll never change, always with a finger in every pie. Harmonia had a finger in every pie too, but *she* had lived in Mexico and gone to school at the height of the Generalitat—as opposed to when the whole country was fast asleep, as Natàlia often liked to say. "Your education doesn't justify your restlessness," Harmonia wrote in response to a letter from Natàlia listing the many occupations she had while living abroad, including as the lover of a well-known painter. Unsurprisingly, Natàlia never ate better than she did in that time, once even giving herself indigestion after consuming half a kilo of pâté de foie in a single day.

Harmonia was just as sure of herself as ever and spoke in the same commanding tone that had intimidated Natàlia all those years ago. You could tell, Natàlia thought, that Harmonia had lived during a period—albeit a brief one—when things tended toward equality. This was why Harmonia could live her life as she pleased in Barcelona, why her skin was thick enough to endure any and all kinds of criticism—be it from her mother or from God. Natàlia didn't have Harmonia's mettle, which was why she had gone to London and Paris "to get up to no good," as Encarna would have put it. I am the reluctant daughter of Francoism, she said to Jimmy one time, to which he responded, And we are all the reluctant children of the atomic era. This is when Natàlia realized Jimmy didn't really understand what she meant. I guess if you're taking pictures now, Harmonia said, I could put you in touch with a couple of new magazines. *She doesn't believe me,* Natàlia thought to herself. Come to think of it, do you know the editor Arcadi Segura? Natàlia had met Segura on a wild night in London at the house of Mexican novelist Emiliano Echevarría. Arcadi had gone there straight from the annual meeting of the Anglo-Catalan Society and got roaring drunk. Stark naked save for the barretina on his head, he had sung "L'emigrant" with his arm around a Jamaican woman called Nailini. The following day, Natàlia and Segura went to the National Portrait Gallery, where they paid homage to Virginia Woolf. Yes, she certainly knew Arcadi. They wrote each other a couple of letters, both of his clearly under the influence. And yet Segura had managed to convey to Natàlia the historical dismantlement of their home country, even in letter form. I know Segura is looking for a photographer to shoot some covers for a new series he's heading up. Go and see him, tell him I sent you. Harmonia offered Natàlia a glass of whisky. I take it you heard what happened on Saturday, she said. No, replied Natàlia. Unless you mean Puig Antich's death. Let's call it what it is. An assassination. It's been a dreadful few days, I barely slept a wink on Friday night, Harmonia continued. Did people here not do anything about it? Natàlia asked. Harmonia gave her an acerbic look. Your friends are the ones who didn't do anything. You might even say it was the communists who killed Puig Antich.

And so the scapegoating begins, Natàlia thought. Don't you think you might be exaggerating a bit? As far as Harmonia was concerned, there was no such thing as shades of gray, only black and white. You weren't here, so you can't judge, Harmonia continued. The communists gave as much of a damn about Puig Antich's death as they did about Grimau's. Puig Antich was an anarchist, as you're well aware. And you—did *you* do anything? Natàlia would've liked to ask, but she didn't have the courage.

Sílvia got out of bed early that morning, a rare event. She even let in the housekeeper Felisa when she rang the doorbell at 8 a.m. bearing bread and a copy of *La Vanguardia*. Sílvia Claret wanted to go to the gym and, time allowing, the salon. *I need to get my legs and mustache waxed.* She was happy, because Natàlia was back, *the cheek on her, she could've stayed with us instead of holing up at Aunt Patrícia's house—it's so old and musty there. For the main course, we'll have pork in almond sauce. But what about the entrée?* While Felisa prepared breakfast—Sílvia had read somewhere that the best way to lose weight was not to cut carbs but eat grapefruit, "eat one grapefruit before every meal"—she went to wake up Lluís— You're going to the Matadepera site today, don't forget—and Màrius—Would you please remember to turn off the record player. She picked up two of his motorcycle magazines from the floor. Felisa had already set the table in the kitchen-diner. Remember, Mr. Lluís will have one soft-boiled egg and a glass of orange juice for breakfast. We're out of oranges, ma'am. Didn't I tell you to buy some more yesterday? Sílvia asked. *The woman is playing me for a fool. She's utterly useless. I don't know why I keep her around. I'll have to bring it up with Lluís. But what about the entrée?* Sílvia took a sip of grapefruit juice—*goodness, it's so bitter!* She smeared margarine on a piece of toast, always with an eye on the calorie chart—*I'm still within the limit.* She didn't care much for jam. She spread strawberry jam on Lluís's toast with the butter knife. Just a thin layer, he always said. *Where should I go—the market or the grocery store? Maybe the market. After all, we have guests. My sister-in-law is back from England!* Màrius bolted down a slice of bread and downed his café au lait with a drowsy look on his face. Honey, can't you see it's scalding? He didn't even bother to toast the bread. If you give me a minute, I can butter a piece of toast for you, Sílvia said. But Màrius was already leaving the kitchen. Sorry, in a rush, need to get the tires changed on the motorbike before school. Give me some money, will you, Ma? Again? Who else am I supposed to ask? Màrius shrugged and picked at the pimple on his face. Sílvia fetched her wallet and handed her son a blue note. That's the last you're seeing from me.

She heard Lluís step into the shower. *Rats, I forgot to get his special soap* . . . Sílvia closed her eyes. Seconds later, as if on cue, she heard *Sílvia!* booming from the shower. Sílvia went to the master bathroom. I forgot, Lluís. I'll swing by Sears today and get you the kind you like, for sensitive skin. It burns, damn it! The stream of water swallowed Lluís's last few words. *Now where was I? Oh, right. The entrée!* But seeing as she was there, Sílvia decided to tidy the bedroom. Lluís had a maddening habit of dropping his clothes on the floor on his way to the bathroom. Silk pajama top over here, bottoms over there, yesterday's shirt and socks. Lluís insisted on wearing fresh clothes every day and changing his shirt in the morning and afternoon. He claimed the collars got dirty from rubbing against his skin. Yet, the shirts Sílvia loaded into the washing machine were always spotless. She didn't even have to apply that gel she was always seeing ads for on TV. Where the hell did you put the sponge? she heard Lluís ask. It's right here. Go on, stick out your hand! Sílvia went to Màrius's bathroom to wash. She walked in just as he was zipping up his fly on the way out. She asked him to please clean the hairs out of the drain. It turned her stomach to have to scrub the bathtub with all those strands bunched in the catch. It's not my fault I was born hairy, Màrius said, and Sílvia went, Oh, go on already, will you? And don't forget to be home in time for lunch. Your aunt Natàlia is coming over. She's back? As of yesterday. She called to say she was coming over. Màrius was five years old when Natàlia had left, and he barely remembered her. You used to laugh so much when she nibbled your cheeks—don't you remember? Màrius gazed at his mother with indifference. Sílvia walked into the bathroom and smiled when she saw a bottle of lotion for acne-prone skin sitting on the glass shelf.

Sílvia Claret had trouble keeping her weight down. She'd got her figure from the Claret side and would always have cellulite on her waist and rear, no matter what she did. Mundeta, on the other hand, had been slender and petite, much like her mother and grandmother. A brunette like her father—You look like a silk-stocking gypsy, her mother was always telling Joan Claret— Sílvia had curly hair. This had driven her mad back when straight hair was all the rage. She had done all she could to tame her locks—with a flat iron, a clothes iron, a hair-straightening cream that stank to high heaven . . . But nothing seemed to work. At least natural hair was in now, and she no longer had to suffer at. the hands of stylists. I need to get my mustache waxed, she repeated, studying herself in the mirror. She swallowed her lips to get a good look under her nose, then ran her finger along her upper lip: a slight fuzz. Sílvia was hirsute. Màrius had also taken after the Clarets and had hair all over his body. All the same, Sílvia was proud to look like her father, with the same slender eyes. Sílvia wished she could have been more like him in fact, a fine tennis player with a strong will who did whatever he pleased. Joan Claret came from nothing, but he had money now, and lots of it. Papà is a powerful man, Sílvia bragged to her friends. My favorite thing about you is your dad, Lluís told Sílvia one day. Joan Claret has brass balls. I admire him because he hasn't failed and has no intention of doing so, and because he pulled himself up by his bootstraps. Sílvia had always been her papà's little girl. I'm going to raise you like a queen, he told her when she was a child. You'll be the most sophisticated *cocotte* in all the land. Men will throw themselves at your feet. Joan Claret was fond of Sílvia because they had the same slender eyes and curly hair, and because she was clean and put-together like his mother, who had lived on Carrer Aragó and died during the war. Joan Claret would go to great lengths to buy her the prettiest, most expensive clothing: dresses of poplin and organdie, velvet ribbons, mohair jumpers, perlé socks, and patent-leather shoes—I want my daughter to be the loveliest girl in the house. You'll be a great dancer someday, he said. Joan Claret was a canny entrepreneur and good at the helm. Once his small empire had prospered, he pivoted from patents to the real-estate business—which died on the vine on account of the hotel in Lloret and Joan Miralpeix—to saving an advertising agency from bankruptcy and turning it into the second most successful business of its kind in Barcelona. He had also opened two lingerie factories in Berga, in his wife's name, and was said to have double-dealings in Andalusia. Sílvia fell for Lluís because he was as much of a man as her father, as strong-willed and resourceful, and because he looked just like Clark Gable in *Gone with the Wind* when he half closed his eyes. The day she saw Lluís in Gualba, he was standing at the foot of the stairs as she walked down the steps, and she thought to herself, Look, I'm Vivien Leigh walking down the staircase and he's Clark Gable waiting at the bottom. She met Lluís at the masia in Gualba, a large country house belonging to the Miralpeix family, the day Patrícia invited her friend Mundeta Ventura, Joan Claret's wife, to visit with her four children. It was the anniversary of Mother Carrió's death—a nun and a close friend of the Miralpeix family whom they were trying to have beatified—and they sat together to eat a Three Kings Day feast, quite possibly their last all together. Lluís paid no attention to Sílvia. He clearly thought of her as a little girl and was even rude a couple of times. "Women are twits, you're no good for anything." But the way he said it, half closing his eyes, sent her head over heels. When they parted, Lluís gave her a bunch of marigolds, "an unscented flower."

Sílvia was stout, though this hadn't always been the case. It was different before, when she used to dance. If we get married, Lluís said, you'll have to quit dancing. And she did, even though Magrinyà had told her it wouldn't be long before she was a soloist for the Liceu dance company. She danced to *Concierto de Aranjuez* and learned to play castanets very early on. But these days, whenever she heard some familiar refrain from *The Nutcracker* or *Swan Lake,* her eyes misted over. "Before meeting Lluís, dance was my life." Her father was right when he said, Please don't give up dancing, pumpkin. Yet she had, and there was nothing she could do about it now. Nonetheless, when no one else was home, she turned on Radio 3 and crossed the dining room *en pointe*— knees locked, legs firm—then folded back to front into a *développé*—waist lifted, shoulders rolled back—while admiring herself sidelong in the foyer mirror. She could still do a *pas de ciseaux* and a double *frappé,* arms aflutter like the wings of a dying swan. Sílvia debuted the same year she married Lluís. She said goodbye to a life of dance by attending a performance of *Les Sylphides* at the Royal Opera House in London. Lluís sat in the booth with her, stroking her hand, which was warm to the touch. Sílvia forgot all about ballet during their first years of marriage. This was before they moved into the maisonette, when they lived in a smaller flat in Guinardó. But she had Màrius, whose eyes melted her heart, as well as various household items—bedclothes, a dinner service, pots and pans, all beautiful and brand-new. She liked going to the market and talking about her *husband* or when the door woman said, "Good morning, Mrs. Miralpeix." In those early years, Lluís treated her like a queen. She had everything she could want—dresses and stockings, leather shoes that matched her purse—and he spoiled her just as her father had. Sílvia felt safe in his arms. They held hands in the cinema and restaurants, and he introduced her to all his friends. "This is my wife," he would say, and she'd feel like a grown woman. With the help of his father-in-law, Lluís was able to stop working for his father, Joan Miralpeix, and set up his own architecture firm. He's a sharp one, your Lluís, Joan Claret said. They played tennis and he won. Son, the future belongs to the young. Between the pregnancy and knitting sweaters for little Màrius, between cooking lessons and waiting for Lluís, who always came home late, Sílvia didn't feel time passing. Days slipped away from her, then years, and if someone had asked how she was doing, she'd have said: "Happy, of course. Why do you ask?" But then, when she stepped into the elevator and saw her reflection, she would start dancing, only to halt mid-flutter, fix her eyes on the eyes of the woman in the mirror, and say: You're ridiculous. When she used to kneel at Mass—they stopped going because Lluís said he'd had enough of that old-fashioned, authentic Spanish nonsense, they needed to get in step with Europe—she would slide her fingers along the pew in front of her, making them dance *Swan Lake* from start to finish—*développé, ciseaux, frappé.*

Sílvia's nerves were always frayed, and she often cried for no reason. Her grandmother Ramona, Mundeta Sr., claimed Sílvia's anxious disposition could be traced to the fact that she was in utero when her mother had searched for her husband all over the city like a madwoman. It was the war and Mundeta Ventura believed Joan Claret had been killed in an air raid, so she set off alone, scouring hospital after hospital for his body. Sílvia was born in August 1938, about five months after that dreadful scare. People always asked, seeing her hands and feet twitch oddly: Are you sure there's nothing wrong with her? Her little body sucked up all that fear, declared Grandmother Ramona, who knew everything. The first word Sílvia learned to say, at only sixteen months old, was *fear*. Sílvia's mother didn't want any girls, and yet somehow she wound up with three. She hadn't wanted any girls because she believed women were fools and men had better luck in life. Sílvia cried easily and a lone tear could often be seen rolling down her cheek. When she was older, Joan Claret told her, You mustn't be soft. I like my women strong. How else will you win over the men your dear old papà brings home for you? But she couldn't help herself. The minute something emotional happened on-screen at the cinema, her eyes welled up like a silly little girl's. To make matters worse, she was always forgetting her hanky—why do I even bother crocheting borders onto your handkerchiefs? her grandmother Ramona would ask her. Yet Sílvia forgot hers, which meant she had nothing to dry her tears or blow her nose. More than once, she'd had to go to the cinema lavatories to blow her nose on toilet paper, which was nowhere near as soft then as it is today and came in far fewer colors. *Natàlia, though, Natàlia is strong,* Sílvia thought to herself, even though she didn't approve of how she had stormed off—on bad terms with her father and her mother still living. After he gave her the marigolds, Lluís ignored her for a couple of months, *and to think he even touched my breast beneath a chestnut tree in Gualba.* But a week before her debut he sent her an orchid, and the night after the show at the Liceu he telephoned to ask her out. It was a very short engagement—he had kissed her that very night at the Liceu—and before long Lluís was on his way to Carrer d'Aribau to meet the Clarets and face the question, Tell me, young man, what are your intentions? Lluís worked with his father, who was an architect like him and the brother of Patrícia Miralpeix, You know, your wife's friend. Joan Claret leaned back in his armchair and said, I hear you play tennis. And so on and so forth, and so swiftly that Grandmother Ramona had to race against time to finish the lovely lacework she had started for Sílvia's trousseau. The day the wedding dress was unveiled, Sílvia's mother, Mundeta Ventura, hired a window-display designer, who laid out the bridal garments on one wall and the family linen on the other. The pieces were hung from a single corner, and so daintily they looked as if they were floating. There were half a dozen regular table covers, with another set in linen, hand-embroidered with lace trim, one set for eight in linen, one set for twelve in linen with hand-embroidered cross-stitch, one set for twelve in the style of Lagartera, all white, four embroidered sets—two by Sílvia—two in organdie with shadow embroidery—also by Sílvia, in school, a keepsake—two sets for two and another for eight in the style of Lagartera, but in color. Then, half a dozen sets of regular monogrammed bedclothes, two with colored turnovers and scalloped edges, two with crocheted details in color, two in linen with hand-embroidered cross-stitch. Two dozen monogrammed full-size towels, a dozen smaller towels, half a dozen hand towels, two dozen kitchen cloths, and half a dozen dust cloths. On the other wall hung the bridal garments, over which everyone oohed and aahed—six nylon slips, six nightgowns, six patterned batiste pajama sets, six matching chemise-and-robe sets in raw silk with lace detailing, a black gauze nightgown, a set of satin pajamas, two winter robes, silk stockings, socks, handkerchiefs, and a white openwork shawl passed down from Sílvia's grandmother Ramona. And the Manila shawl passed down from her other, late grandmother. The jewelry, the silverware, the crystal . . . They had a wedding registry in Vinçon for the porcelain dinner service and in Can Bagués and Can Pallé for the silver, as well as in Grifé and Escoda. The bridal-shower guests were entranced, and the women all exclaimed, What fine threads! and smiled at the bridal nightgown, which was embroidered with roses, and had a décolleté and a tail—that's right, a tail. Presents poured in from every side—the Clarets only sent a few, though there were dozens from the Venturas and Miralpeixes. Aunt Sixta, for example, gave them three silver goblets, and Patrícia half her silverware—she had already pawned the Limoges dinner service by then. Sílvia missed her family in the early days of her marriage, her papà above all, and stared wistfully at the porcelain doll she had brought with her from home. A Marie Antoinette doll her grandmother claimed had been confiscated from the Bertran i Musitu estate by a commie friend of her father's who would go on to join the Falangist party. *Grandma Ramona couldn't stand Papà and never missed an opportunity to say an unkind word about him.*

Lluís was done showering, which meant he must be in the kitchen, having breakfast. Sílvia could tell he'd shaved because the bathroom was peppery with Varon Dandy cologne. Sílvia pulled out a shirt for Lluís—what will it be today, beige or salmon?—and then asked him, Are you going to tell Natàlia? Tell her what? About your father. Of course I'm going to tell her.

If she asks. I imagine she'll find it strange, him not being there, Sílvia said. Pass me the beige trousers; I'm going to wear the khaki shirt today. Didn't you say you wanted the salmon one? No, he said. Lluís finished dressing. He ran the palms of his hands along his widow's peak—*I'm going bald.* Don't go to the club today, Sílvia said, or you'll get home too late. Natàlia called, she's coming over for lunch. The woman wastes no time, he said. We're family, Sílvia replied, and then finished tidying the bedroom: She stripped the sheets off the bed, opened the window to let in some air, closed the drawers, collected the dirty laundry from the floor, and arranged the slippers on the shoe rack. Just as she was standing up, she spotted a hole in the carpet: *The man's neat as a pin, but for some reason, he's incapable of using an ashtray.*

Sílvia dictated her shopping list over the phone. Get the pork at the market, she told Felisa. It'll be less expensive there. She finished getting dressed. *I can't go to the gym or the massage parlor, or else I won't have time to get anything done. But what about the entrée?*

Lluís Miralpeix went to fetch his car from their garage—*The brake's sticking, I should have it looked at.* When he slid into his Simca 1000, he felt his midriff form into rolls: *It's been too long since I played tennis. I'll go tomorrow.* He turned on the engine. Something was niggling at him, though he couldn't put his finger on what. He had plenty of work on his plate. The two-story chalets were a hit, especially the ones in Vallès, where it was exceedingly humid. He had built the houses about three meters above ground. The lower level, in exposed brick, served as a wine cellar. A staircase led to the first floor, which boasted a kitchen, a lavatory, a bedroom, and a dining room with a working fireplace. The sitting room was upstairs, where the ceiling was dotted with skylights. "Every space has its own ambience. For a low price, clients can enjoy both a wine cellar *and* a study." People were buying land—money seemed to be worth less and less these days—and they liked this architect with novel ideas who treated them like royalty. A house with a wine cellar—it was their life's dream! Small property owners went gaga over it. There was no denying that Lluís Miralpeix had a way with these men and women who had got rich rather suddenly, and he knew just what to say to dissuade them from the Swiss-style chalets, which by then were no longer called *torres*. Wood's too expensive, and where do you expect me to get hold of slate? he would ask. Now and then, some bullish woman, usually covered in bracelets and earrings, would insist on a "postcard chalet." Steep roof, wooden walls, mansards . . . Lluís suspected these people liked to visit Switzerland to stock up on chocolate and, while they were at it, deposit some gold in the bank. For the fat cats who walked into his architecture firm wishing Barcelona were cold enough to justify furnishing their flats with parquet floors and thick sheepskin rugs, Switzerland was the dream. And Lluís, who loved his job, had to steel himself whenever an avalanche of bad taste breached his sanctuary. His sanctuary, or *sanctum sanctorum,* was the firm where he employed more than twenty people, among them architects, engineers, drafters, secretaries, and typists. There were also one or two architecture students, carefully screened for political involvement—this was not for nothing, as Lluís found that the political ones usually lacked follow-through. The architects drew up blueprints and he signed off on them, because his real passion was traveling around Catalonia for inspiration. We don't know enough about our own architectural tradition, he would assert. The open-plan galleries and spatial layouts of our masies are almost perfect. He traveled as often as he could. When he saw the ambition and harmony of the new UNESCO Headquarters in Paris, he was transported. In his view, Walter Gropius was a master whose only desire was to uncover the link between art and technology. Partial to clear surfaces and clean lines, Lluís believed in the liberal use of windows and stilts. For a while he was convinced the only way to save Barcelona from architectural ruin was to pry it free from the grips of Gaudí and impose a more rational design. But in the end, he always reached the same conclusion: the country was overrun with morons who knew next to nothing about architecture. "They're only interested in making money fast. What they don't realize is that taste always wins out in the long run. Spain is never going to be allowed into Europe," he said.

Lluís had been a model student at Jesuit school, and it wasn't easy for him to "clear away the cobwebs of irrationality still cluttering my mind." To this day he doesn't understand why his father, who hadn't been a believer then and wasn't especially devout now, sent him to study with the Jesuits when he was a child. For a short period, while he was still in school, Lluís intended to join the priesthood and led a life of spirituality and seclusion. His mother laughed when she found out—"Lluïset thinks life is a ladder and wants to climb up to the highest rung." Lluís hated his mother because she never congratulated him when he got good grades, never cheered him on, never thought him brilliant or clever. Judit loved Pere and only Pere, and maybe Natàlia a little too. With hard work and ingenuity, Lluís managed to achieve everything his father hadn't: a name for himself and the respect of his colleagues. Lluís had succeeded, and that was a fact. So he resolved to flaunt his success and talk about it every day, especially to his mother. He would sit in the conservatory, within earshot of her, and say as much to anyone willing to listen to his tales of professional triumph. And while his words were addressed to someone else, they were meant for the woman in the armchair with her smooth brain, dead eyes, and childlike smile. It was to her that he explained how he'd built his first house, raising it from the ground up with nothing but his quick wits and his own bare hands. How he drew the blueprints himself and planned out every room. How people sang his praises and how someone had recently asked to publish his design in an architecture magazine run by the Opus Group—they're at the top of the game right now, you know. Lluís recounted the tennis matches he won—I demolished the guy—how much money he made that month—Sílvia is the classiest woman in town—the cars he was going to buy. But the woman with emerald eyes just sat there: hands still, eyes vacant, a dumb smile on her face.

Lluís soon forgot all about that, for Judit was dead and buried and he was close to the top rung. Lluís was a practical man; if something upset him, he pushed it right out of his mind. In life you've got to hold fast to two things, he said, three things at most. He was a rationalist, and it hadn't taken him long to realize God didn't exist. Religion is for suckers, women, wimps, and losers, he declared. "It's the twentieth century. We've walked on the moon. Before we know it, we'll be walking on Mars. But we live in a country of zealots." So-called idealists drove Lluís up the wall; if you asked him, both the right wing and the left were a plague that ought to be stamped out. "The era of politics and 'isms' is behind us. The time of religious and ideological rubbish is in the past. The future is technology, and scientific progress." Lluís liked cars—he never missed a Grand Prix or Formula 1 race—and dreamed of owning a Jensen-Healey, an English two-seater sports car. *When I get one, Sílvia can have the Simca, now that she finally has her license.* When Lluís drove his car, he wasn't Lluís Miralpeix, architect—he was a child. The sheer satisfaction of his mind going blank, the wind tickling his ears, the whoosh of cars vanishing behind him as he charged forward and was engulfed in darkness. The cars in his rearview mirror shrank into little black dots, their tiny headlights blinking and then fading as he barreled into the night, master of all. It was intoxicating, breaking off from the world like that. In those moments, Lluís didn't give a damn about life or death; he didn't give a damn because life and death didn't exist, and nor did his senses. He wasn't so much a body as a breath of air, a gust of wind, a soul reigning over everything. The needle on the speedometer crawled past 100 km/hr, then 120, and 150, maybe even 180, as his foot pressed down on the accelerator and he slid like a canoe over silky calm waters . . . He glanced sideways at the other cars, the ones slowing him down—in the end, he, Lluís Miralpeix, always won. Then, exhausted, Lluís would rest his arm on the open window and at last let them overtake him. He gazed at them with disdain: if he wasn't speeding, it was only because he didn't want to. Even though he frequented the bars on the side of the Sarrià highway, he preferred cars to women. He had two or three girls on the go at a time. That way he didn't risk doing anything stupid, he told himself. If one of his lovers got jealous of the others, he left her. "I don't want any messy business."

Films were another of Lluís's passions. Whenever he had the chance, he would visit Perpignan or Ceret and watch as many as six in a single day. He liked American movies, especially the violent ones against violence, and the odd Italian film. Sometimes he and his friends, Albert Mateu and Quim Renau, got together to watch porn. A Swiss man, the cousin of one of his clients, imported them at a fair price. They watched the films on Sunday afternoons or, in the summer, in Pineda, where the three men and their wives met up—Quim and Mateu's wives were friends of Sílvia—and split their sides laughing. "They're all the same," they said. "Watch too many and it gets a bit boring." If there was one thing he had learned from the Jesuits, it was that you had to look after your body—and soul—in order to succeed. He went to the Tennis Club whenever he had the time. But recently, he'd been exercising less and less: It was exhausting, he had a fatty heart, he was getting old.

Sílvia told the hairdresser not to bother with a perm—she was in a hurry. Just wash and set. She also asked her to heat the wax for her mustache and eyebrows. No, not the legs. I'm late enough as it is. Eyebrows first, Sílvia reminded the hairdresser. You know how sensitive my skin is. It goes red like a tomato. Sílvia sat beneath the hood dryer with clips all over her head, topped by a pink hairnet. This was her favorite part of going to the salon. The warmth made her drowsy, and she often fell into a gentle slumber that reminded her of the naps she took as a little girl. She opened *Garbo* and quickly leafed through it. There was a piece about Maria Schneider from *Last Tango in Paris*, the actress with the baggy eyes, olive skin, damp hair, and large breasts that sagged a little. Maria Schneider had lost her head over a girlfriend and stood up a movie director in Rome, right in the middle of a shoot. *I don't see why they don't just come out and call her a lesbian,* Sílvia thought. *The woman is dirty—not dirty in the sense that she's unclean, but dirty in another way. I can't really explain* ... Sílvia went on leafing through the magazine. Ronald D. Nadler, an American professor, had discovered that male gorillas were not actually aggressive. "Males Less Ferocious Than Portrayed" read the headline in Spanish, and a bit further below, "female gorilla pursues male for lovemaking." Dr. Ronald D. Nadler confirmed that the gorilla, "long depicted as a ferocious animal with an insatiable libido, may in fact be the opposite, recent studies reveal." The American professor was pictured in the article: abundant hair, Groucho

Marx mustache, sensual lips that looked as if they had just eaten sobrassada, and an aquiline nose. *A prime specimen,* Sílvia thought. His low-cut top revealed a tuft of flaxen chest hair . . .

> "Instead, when it comes to mating, the female heads the chase, actively pursuing the male to initiate copulation. The male is rarely the one to approach the female. The female almost invariably takes the initiative, throwing herself re-peatedly at the male, pushing him continually against the wall, sometimes even punching him until he is cornered. While in pursuit of the male, the female emits a soft, high-pitched sound similar to that of a smug baby pigeon. The male not only responds passively to the female's courtship," Professor Nadler continues, "when presented with the op-portunity of daily access to the female, the male gorilla responds positively once or twice a month at most. A banana seems to bring him much more satisfaction than the atten-tion of his female counterpart."

. . . The magazine had fallen from Sílvia's hands. A thick fog clouded the print and her eyelids blinked shut again and again. Her head knocked against the hood of the hair dryer. She dreamed Professor Nadler came in pounding his chest while Maria Schneider cooed like a turtledove with her breasts hang-ing out, before pouncing on a gorilla and making love to him as if she were riding a horse. Professor Nadler took notes as she, Sílvia, enjoyed a delicious banana. Her dream ended when her head hit the dryer. She'd even drooled a little. The trainee picked up the magazine and gave it back to her. Sílvia called out to the manicurist and asked her to do her nails in mother of pearl. As they trimmed her cuticles, Sílvia thought to herself, *I know what to make as the entrée: prosciutto and melon. I'll have to check if there's any melon at Tívoli.* The idea had come to her after reading the story about the gorilla who loved bananas.

I wish you'd told us. We'd have fetched you from the airport, Sílvia said, kissing Natàlia on both cheeks. *She's got older,* Sílvia thought, *though just as disheveled as ever.* The boys aren't home yet. Come on, let me give you the grand tour. Upstairs were the dining and sitting rooms, the library, the eat-in kitchen, the foyer, and the bathroom. A black iron chimney hung from the dining-room ceiling, dividing the space in two. The ceiling in the sitting room was slightly higher, and the floor was made of wood. Scattered around it were large cube poufs upholstered in various shades of corduroy. A dark pinewood table flanked by two long benches stood in the carpeted dining room. The inbuilt shelves were stacked with art books and a collection of small ceramic owls. This is all Lluís, of course. He has excellent taste, as you well know. Sílvia was giddy and showed Natàlia every detail: Judit's piano, with a tall glass pitcher on top—poor Mamà, Sílvia sighed, such a tragic end—prints of works by Mondrian, Hoyland, Nicholson. Cool lines, steely colors, large white walls. The library was next to the dining room. The bookcases were walnut, as was the imposing desk, while the armchairs were black leather. This used to be Papà's study, now it's Lluís's. On one wall hung pieces by Maurice Utrillo and Raimundo de Madrazo y Garreta. The shelves were lined with books about art and architecture, as well as the entire Espasa encyclopedia. All in all, the atmosphere in the library was rather somber compared to the living and dining rooms. The bedrooms were downstairs. They whisked past

Joan Miralpeix's—Sílvia noticed Natàlia didn't ask about him—
then lingered in Sílvia and Lluís's, its walls white and a large
piece by Paul Klee hanging above their headboard. The furniture was spare, the wardrobe inbuilt, and the bedspread electric
blue. Beside their bedroom was a master bathroom with bottle-
green tiles, sinks like baptismal fonts, and a large mirror that
took up half a wall. Then came Màrius's room. It's always so
messy in here, Sílvia complained. Inside there was a pinewood
desk, a record player, record sleeves strewn here and there, three
white shelves full of books—he's into poetry now, if you can believe it. Natàlia picked up a heavily thumbed book from the
floor, *Nueve novísimos poetas españoles,* and an album by Blood,
Sweat & Tears that had practically vanished beneath his bed. On
the wall posters of Che and a Japanese motorcycle trial hung
next to a print of *Ophelia* by Everett Millais: a pallid girl the color
of death and circled by flowers—hands open, lips parted—
floated in a stream amid ferns and dead trees. Lluís can't stand
the painting. He says it's unoriginal. But Màrius thinks it's beautiful. Natàlia recited:

> *Sur l'onde calme et noire où dorment les étoiles*
> *La Blanche Ophélia flotte comme un grand lys . . .*

What? Sílvia asked. Nothing, don't mind me . . . Màrius has been
reading a lot of poetry. He and Lluís are always fighting because
Lluís wants Màrius to make up his mind about what to study at
university. There was a big to-do the other day because Màrius
said to him, What makes you think I'm going to university? You
know, I'm worried Màrius is doing drugs. He keeps such strange
company. Sílvia continued the tour of the maisonette, the guest
room, Màrius's lilac-tiled bathroom . . . Come here, Sílvia said, I
want to show you something. They walked to the study, and Sílvia pulled out a folder with purple marbling from a drawer in
the walnut desk. She opened the folder and showed Natàlia a

couple of white sheets of paper, *mon chou, je ne t'oublie pas* . . . Lluís
thinks I don't know about it, but I'm always going through his
things. You haven't said anything? Natàlia asked. For what? I'd
rather things stay the way they are. It's peaceful at home now.

Sílvia went to the kitchen with Natàlia to check on the pork.
We have one of those modern stoves with an oven—it's life-
changing. Sílvia wouldn't stop talking. You must teach me how
to bake one of those delicious English cakes. She cracked open
the oven—I can't really see inside, even with the light on—and
used a fork to check if the pork was done—no, needs more time.
Pork in almond sauce, in your honor. You add a pinch of salt and
a crack of pepper, then give the pork a little score and roast it on
low until it's cooked through. Then you add sliced almonds sim-
mered in milk—don't forget to make sure the sauce gets in the
grooves—and pop it back in the oven. You wouldn't believe how
hard it was to find melon, Sílvia continued. They're not in season, so I had to go to Tívoli, the fruit store. Of course, you should
always eat melon first, or you might get an upset stomach. And
the way it pairs with the ham—I bought Parma—is phenomenal.
Classy, huh? Sílvia asked. Trust me, we follow the latest trends in
this house. We've changed a lot. I'm sure you'll find things here
aren't so different from in England. Sílvia sat across from Natàlia.
Now, tell me, what have you been up to all these years? But Lluís
had just walked in, and even though he and Natàlia had only
seen each other a couple of times in the last twelve years, there
was a chilliness to their greeting.

They were at the dining table when Natàlia noticed it was
only set for four people. *Dad must be in Gualba.* They started with
an aperitif. Lluís had whisky and she and Sílvia white vermouth—
one sweet, the other dry. Sílvia placed a couple of small dishes
on the table—Some snacks while we wait for the pork to finish
roasting—stuffed olives, cubes of Gruyère, and fried shrimp. Sílvia was the chattiest of the three and went into great detail about
the many diets she had tried. During the occasional long silence,

when it seemed no one knew what to say, they usually fell back on the subject of Màrius, his studies, and the motorcycle. Don't you think motorcycles are sexy? Sílvia asked. I'd ride one if I were younger. You, Lluís teased with a smile, the woman who's scared of elevators? Sílvia looked at Natàlia. Don't listen to him. He just wants to make me look bad. Lluís was in a mood. He leaned back in the black cattail chair, hand in pocket, while sipping at a glass of bourbon. Are you back for good? Lluís asked Natàlia, after a while. It was funny, Natàlia thought, how everyone wanted to know the same thing. Before she had a chance to answer, Màrius walked in. *He's the spitting image of the Clarets,* Natàlia thought to herself. Like a teenage boy in some Venetian painting, a Bellini—tousled hair the color of charcoal, strawberry lips, black eyes, rosy cheeks, and a stiff, guarded demeanor. His face was unfinished but beautiful. He had dark bags under his eyes, the Miralpeix trademark. There was something unsettling about him. Maybe it was his gaze, which was as elusive as his grandmother's, somewhere between childish and wary. It was as if his eyes refused to settle on the physical objects around him and instead looked straight through them. *His eyes are at once innocent and wicked,* Natàlia thought. Since she was seated, Màrius kissed her on the forehead. Then, without once looking at her, he sat across from her at the table. That's no way to greet your godmother, Sílvia said. Don't worry about it, Natàlia replied. How else should he greet me? I haven't given him much to remember me by. Màrius stared down at his plate and shuffled his legs from side to side. He had a large whitehead on his right cheek, which he rested on the palm of his hand. It was still visible, even though he had popped it earlier that morning. They talked about Aunt Patrícia for a while, poking fun at her colitis and at the latch on the door. She's scared someone will break in. Or that a strange man will abduct her, Lluís joked. Sílvia said they had to admit Patrícia had changed a great deal since Esteve's death. She told me she knows the truth about life now and that she feels as if she was robbed. She doesn't drink Aromes de Montserrat anymore, not since acquiring a taste for Cuba Libres and Jumilla wine. She has her hair dyed every week—I'm sure you noticed when you saw her. She's even started smoking and getting her nails done. After lunch she and Encarna will go to Can Jorba or El Corte Inglés and wander around the department stores without buying a thing. One time I saw them at Moka eating an ice cream as tall as a cathedral. I know, it's crazy. She even goes to the cinema at night. The woman is throwing money away. This, in Lluís's opinion, was the crux of the story. She doesn't charge her tenants enough. I've told her to sell the other flats, maybe even as office space. But the woman is stubborn as a mule, says she has plenty to live on. We'll see how she feels when the well runs dry. Esteve's annuity isn't even enough to pay for a retirement facility like Llars Mundet. She's careless, Lluís concluded. I guess Dad must be in Gualba, then? Natàlia asked. Màrius looked up and made an almost imperceptible movement. Sílvia glanced at Lluís out of the corner of her eye. Lluís confirmed their father was in Gualba. I suppose it's for the best, Natàlia said. I get to put it off a bit longer. I don't feel like seeing him just yet. What's he up to these days? Has retirement aged him? No, Lluís said a bit brusquely, but Natàlia wasn't listening; she had turned to face Màrius, and they were discussing the Rolling Stones. They're losing popularity in England. Kids there can't get Jimi Hendrix out of their minds, and they think Zappa is a joke. No, they can't be, Màrius said. I've listened to *Goats Head Soup*—it's a masterpiece. The only reason those men can play music at all is that they're on drugs, Sílvia said. So what? If it helps with creativity. Besides, what do you know? Màrius asked his mother. I know what I've read, honey. Last year they arrested whatshisface—Keith Richards, Màrius interrupted. That's right. They arrested Keith Richards after drugs were found in his house. Mom, no one cares . . . While Sílvia and Màrius argued, Lluís realized why he had been in such a foul mood that morn-

ing: Natàlia. Yes, Natàlia, showing up out of the blue, ready to
stir the pot. They retired to the sitting room for coffee, which
Sílvia served on an oval tray. They sat on the corduroy poufs
around a low glass table. On top of it was a large object. What's
this doodad? Natàlia asked. A lighter, Sílvia answered. It's designer, Lluís added. Sílvia was on the floor, propped against a
faux-silk cushion. She wore peachskin trousers the color of pa-
paya and a black blouse. She had on several pendants, including
a small ivory horn—she joked with her gym friends that it was a
reminder of her philandering husband. Natàlia asked after Sílvia's family. Anything new? Sílvia sighed and said, So much!
Grandma died, as you know, and Gèlia drowned in Calella last
year. My parents were devastated. Mamà aged twenty years in a
week . . . You know they left the place on Carrer Aribau, right?
They bought a flat in Pedralbes . . . Papà's business is booming . . .
I never know what Nasi is up to, or where he is—Brazil maybe,
or Chile. He hasn't written in a long time. Grandma died with a
broken heart. Sílvia perked up. Oh, yes! Mundeta is getting married. Finally, Lluís said. She's changed a lot, Sílvia continued.
She left home during that big hoo-ha at the university and became a bit of a hippy. Now she's working at a school. Who's the
lucky guy? Natàlia asked. A lawyer who's also in politics. His
father is one of the founders of the Democratic Union of Catalonia, Lluís said. Her fiancé has been to prison a couple of times.
Very pro-Catalonia, Sílvia added. Natàlia smiled. Mundeta is
marrying someone in the UDC? Didn't you tell me in a letter
that she was a borderline Trotskyite? It's all the same to me, Sílvia said. Except it isn't, Natàlia replied. Lluís, who was nursing a
glass of Torres 10 brandy, said both sides engaged in old-world
politics. What people want is good, comfortable living. You were
in England, you should know. It's "welfare" politics that counts.
And neither the right nor the left can pull that off. I see you
haven't changed, Natàlia said. Still refusing to pick a side. Lluís
downed the rest of his brandy, I just want to be able to say hello

like an ordinary person and go back to minding my own business. The days when people only greeted each other one of two ways—with raised fists or straightened hands—are long gone. That thief Puig Antich—Màrius cut in, He wasn't a thief, Dad. Whatever. That anarchist Puig Antich poked the bear. He was a moron—Màrius turned to Natàlia. Dad is still a centrist, as you can tell. Do you support the death penalty? Natàlia asked Lluís. Listen, he said, I'm a man of Europe, not some backward Spanish jingoist. What if someone rapes you in the street? Sílvia wondered aloud. What are you supposed to do then? Lluís laughed. Don't go getting any ideas, sweetheart. In any event, those zealots are going to make a mess of things and ruin our chances of joining the Common Market. You don't care that Puig Antich died, do you? Màrius asked. OK, that's enough politics for one day, Sílvia said. Let's end lunch on a good note. Then she turned to Natàlia: Are you doing anything tomorrow? We could get together . . . I'm going to meet up with an editor. I need to find a job. Lluís said nothing. Oh, a job—how wonderful! Lluís turned to Natàlia. This one has got it into her pretty little head that she wants to join the workforce—when she could be enjoying the joys of *dolce far niente*! As Lluís said this, he stretched out his arms and yawned loudly. You'll have to excuse me, it's time for my nap. I'm useless if I don't get my ten minutes in after lunch. He turned to Natàlia. We have more than a month of Sundays to catch up.

Natàlia thinks it's sweet that you like poetry, that you're so committed to the form, Sílvia said to Màrius, who turned red as a tomato, all the way to the tips of his ears. I'm not exactly committed, he said, holding his hand over the pimple on his cheek. On weekends, a group of us visit Roser Roura at her flat in Begur and read poetry together. Roser Roura is a divorcée and mother of four, Sílvia clarified snidely. Roser Roura is an extraordinary woman, Màrius snapped back. Do you write poetry? Natàlia asked. Some friends and I wrote a *Manifiesto*. In Spanish? Natàlia pressed. Yeah, in Spanish. We also read Verlaine, Rimbaud, Baudelaire . . . What's your *Manifiesto* about? About literature, about how we've outgrown every poetic form that has been used until now. About needing to leave behind social and political poetry. Roser Roura says poetry is about something else . . . Natàlia stared at Màrius's strawberry lips and remembered a poem by the other Màrius: "Now that the mighty arms of the furies raze / to the ground the city of ideals we wanted to build . . ." His lips were sensual, young. He's in love with Roser Roura, Natàlia thought, they may even be sleeping together. Màrius leaned his face on his hand so that his pimple was completely hidden. Natàlia nearly missed Sílvia's question: I bet we seem different to you, don't we?

PART TWO
PERFUME OF AUTUMN

We never entered.
We were sloughing off our skins, and had
no interest in the tatters of the old one.
Our nostrils were filled with the fear which was
the perfume of that autumn.

GABRIEL FERRATER, "In memoriam"
(tr. Christopher Whyte)

Aunt Patrícia had never been pretty. Her skin was dry, the color of parched soil. You look like you're from the drylands, Esteve always told her. Broad-shouldered, with eyes that were like drill holes from up close and vanished beneath a pair of bushy eyebrows from afar. You Miralpeixes look like hardliving people, Esteve used to say. From the bags under your eyes, anyone might think you had crawled out of the gutter. She tried lightening the dark, wrinkled circles with a rosy powder, but it was useless—they always showed through as the day wore on. You people wither before your time, Esteve added. Her nose didn't end in a hook so much as hint at one, and her cheeks were taut, as though the skin had bunched behind her ears. Patrícia's prettiest feature was her hands, "the object of everyone's envy." They were long, slender, pale—their pale elegance contrasting with her weathered complexion. "Your hands are exquisite," Esteve would tell her whenever he went through a phase of wanting not to offend her. "We usually see hands as purely functional vertebrate extremities: we use them to grasp objects, scratch ourselves, button up our clothes, point, caress. The only time you notice someone's hands is when they're beautiful. That's why everyone always looks at yours." Esteve dedicated a noucentista sonnet to Patrícia that began: "La meva vida i el meu cos / les teves mans han buscat / com un vaixell ancorat . . ." *Like an anchored boat, your hands have sought out my life and body.* One time, when he had money, Esteve bought her a couple of rings, one with a gemstone the size of a chickpea.

Patrícia's hands were melancholy, at times a bit distracted—"a prude's hands," Lluís called them—modest, and somewhat underused. "I bet her hands wouldn't be so smooth if they were always in bleach like mine," Encarna said. They were hands that coddled other people's children, the hands of a barren woman who stroked flowers on spring evenings and ran her fingertips along the fallen leaves of plane trees in autumn, hands that searched for a point on the horizon, that parted Judit's prematurely white hair and tenderly patted it down, closing her eyelids when she breathed her last, hands that probed the mysteries of pain and made the sign of the cross while damp with holy water, that gripped each other on dark nights of air raids and gave out sweets to the children of the poor, hands that patiently unlaced her corset when she was fat and lathered her body in lotion now that she was slender. Those same hands trembled with passion and despair when they smashed the cherub's mouth one hot night when she felt she might be going mad . . . A distant passion that died on the wind, like the sound of a hunting horn. Her hands parted like a virgin about to surrender, then closed like a dying man who has accepted death. But the cherub didn't have a mouth and could no longer smile. Now Patrícia wore her nails long, manicured—mahogany to match her hair—and they were skilled at solitaire and nimble at uncorking bottles of wine. The cherub was gone, as was the garden where she had known sorrow. These same hands traced the monogrammed letters on her sheets at night and made morning plans to hunt down the specks of dust that filtered through the shutters into her bedroom as rays of sunlight. Patrícia's hands look like they belong to someone else, Sílvia said—they're the hands of an artist.

Now Patrícia says she drinks to drown her sorrows. She knows it isn't a sin: Jesus turned water into wine during the wedding at Cana; Jesus spoke a great deal about wineries and winemakers; Jesus made the wine his blood at the Last Supper. Patrícia had read it in the Bible: "No one sews a patch of un-shrunk cloth on an old garment, for the patch will pull away from the garment, making the tear worse. Neither do people pour new wine into old wineskins. If they do, the skins will burst; the wine will run out and the wineskins will be ruined. No, they pour new wine into new wineskins, and both are preserved." Jesus Christ poured wine on wounds and did not force anyone to fast. Those who take Christ into their hearts are not sad. Patrícia had been awfully sad, but she isn't anymore—now the wine melts away her sorrows. She wants to banish her sadness, which is like a flock of pecking crows circling her day and night. She used to only drink Aromes de Montserrat. These days she pre-fers wine, warm Jumilla wine that reddens her cheeks and settles her throat. When she drinks, the crows scatter and keep their distance. Patrícia drinks to be happy but instead of happiness she feels a deep sorrow, deep like a night thick with swooping crows. She doesn't want to shed a single tear. She doesn't know why, but lately she has been visited by the dead. The men and women in her life who have died sit beside her to chat. There's Paquita, whose moon face twists into laughter; Judit, whose eyes are both present and far away; Kati looking at her wryly with her waxed eyebrows and tricot outfits; Mundeta Jover, whose long hair is like a bird's wings, her hands beams of moonlight; and Esteve, who doesn't even look at her . . . They all speak over each other, their murmuring voices coming and going as if she were walking in and out of her bedroom, and sometimes the voices are like echoes, sometimes they are right in her ear. Kati: Patrícia, you're alive and well and yet pushing up daisies. Mundeta: Come with me, Patrícia, what's the point of suffering? Esteve: You speak eastern Catalan. Tell me, does *ressò* rhyme with *cançó*? . . .

. . . poet, Poet with a capital P, Esteve called himself. Even when they were at their most down and out, he still sat at the table between original pieces by Casas and Nonell, surrounded

by the hand-embroidered, cross-stitch tablecloths, the silverware—
when it wasn't at the pawn shop—and the Limoges dinner service. Patrícia would ask him, What would you like for dinner?
and Esteve would say, The Poet would like pheasant, *huîtres
vertes de Marennes, dessert assorti,* and a bottle of 1891 Bordeaux.
Then Patrícia would turn to the housemaid and tell her, Mr.
Miràngels will have a one-egg omelet. The housemaid, if she
didn't leave them to work for a better family, served their supper
in gloves and a bonnet, a black uniform with white lace at the
neckline and cuffs, and a fine white apron. There were many
nights when Patrícia did not eat—though this wasn't necessarily
a bad thing, since in doing so she lost weight—while the housemaid ate a two-egg omelet, so that she wouldn't leave the Miràngels for another family. Esteve would say, You may be a country
girl, but my relations are counts and marquises. I can't stand
such misery . . . They were starving because her father, heir of
Casamitjana, one of the best houses in Gualba, had cut out his
three children. "Such an esteemed house fallen from grace. I
wonder what bird of ill omen entered that home," whispered the
gaggles of old women. "One daughter a whore, the other married
to a charlatan who fancies himself a nobleman, and the son, the
heir, wandering around God's green earth, neglecting the estate."

And it was true, Casamitjana was one of the finest estates in
all of Gualba, with land as far down as the foothills of Montseny.
Patrícia's great-grandfather was awarded a cross of military
merit by Isabella II of Spain for his service in the First Carlist
War. He had died right outside the masia, and to this day there is
a record of his bloodstain: a rough black patch edged in gold that
the elder Casamitjana commissioned from a religious artist in
Barcelona, in honor of the family hero. For a long time, his medal
sat on a scarlet velvet cushion in a glass display case in the piano
room. Casamitjana had produced two other heroes as well, both
in the war against the little French general: the family claims a

relation to Father Joan Salarich, "illustrious poet and valiant nobleman, executed by Napoleon's battle-hardened army," and to Mother Carrió, a saint. Well, not yet, though rumor had it the Pope would beatify her soon enough. Mother Carrió was a nun and hero of the Napoleonic war. It's said that during the siege of Zaragoza,

> Mother Carrió prevailed thanks to her self-sacrifice and heroism, ministering with extraordinary care to countless wounded and traveling to dangerous places in service of her charitable missions, accompanied by other nuns. In one assault the hospital caught fire, and with extraordinary effort and encouragement from their superior—this superior being Mother Carrió—the nuns were able to save a few patients (the account fails to mention that many of these helpless creatures were cruelly violated, while others simply vanished, their fates unknown). This tragic war was followed by a famine that killed some of the patients they had rescued, as well as nine sisters. Out of the twenty-one nuns who set out in the beginning, only three remained.

It was in these critical circumstances that Mother Carrió and the two remaining nuns traversed enemy fire to the site from which General Lannes (who had been apprenticed as a dyer and fought closely with Napoleon during the Coup of 18 Brumaire) lay siege to Zaragoza. There she was able (we still don't know how) to convince them to hand over a few essential resources. Mother Carrió's sway over the general was so great that she succeeded in preventing several more of her distinguished patriots from falling under enemy power.

Given their lineage, it was only natural for the elder Miralpeix of Casamitjana to be suspicious of the newcomer, this impoverished scion with his baseless airs of grandeur. Miralpeix Sr. summed him up with a single phrase: The man's a layabout.

"What can he possibly have to offer you?" he asked Patrícia. "Don't you see he wants you for your fortune?" Her father threatened to cut her off if she married Esteve, leaving her with nothing—no trousseau, no crystal that chimed when you flicked it, naught. But marry him she did, and still inherited her grandmother's slip, her mother's lace shawl, the bridal nightgown that had belonged to her great-grandmother, grandmother, and mother before her; the satin robes, the Japanese kimono with silver embroidery, the damask table linen and a set of sewing threads, the twelve dozen handkerchiefs, the silk undergarments, her aunts' Manila shawls, the gauze robe with lilac marabou edge . . . In other words, everything the heiress of a house as esteemed as Casamitjana could possibly hope for. Patrícia also had her eye on a satin bedspread printed with large blue flowers she had seen in a magazine in Paris. Patrícia was in love with Esteve when she married him, there's no denying it. He was so well-spoken, with his rounded *o*'s and that turn of phrase he used to express disbelief: when Esteve said *poc que te crec* very fast, it sounded to Patrícia like a train chugging down the tracks . . . Besides, Esteve wrote poetry and kissed her earlobes. And his kisses sent a warm feeling up her legs and all the way to the top of her head . . .

. . . all their troubles began, Patrícia would tell you, when Esteve insisted they move to Barcelona. One fine day her brother Joan had simply left without a trace, making her the heiress of Casamitjana. "We threw such dinner parties! We'd leave the doors wide open, and the house would fill with people. Poor men and women from around the region came to the masia to eat turkey and capon, and the wine flowed freely. One time a traveler wandered in, thinking it was an inn. We were powerful and spared no expense. It was a time of merriment and joy . . ." When she spoke about it, no one could tell if Patrícia was lying. But Patrícia, who loved fresh-cut fields soaked in sunlight and dark, humid forests of centuries-old trees, who loved the estate's cypress-lined paths and the black poplars that kissed the Gualba riverside, she hadn't been raised for the country or the city. In the country, she languished. In the city, people thought her provincial. She could cook, play the "Turkish March," and cross-stitch, and that was about the extent of it. She was fat and ugly—so fat she had to sit on two chairs. A pair of Isabelina chairs were placed side by side in the piano room, never to be moved again. One fine day, Horaci Mir arrived in Gualba in the company of a tall, corpulent man with brown hair and a ruddy face. He was a poet and friend of Horaci, a poet in his own right who was engaged to one of the poorest girls in the region, a close friend of Patrícia. The poet's name was Esteve Miràngels. His family had been bankrupted by phylloxera. He was from l'Empordà on his mother's side, and neck-deep in debt. Esteve had asked his friend Horaci: Who is the richest girl in Gualba? And Horaci had asked his fiancée: Who is the richest girl in Gualba? And his fiancée had said: Patrícia Miralpeix of Casamitjana; her brother is a waster, and his father cut him out.

. . . and so they married, and the wedding was a lavish affair. They say half the region attended and the other half died of envy. Esteve wrote a long, hendecasyllabic poem for the bride and the bride wept for joy. That night Patrícia wore the nightgown that had been her grandmother's, and great-grandmother's, and her mother's as well. It didn't fit her and needed to be let out at the seams: Patrícia's foremothers had been quite a lot thinner. Patrícia got undressed in another room, then came back in the white floor-length nightgown, naked underneath, her eyes cast down. In the area of her lower belly, around crotch-height: a hole so miniscule not even a cherrywood branch would fit through it. At first Esteve was perplexed. Then furious. Finally, he burst out laughing. He chortled loud and hard, and his laughter haunted Patrícia for a long while. Esteve kept laughing as he tore off her nightgown, gripped her shoulders, and pushed her onto the bed. Patrícia squeezed her thighs shut, her hands—so beautiful and white—clasping the hand-embroidered sheets. But Esteve was already on top of her, elbow digging into her neck and knee at her crotch, trying to pry open her legs. The pressure lasted only a moment, but to Patrícia it felt like an eternity. Finally she gave in. His leg squirmed between her legs and something stiff pushed into her inner thigh. Esteve nibbled her all over and said, Pubilla, my sweet heiress, I shall make you all mine. She closed her eyes, maybe even prayed. They rolled around the rumpled sheets, which had been her grandmother's and great-grandmother's before her. The satin bedspread printed with blue flowers slipped away. Patrícia screwed up her face and let herself go. The bed, which was improbably tall, lurched, and it felt as if the springs might give and send them both onto the floor at any moment. As the satin bedspread printed with blue flowers tangled around her legs, she felt a warm liquid hit her lower belly.

Patrícia's father was rather miserly, and the maids the sole beneficiaries of his generosity: he had children scattered all over Gualba and Sant Celoni, and all his former lovers wore cultured pearl earrings in memory of their fugitive intimacy. As is to be expected, father and son-in-law did not see eye to eye. They argued constantly, and things grew even more heated when the conversation turned to politics, with the fall of Prime Minister Miguel Primo de Rivera. Esteve was a Catalan patriot and Patrícia's father was not; or rather, Patrícia's father believed work to be the primary source of wealth and said he could not abide layabouts—this was directed at Esteve, who seemed always to be wandering around the country estate twiddling his thumbs. They agreed on one thing only: that the crop-contracts law, which protected tenant farmers, had been cooked up by a band of imbeciles. Patrícia's father was a member of the Catalan agricultural association, L'Institut de Sant Isidre, and sent money to the campaign in Madrid lobbying against this new law.

Esteve and Patrícia had spent long stretches of time in the flat on Gran Via, between Bruc and Girona, which he inherited from his mother. Two years before the war started, when Miralpeix Sr. realized they would give him no grandchildren and decided to cut out his daughter, they moved there for good. He left his fortune, including the house and land, to Hospital Sant Pau and the Little Sisters of the Poor. When the heir of Casamitjana saw he wasn't long for this world, he had a pang of remorse and made a pair of minor adjustments to his last will and testament: the house in Gualba went to his two eldest children, Patrícia and Joan, while the forest in Turó de l'Home went to Paquita, his youngest. Miralpeix Sr. had a washroom all to himself—he carried the key with him at all times—and when he died—they say it was a horrific death, that he swam in shit for three days and three nights, and that no one, not even the maids or any of his relatives, could bring themselves to clean him up—Esteve nailed a sign to the washroom door that said "House of Slop." Without the forest or the fields, the property in Gualba gradually deteriorated—the orchard boundary crumbled, paint flaked off the walls, plants withered, and the cypress trees shriveled. All that was left was the old groundsman, who minded the animals. Later, when Esteve Miràngels was an old man, he sold Patrícia's part to his brother-in-law, Joan Miralpeix, who agreed to buy it because he believed no sister of his should go hungry.

Esteve had slowly exhausted his remaining sources of income. The vineyards he'd inherited from his father, the wheatfields—which "brimmed with golden ears," as he wrote in one of his poems—the house in Begur . . . After the war ended, he would walk to L'Ateneu every day and sit by the pond among the cats and turtles, hobnobbing with the relics of a dying world. He wrote poems—he struggled with open and closed vowels—that some blundering, starved musician would adapt into sardanas. At the Gran Via flat, Esteve was able to stop time: he adored the original paintings, the collector's-edition books displayed in glass cases, the library, the Sèvres vases and velvet drapes. He and Patrícia barely ate, but they had a housemaid who opened the door for them in a bonnet and lace apron. Whenever they owed her several months of back pay, Patrícia would pawn some of her silverware. Every now and then, Judit would send steak and vegetables, as would Mundeta Ventura, who never forgot the sacks of potatoes Patrícia had sent her from Gualba during the war.

Esteve refused to work "because no one had, or ever would, boss him around." Before long Patrícia was on first-name terms with every broker at the pawn shop. She pawned the silverware, the crystal—the kind that chimed when you flicked it—the rings Esteve had given her, and her mother's ruby necklace. The prisms fell from the dining room chandelier, her great-grandfather's clock stopped ticking, the bridal chest was worm-eaten, and the velvet drapes warped, the mahogany table wobbled, the dinner service was chipped, and there were chunks missing from the modernist figurines. Patrícia awoke several nights to a faint rustling sound: the mice were gnawing at the satin Empire-style chairs. Patrícia did all she could to convince Esteve, who was on his deathbed and riddled with disease, to let her pawn the Casas and Nonell paintings. They never got them back; Esteve Miràngels, noucentista poet, died with this disillusionment inside him. During the war Esteve had his neck saved by Kati, "who went as red as a radish the moment things got serious," after the groundsman of the masia in Gualba started making things hot for him. According to legend, Esteve hosted a party at the house in March 1936, perhaps in celebration of the elder Miralpeix's passing. He lied to his friends, saying his wife had inherited everything, including the forests and the land, and then invited them over for a feast. Spurred by the desire to flaunt his vast wealth, Esteve had the groundsman wear livery and gloves and serve them dinner on a silver platter. Later, when Esteve was three sheets to the wind, he ordered the groundsman to dress in a tattered bridal nightgown with a hole in the center. His friends cried with laughter. The groundsman never forgot this and in 1937, with the support of the Committee of Anti-Fascist Militias of Sant Celoni, had Esteve Miràngels thrown in jail. Kati, a friend of Patrícia, pulled strings in the Department of Justice of the Generalitat, and the whole thing was chalked up to a harmless joke. But when Patrícia and her husband sheltered from the air raids of 1938 in an aunt's house in Gualba—by then their property had been confiscated—the groundsman made Esteve dress as a footman and serve him at the table while his militant friends roared with laughter. Esteve never forgot this either. When the Nationalists arrived in Barcelona in 1939, Esteve Miràngels, of noble lineage, turned him in. The groundsman died of typhus in 1943 at the concentration camp in León to which he was deported.

Esteve died before Judit, and his was a slow, agonizing death. He would rant and rave, Get her off of me, get her off! harking back to a time when Patrícia had needed two Isabelina chairs to support her weight. Esteve lost control of his bowels. Your husband has always been a filthy pig, said Sixta, a relation of Mundeta Jover, who lived around the corner from Patrícia. Patrícia cleaned up after her husband every day while Esteve wept: Look at me, pubilla, look at what I've become. You're a saint. I don't deserve all you do for me, Patrícia. Wouldn't you do the same? she asked him in a sudden surge of tenderness, smoothing the bedsheets with her angelic hands. No!!! the dying man screamed. Sixta came back and said, When his nose gets narrower, that's when you'll know his time has come. And Mundeta queried, You do realize you have to plug all his holes? Mundeta, Sixta, and a pair of neighbors sat together and whispered to each other. Every now and then, when the sick man gasped, the women crowded around him: Hurry, it's his death rattle. They'd shush each other, prick their ears, and then listen to him gasping. But then his breathing steadied, and the neighbors would say, No, not yet, then sit back down to carry on gossiping. Patrícia was terrified Esteve would die at night when she was alone—the housemaid had left them—so she had him taken to L'Aliança, where they washed him and brushed his hair, leaving him "clean as a whistle, all nice and fragrant," then plugged catheters all over his body, even his rectum. Ay, pubilla, they're violating me! the poet screamed from his deathbed. At first Esteve clung to his agnosticism and refused last rites, but Patrícia—and the fear of nothingness—convinced him otherwise, and he took Holy Communion. Father Dalla, a chaplain and patriotic poet, administered the Eucharist. The dithyrambic poet Horaci Mirs wrote a florid obituary for his friend, which ran in several regional journals. He looks like he's asleep, Sixta noted with a sigh. He's very debonair—they've done a fabulous job, Mundeta said. Don't worry, he didn't suffer, added her daughter, Joan Claret's wife. Patrícia attended the burial dressed head to toe in black and swathed in the black veil that had belonged to her mother, grandmother, and great-grandmother before her. She said a solemn prayer for the soul of her dead husband. Horaci Mir's wife observed, Dreadfully pale, isn't she? Yes, Sixta replied, but did you notice she hasn't shed a single tear? And the two women glanced sidelong at one another. When the men went to the cemetery, Patrícia stayed back, claiming she wished to be alone. She entered her flat and drew the latch on the door. The sound of the locking mechanism startled her. The dining room was quiet and gloomy. A low light fell on the objects inside. Her great-grandfather's clock was silent. She ran her finger along the velvet drapes, the silver fruit bowl, and the Empire-style chairs, the ones with nibbled satin. She opened the display case and took out a crystal wine glass, the kind that chimed when you flicked it. She went to the kitchen and opened a bottle of champagne that Esteve had reserved for guests. And she drank the whole thing in slow, dainty sips.

Patrícia called out to Encarna, Won't you have a glass of dessert wine? Encarna was getting married the next day. Patrícia said, Come on, let's celebrate. Don't you think we should tell Natàlia about her father, Mrs. Miràngels? Oh, hush. Lluís promised he would do it himself. Why make more trouble? Encarna took off her apron and hung it behind the kitchen door. Every night before bed, she enjoyed a small glass of ratafia with Mrs. Miràngels. I feel sorry for the old thing, she told herself. She's going to be all alone now. But Encarna had a life to live, for Pete's sake. Besides, Jaume was handsome and owned a flat. I promise I'll visit, Mrs. Miràngels. Oh, tosh, you're going to forget all about me. Encarna studied her hands. Even though she had moisturized them several times that day, they were still chapped and wrinkly from the bleach and powdered dish soap. Don't drink too much now, Mrs. Miràngels. It isn't good for you. Encarna said the same thing every night, and much like all those other nights, Patrícia had already polished off two glasses of Jumilla wine and was starting on her third. Encarna poured herself some ratafia. You forget that my stomach is young and my liver tough as nails. Encarna lowered her head and said nothing—what was there to say? *Hermano, bebe, que la vida es breve,* Patrícia teased. Bottoms up, life is short . . . She ought to have asked the hairdresser to do her hands too, Encarna thought. She wouldn't have time tomorrow. She had a couple of errands to run in the morning. She needed to pick her dress up from Pronovias at eleven—they swore they'd have it ready by then—and the wedding ceremony was at six that evening. The Pronovias salesgirls were a bunch of twits—couldn't they see the chest and ass on her? They kept on bringing out petite sizes. What about women like her who got married later in life, hmm? Fashion workers seem to think all women are stick figures . . . In the end, they had to let out the dress, taking it apart at the seams and sewing it back up again. They said you wouldn't be able to tell—let's see about that. Her sister Rosalia thought she was nuts. Getting a wedding dress tailored like you're still twenty years old! You should've had them make you a two-piece suit and black waistcoat—not this sappy nonsense that isn't the least bit flattering. People are going to think you're in costume and laugh. But Encarna wanted something romantic, and she'd fallen for a mousseline gown that was tight at the waist and flared at the bottom, with wide sleeves and a lace neckline. It's like Romy Schneider's in *Sissi: The Young Empress,* the Pronovias salesgirls told her. On her head she would wear the lace veil Mrs. Miralpeix had given her—it matched the neckline. I haven't worked like a dog, pinching pennies my whole life, not to have the wedding I want, she grumbled. Patrícia agreed and finished off her third glass in one gulp. Yes, Encarna was absolutely right. When people get married—*if* they get married—they ought to have the wedding they want. Although sometimes I do wonder if we're better off left on the shelf—what good has being wed done me? Don't talk like that, Encarna objected. Mr. Miràngels was a fine, educated man. Yes, he was very fine, but we barely had enough to eat. Here come the waterworks, Encarna thought. I used to wear silk hosiery, you know, Patrícia continued. Except it was full of ladders. I want you to be the most sophisticated woman in all the city, Esteve would say and buy me silk socks and gauze stockings that instantly snagged, then refuse to replace them. Everyone in the neighborhood laughed at my darned stockings. Esteve used to take her to the Liceu to watch *Madama Butterfly* and *Lohengrin* and then vanish during the interval. On top of that, she would see several pairs of opera glasses scanning her booth . . . Patrícia laughed, and her laughter was quiet, restrained. Did you know that Esteve ran off with Mr. Claret's tart? That's Sílvia's father, by the way. Well I never! Encarna said, although she knew the story inside out. That's right. Her name was Dorita, and she would perform onstage dressed as a peacock. Swaddled in feathers, she plucked them out one by one until she was stark naked. Heavens! Encarna exclaimed. Encarna let Patrícia talk. *Here comes the drama.* You'll feel lousy tomorrow if you're not careful, Mrs. Miràngels. But Patrícia carried on. Mundeta Sr., God rest her soul, found out about her during the war when a short, ordinary-looking woman knocked on the Clarets' front door. She spoke like a *xava,* in a mix of Catalan and Spanish. I know my Juanito lives here, don't lie. I want to see him. Mundeta was dumbstruck. Patrícia chuckled again as she sipped her fourth glass of Jumilla. It was May 1938 or thereabouts. Mundeta Sr. had come down from Siurana and Joan was in San Sebastián. It was a good thing she was the one at home and not her daughter: Mundeta Ventura was pregnant and seeing that woman on their doorstep would've given her an awful scare. Did you know Mundeta Jr. almost lost Sílvia, her baby? She thought her husband had been buried alive in that famous air raid on the Coliseum and nearly miscarried. Mrs. Miràngels, if you keep on like this you won't be able to stand on your own two feet tomorrow, Encarna said . . . Never mind that, I want to tell you how Esteve met that bimbo, Dorita. As I was saying, Mundeta Sr. stood there wondering what to do about the banshee shrieking at her front door. My daughter might come home any minute, she thought to herself, then decided the matter ought to be handled by a man. So she grabbed Dorita and went looking for Esteve, who was at L'Ateneu. And that, Encarna, is how Esteve met Dorita, *"an authentic, sizzling rumba dancer from the Dominican Republic."* That tramp may have danced rumba at La Bohèmia, but she was born right here in our city, in Barceloneta. Mundeta, who knew about these things, said Dorita didn't hold a candle up to Raquel Meller, whose performance of "El Relicario" at L'Arnau was just divine. Maybe she was trying to make me feel better. You mean the one Sarita Montiel sings in *The Last Torch Song*? Encarna asked. Yes, Patrícia said, the one about *el día de San Eugenio*. Encarna grew animated. The dessert wine warmed her stomach and stirred her hips. She bellowed, *"yendo hassia al Pardo le conossí!!!"* and then Encarna and Patrícia sang together, *"era torero de más tronío, el más castisso de to'o Madriiit, iba en calesa, pidiendo guerra, y yo al notarulu m'estremessiiiii."* Encarna shook her breasts like a pair of bell clappers, while Patrícia, cheeks red and eyes closed, shimmied her body all over, *"bajo del cotxa y muy garbosu vino hassia miiii."* Their voices drifted up the lightwell. Over the rush of open taps, the clink of forks beating eggs, the hiss of a pressure cooker, and the split-splat of oil in a pan rose the sound of two raspy voices, *pisa morena, pisa con garbo, que un relicario, que un relicario, te voy a hacer.* The pipes leaked. There was the smell of fried fish and steamed Romanesco broccoli. Dorita was low-class, you know, Patrícia said. A Jezebel who thought she could shake her ass to rumba and conquer the whole wide world. Do you think an ass shake is powerful enough to conquer the world? And Encarna said, I guess it depends how well you shake it. It's an art form, you know. Is this how it's done? Patrícia asked, her body tipping to the left. Easy there, Mrs. Miràngels. If only I had shiny peacock feathers, a shimmering sequin dress, and could drape myself in mohair . . . Patrícia sat back down. No, Dorita wasn't sophisticated in the least, but Esteve fell for her anyway and even dedicated an entire book of poems to her. He didn't like the name Dorita, so he changed it to Teresa. The dedication read: "After Teresa from Eugeni D'Ors, *La Ben Plantada.*" He published the collection himself at a print shop run by a man who frequented L'Ateneu and could hardly publish in Catalan because all the Catalan writers, the good ones anyhow, had jumped ship . . . You know what Esteve couldn't live with? The fact that he never found success. People say I'm a me-diocre poet, he used to cry. Me, a genius! Encarna started to get up. Come on, Mrs. Miràngels, or you'll have an awful bellyache tomorrow. Wait a second, Patrícia said and waved at Encarna to sit down. Like I was saying, Esteve dedicated a book to Dorita called *Sonnets for Teresa*. Meanwhile, I still had to remind him that *ressò* didn't rhyme with *remor*! Because he couldn't tell the difference between open and close vowels. But you're from An-dalusia! What would you know about open and close vowels? Patrícia couldn't stop laughing. Wait a second, wait, Encarna, let me finish the story. That tramp, that *vedette*, got a book of sonnets. She was a cow.

Encarna corked the bottle of wine. That's enough now, Mrs. Miràngels. It's time to go to bed.

That was why Encarna wanted to get married—*I'm sick and tired of listening to the old drunk's sob stories. I already did my time, put-ting up with Natàlia's father's eccentricities.*

Patrícia woke at midnight with colitis and a splitting head-ache. Her hand clutching her belly, she had the urge to run to the bathroom, but didn't make it in time and soiled herself instead. *I'll have to put a chamber pot under the bed.* Patrícia tiptoed to the kitchen to fetch the cleaning rag—she mustn't wake Encarna. A fine, persistent drizzle fell outside, and the sky was a solid gray mass. Patrícia scrubbed the bedroom floor and changed out of her nightgown. She opened the mirrored wardrobe and felt around for her stack of old nightgowns, the ones mended a thousand times over. Her silk and gauze bridal nightgowns, which she had worn once or twice at most, were in a separate stack. She soaked the soiled nightgown in the bidet with some powdered soap, *I'll get out of bed early tomorrow morning and rinse it before Encarna wakes up.* She glanced at herself in the bathroom mirror: *I look out of sorts.* Patrícia was under the weather: she had heartburn, a throbbing headache, and her tongue felt like a wad of cotton wool. She had to relieve herself again. This time, thankfully, she made it. She hitched up her nightgown and sat on the toilet. Liquid splashed into the bowl and the stench perme-ated the washroom. At least her stomach wasn't rigid anymore. *My belly feels empty.* She wiped herself carefully, pulled the chain, and washed her hands with a special tropical-scented soap that she kept wrapped in onionskin paper in her nightstand drawer so that Encarna wouldn't use it. Her tongue felt tacky, as if her mouth were full of sawdust. She lumbered back to the bedroom.

She placed her hands on her lower back. *I'm so tired. I'll never drink again, I swear.* A picture of Mother Carrió glowered at her from the nightstand. I don't believe you, it said. Your loss, Patrícia thought, turning the picture around. She heard the street door, a thud, and the slide of the locking mechanism. *Natàlia's home.* Then she heard a smaller door open and immediately close again. *Good girl, she remembered the gas.*

Patrícia knew full well what happened when she drank: *I think too much, and it makes my brain hurt.* While the wine was trickling down her throat she felt deliciously warm, as though her mouth were filled with all the sweets in the world. Her body came back to life, and she could feel blood coursing through her limbs. *Everything is twinkling,* she thought, and her head clouded with joy. *Everything is the color of mist, and I feel so happy I could cry.* Patrícia knew she always told Encarna the same old story: about Esteve's fancy women, the runs in her sheer stockings, the mended slips. "I don't care if people know about it. I don't care if they think I'm a fool," she said to herself, weeping between each glug of wine. Then at night, when the light filtered through the shutter slats and the shadows of the streetlamps loomed into her bedroom—*it's death closing in*—when she heard the intermittent rumble of cars and buses crossing Gran Via, at night Patrícia felt truly sad. She felt sad because she thought about her secret, a secret she had never shared with anyone. She thought about Gonçal.

Gonçal Rodés was a poet like Esteve. He had honeyed eyes and a smile from ear to ear. His cheeks were slender, a little sunken, and his hair flopped over his forehead. Now and then he listened wincingly to the nonsense coming out of Esteve's mouth, an alarmed look in his eyes. Gonçal was gentle to Patrícia. The two had whiled away many an hour in the conservatory while waiting for Esteve. They talked: Gonçal was from Cerdanya and adored the Cadí mountain range. It's never the same color, he told Patrícia. On summer evenings it's flaming copper and at night like the plumage of a falcon; in the mornings it's mint-green, and at noon the color of fresh grass. It changes in winter too—bright white and slate gray, or ashy with stars . . . Patrícia would close her eyes and think of the newly cut fields and dark forests that edged Turó de l'Home, of the oaks and holm oaks around the masia in Gualba, of stormy nights when the sky was both a deep black and a brilliant white. Every so often Gonçal read her a poem she found beautiful, though too complicated to understand. It's a symbolist poem, Gonçal would say, and she would melt and nod, yes. Gonçal never shouted, not like Esteve, and he said things like "pardon" and "may I." Gonçal was different, gentle as a cloud. *He isn't the same kind of man as my father or Esteve,* Patrícia thought. He always asked to wait for Esteve in the foyer, but Patrícia would usher him into the conservatory, where he kept her company, talking while she crocheted. They would go down to the garden together, where the pebbles crunched underfoot. Gonçal stroked the coppery ivy, then picked a lemon and smelled it. He ran the lemon all along his face. "The perfume of autumn," he said. "This is the scent of Barcelona." Occasionally they would sit in the piano room, and she would put on the pianola. They'd listen to Mozart and it was as if Gonçal were somewhere else. Patrícia didn't make a sound in those moments, respecting his silence. The only person Esteve treated with any courtesy, she noticed, was Gonçal. When he came over for lunch, they brought out the crystal and silverware. *He wants to impress him,* Patrícia thought. Esteve viewed Gonçal as a child, and whenever they went out together at night, he even gave Patrícia a kiss.

Would you like some help, Mrs. Miràngels? Gonçal used to ask when he found Patrícia kneeling in the garden pruning the rosebushes. Two of the rosebushes bloomed all year long, their flowers dainty and blood red. Gonçal liked strolling through the Miràngelses' garden; he went round and round, looking out at

L'Eixample courtyards with his alarmed eyes. All these courtyards should be turned into gardens like yours, Patrícia. There
ought to be entrances on every street corner, and inside, trees
upon trees. Gardens for everyone. There's no need for buildings
to be four stories high—though later they would be as tall as
six—or for there to be warehouses and factories. But they made
a mess of everything, and your garden, Patrícia, is like a flower in
the desert. This city doesn't love life, Gonçal used to say. This
was when Patrícia thought to herself, in a very imprecise way,
that everything had been spoiled. And what was to blame if not
the wickedness of mankind? Other times, Gonçal Rodés would
breathe deeply and say, Can't you feel the sea breeze? And Patrícia would take a deep breath too, but instead of sea breeze she
got a noseful of mint. It's simple, Gonçal said. Just look at how
the leaves are moving, and Patrícia would look at the leaves on
the lemon tree. Don't you see them rustling in the dark? One
evening Gonçal kissed her, and after kissing they gazed down at
their shadowy reflections in the water. Patrícia's lips were still
moist when he said, The cherub's smiling, see? And Patrícia
looked at the cherub: Yes, its mouth was half-open.

Some evenings Gonçal and Esteve played chess as she sat beside them embroidering tablecloths and crocheting items for
other people's daughters. Every so often, she yawned. Esteve and
Gonçal often talked about art and politics. It's hard to put an
image into words, Gonçal said, and Patrícia saw his ears go pink
as pomegranates. And even harder to master those ideas, dear
Gonçal, Esteve replied. You get an idea, it hounds you, obsesses
you, pushes you to translate it into a sonnet, to give it a form—
And weight, Gonçal noted. That's right, weight, but then what
actually comes out is gibberish. What kinds of ideas? Gonçal
asked. I don't know . . . that's not true, I do know. Men circle two
basic concepts, like beasts around a waterwheel. I'm talking
about sex and death, of course. You're forgetting one, Gonçal

said. Oh? Power. Esteve pondered this. Power, you're right. Power dominates sex and also fears death. Yet only a small segment of humanity craves power, the same people who believe death can be controlled. Yes, Esteve agreed, they want immortality . . . As Patrícia watched them, their conversation faded into a whisper that just barely reached her. Serenity, she told herself, that's what Gonçal gives Esteve. And that was all Patrícia could ask for, that and more evenings when the garden and the smiling cherub were swallowed by the night while her great-grandfather's clock ticked away like a beating heart.

Then one day, out of nowhere, the war broke out and Gonçal announced he was enlisting. Esteve nearly cried. He's so young! he said. Why must he be sent to the front? Esteve turned into a bundle of nerves and only relaxed after meeting Dorita three years later. Gonçal came back five years later—he'd been in prison—and Esteve was so overjoyed when he found out that he pinched Patrícia's bottom. Wow, he said, You've lost a lot of weight! Between the war and everything else, Patrícia had become quite waifish.

Esteve went to L'Ateneu to look for Gonçal and invite him to lunch. But the Gonçal he found there wasn't the man he had known before the war. His alarmed eyes had turned inward. His chin had sharpened and his cheeks were sunken. His head had been shaved so that his hair poked out like the bristles on a brush instead of flopping over his forehead. He was no longer in awe of Patrícia's garden, or the pond, or the cherub that smiled when they kissed, and he didn't listen to the sea breeze rustling the lemon tree leaves. He and Esteve argued over the silliest things— mostly the war—and Gonçal slammed the door repeatedly on his way out of the Miràngelses' flat. Eventually he'd come back and the two of them would make peace, then end the evening with a game of chess. The war was complete nonsense, Esteve said. Shut up, Gonçal replied. You haven't been on the front. You haven't seen death with your own eyes. Why did you go? Esteve asked. We could've hidden you here. I volunteered, remember . . . It wasn't our war to fight, Gonçal. You should've just let them kill each other. How can you say that? Gonçal almost shouted, and Patrícia inadvertently began to crochet faster. They fought continually, and many of their evenings went like this. *Things were different before the war,* Patrícia thought. *The world's been turned upside down.* One day Gonçal disappeared and remained out of touch for over a year. Esteve missed him, and it was during this period that he wrote his famous sonnets for Dorita-Teresa, his *ben plantada.* He became an embittered man and harassed Patrícia for no reason.

One Sunday afternoon, Esteve came home in high spirits. Guess what? he asked. Gonçal is back! Then he kissed Patrícia so hard on the lips it almost hurt. Why don't you take Sixta to the cinema? he suggested. I know you find Sundays terribly boring. You shouldn't feel like you have to sit around and watch us play chess. I'll ask Gonçal to stay for dinner, that way you can see him when you get home. You're the sweetest woman in the world . . . You do understand, don't you, why I don't want us to go out and be like all those dreadful Barcelona couples with their dopey faces? Patrícia put on her ash-gray dress and the straw hat with the black velvet ribbon, then wrapped a *renard argenté* around her neck. Since Gonçal was coming over, she decided to wear the gauze stockings a friend had bought for her in Andorra. She lifted her leg—white like a glass of milk and netted with little veins that looked like tiny rivers—and pulled on her stocking. As she slid it up, she felt a small tickle: a tiny hole that swiftly turned into a ladder and ran all the way down to her foot. *My only pair of gauze stockings!* she thought, crestfallen. But she didn't take them off. *I wonder if Sixta will want to get hot cocoa at L'Orxateria Valenciana.* Sixta also found Sunday afternoons dreary, especially as evening started to fall; ever since her husband had been going out with his friends—the soldiers who won the war—she hadn't been able to spend time with him. Esteve snuck up behind Patrícia and hugged her waist, Kiss me, woman. Patrícia eyed her figure in the mirrored bedroom wardrobe. She had slimmed down quite a bit, it was true, but every day she looked a bit more like a Barcelonan. *I'm ugly but agreeable.* Standing in front of the mirror, Esteve kissed Patrícia on each cheek and also checked his reflection out of the corner of his eye—*still handsome.* He walked his wife to the door, and as he waved her goodbye, shouted, "On Tuesday we'll get dinner at Set Portes!"

Maybe I'm not like other women, Patrícia thought as she walked arm in arm with Sixta, who said, You do realize you have a run in your stocking. So? Patrícia replied. At least it's gauze. You're an odd duck, Sixta replied. They sat a while at L'Orxateria Valenciana gossiping about other women's clothes. Look, that one over there has her coat on inside out. She probably doesn't want people seeing how tattered it is. And the *topolinos* look like tanks . . . Fashion trends are in such poor taste these days, Sixta said. You have to move mountains just to get hold of a nice item of clothing. It's the war, said Patrícia. "The world's gone topsy-turvy," Sixta declared, "my husband isn't the same man as before." Neither is mine. At least there's peace, Sixta concluded. They made their way to the Coliseum, where a documentary about Germany was showing before the film. The documentary showed Übermenschen exercising on the riverside: classically beautiful teenagers who were six feet tall or taller, with blond hair and blue eyes like Parsifal, doing their stretches on the grass as the sunlight cast shadows behind them. Their skin was firm and bright and supple. This scene was followed by one of the Untermenschen: barefoot Soviet prisoners in rags trudging toward a concentration camp—short, unkempt, ugly, with weeks-long beards and backs so bowed it looked like their foreheads would kiss the ground. How awful, Patrícia said. They're bad people, there's a darkness to their eyes, Sixta replied. *They have the same look as Gonçal,* Patrícia thought.

———

The movie's opening credits were scrolling when Patrícia began to feel unwell. I don't know what's wrong, she said, my stomach hurts. Do you want to leave? Sixta asked. Patrícia tried to hold on a bit longer but couldn't. I need to get out of here, she said. She gagged, then hurriedly got up to go to the loo—she made the whole row stand, and an old man grunted. She tasted bile. We're leaving, Sixta decided. Patrícia's face was peaky. She felt like heaving again, but nothing came up, only more bile. Was it something you ate? No, it's just that I feel unwell around my time of the month. Sounds like nerves, said Sixta. Patrícia clung to her arm as they left the cinema. *Gonçal is at the flat. Esteve is going to be so upset,* she thought, although she wasn't sure why. They walked faster and faster—they couldn't hail a cab—and she rushed impatiently across the street, on the one hand because she wasn't feeling well, and on the other because of Gonçal. *I haven't seen him in a whole year.* Sixta trailed behind her, prattling on about various herbal remedies: Have some lemongrass and chamomile infusion and you'll be right as rain. It wasn't easy convincing Sixta: You don't need to come with me—go home. I'm just going to get right into bed anyway. But Sixta wouldn't listen. Men are useless when it comes to these kinds of things, she said. But Patrícia dug her heels in—no and no—and in the end Sixta left in a sulk. Patrícia panted up the stairs, heart racing and eyes clouded. Her cheeks were ablaze, and she noticed she was sweating. She opened the door—it was so hard, getting the key in the keyhole—and dashed into the conservatory. I'm going to see Gonçal, she thought gleefully. Her stomach wasn't in knots anymore, and the nausea had lifted.

She was surprised not to find them in the conservatory or the dining room, and she didn't notice the chess pieces lined up neatly on the board. She gazed out at the garden and saw that the cherub was still smiling. She couldn't bring herself to call out to them because she was scared that Esteve would be upset with her, so instead she looked for them in the piano room as well as the room with the Casas and Nonell. She crossed the dark, quiet hall that led to the foyer, and opened the bedroom door, her nerves on edge. Gonçal and Esteve were breathing like *the rustling leaves of a lemon tree,* under the satin bedspread printed with large blue flowers.

PART THREE
HUNTING HORNS

Memories are hunting horns
whose songs die along the wind.

GUILLAUME APOLLINAIRE,
"Hunting Horns" (tr. Paul Blackburn)

On Wednesday morning, Natàlia went to visit Arcadi Segura. Harmonia had called ahead, and he was expecting her. She brushed past a young man of about twenty-five on her way into the publisher's. Who's the boy I just saw leaving your office? Caught your eye, hmm? Aren't you a cougar! It was only five seconds ago that you left Jimmy, and here you are, back on the prowl. Like them young, do you? Oh shut up, don't be stupid. Natàlia said. Who is he? His name is Jordi Soteras. He's a young novelist, fresh out of the oven. Has he published anything yet? A collection of short stories—they're so-so if I'm being honest. He just dropped off his debut novel for us to read. He has another novel too, but he took that one to the competition. The censors are on his case. Too much sex, they say. Gosh. I guess some obsessions never change. So, what did you think? Have you read it yet? Which version? The censored one. I gave it a skim, Arcadi replied. What's it about? Why do you care so much? he asked. I don't know . . . he reminds me of someone . . . He shouldn't remind you much of anyone. He was born in Mexico and moved here to do a bachelor's in philosophy. Father's in exile. Natàlia smiled at Arcadi. Aren't you going to tell me what the novel's about? You're a real pain in the neck. It's about the usual: running away. Running away? Natàlia pressed. Yes, Arcadi said. It's very faddish now, in literature. The younger generation keeps running away . . . It's happening in England too, kids are running off to Kathmandu, or India—Oh please, it's much closer to home than that. Our novelists run away to Europe. Sometimes they run away by sitting at home and flipping through travel-agency brochures. Other times they make flying visits to Italy, London, or Amsterdam—at a push. A handful of them might spend a whole fortnight in Venice. That's not running away, Natàlia said. You're right. Mostly they just write about running away. Natàlia laughed. I had no idea when I left that people would go and make literature out of it. Don't kid yourself. You're from a different era. Arcadi Segura closed his office door, which had been left ajar. I'm talking about mine and my friends' generation, those of us who were thirteen or fifteen when the war ended. Some ran away for good, by suicide. Others ran away by striking it rich, which is another kind of forgetting. Then there are the people who escape via alcohol—and I include myself in that group. My generation didn't run. What I mean is: We didn't leave, let alone turn leaving into a myth. Maybe we thought change was around the corner. But look at us now. Still waiting, and at least one of us is a grandfather! This is why some of my friends have started killing themselves in their fifties . . . What were you waiting for? Natàlia asked. What were we waiting for? Haven't *you* been waiting for something all these years? Arcadi offered her a cigarette. We were waiting for the moment when we could stop apologizing. Isn't that enough? The way these young people are running away—it's all fur coat and no underwear. They're not really running. They're searching. They think, rather naïvely, that by running away they may just find something they haven't been able to get here.

Natàlia had thought the same thing in her day. Paris had felt bright and welcoming that early summer in 1962, when the train pulled into Austerlitz, a filthy station littered with rubbish and dust, the first stop in a city that, for all its hostility, never once caused her to feel judged. Arcadi Segura commissioned a series of photographs from her for a line of pocket-size editions and promised to call the editor-in-chief of a new magazine that was to launch in a few weeks. Then he invited her out to lunch. We'll go to a traditional place. I bet you're just dying to eat some pig's feet, he said. At the restaurant, the tables were half empty and dimly lit. Natàlia was happy. Red-and-white-checkered table-cloths! Don't they make you hungry? Segura smiled. Ever the hedonist, I see! And Natàlia said, Being abroad taught me to appreciate pleasure; it honed my senses . . . How have things been here? she asked Arcadi. As passable as you left them. I saw these huge posters for pamphlets about the revolution . . . And you'll find Marxist literature at the newsstands too, Arcadi said. But if nothing has changed, what are they doing there? You left when they executed Grimau, right? A little before then, Natàlia said. July 1962. And now they've executed Puig Antich. Harmonia says it's the communists' fault nothing is being done. Arcadi laughed. Don't listen to Harmonia, you know what she's like. The woman fought tooth and nail to get where she is, and she couldn't be any prouder . . . None of us wants to admit just how powerless we are. It's been years and we're getting old. Nothing has changed.

Sílvia had said, I bet we seem different to you, don't we? While Arcadi insisted nothing had changed. Things did seem different to her, although she hadn't had the time to work out how, exactly. Was it the language, the newspapers, the cinema, the customs? When she left, the country had been subsumed in a deep calm; she'd only been back three days, and things seemed no less quiet. A lot had happened inside the country, and outside, and of course she had changed as well. She wasn't scared anymore. She had learned a great deal in May 1968, when she and Sergio hid near the Champs-Elysées after a Compagnies républicaines de sécurité attack and he told her people needed to fight to make the world a better place. She'd discovered a whole lot of things, thanks to Sergio. As had her body that freezing winter night in Paris when, in her *chambre de bonne*, he kissed her sex for the first time. An electric charge had rushed up her spine, and her whole body had wanted to open, wanted Sergio inside her. That's when she realized that what they were doing wasn't a sin—it was the start of a new way of perceiving.

Lluís had accused her of being too rootless. You'll never adapt, he said. And maybe he was right, although this hadn't stopped her from missing her country, which was different from missing a person, which left an emptiness inside. Natàlia felt homesick when she was at her happiest. What she missed was a certain aroma, a street, the laughter of friends strolling down La Rambla in waves, the shadows around Santa Maria del Mar, the chilly mornings, the leaves of the plane trees when they fell in autumn. Most of all she missed the colors, and she had thought of them during her yellow days with Sergio ... She'd missed the red and orange streaks on days that forecast high winds, the gray on days of rain, the honeyed days that suddenly ushered in spring. Natàlia eventually admitted to Arcadi that she had left out of fear. Not of her father, or his authority over her—besides, she could've become emancipated from him just a year later. No, the problem was that Emilio Sandoval had taught her to scratch beneath the country's filth, and she was scared she wouldn't be able to stop ... Now she was back, and no one believed her when she said she was a photographer.

The first change she noticed was the noise. Barcelona was noisy, and not like other cities, which clamored with people and cars. Here, much like anywhere else, the cars squealed when braking, exhaust pipes backfired, and motorcycles zipped this way and that. But that wasn't the thing that felt different to her. It was as if the city were shrieking—*shrieking so it won't have to listen to itself.* There were streets with gaping holes where the paving stones had been pulled up, half-built buildings lurking behind scaffolding and nets, walls that resembled backdrops, and the street corners were all uniform. Barcelona was a giant gutted corpse. *Health and safety first*—when she left, construction workers didn't even wear helmets ... What else had changed? Well, the streets were tarmac now and there weren't any trams. Palm trees listed in the squares and there was dust everywhere. Banks had replaced gardens, and the bars where she'd sat for hours, wearing down the velvet upholstery, were gone. El Oro del Rhin, for example, was now a bank with a glacial façade ... El Oro del Rhin: long tables, green-leather sofas, golden mirrors. Natàlia thought of Emilio. Twelve years ago, they used to meet at that bar. It was a five-minute walk from the university, and they would sit there sipping coffee all afternoon. And talking.

Emilio had come up to her at the entrance to the cinema.

Don't I know you from somewhere? And she'd fallen for it. I don't think so . . . Are you a student at the Universitat de Barcelona? No, I don't go to school; I do ceramics, take English and French classes, work in the mornings. No one had ever looked at her the way Emilio did, as if his eyes were fused to her chest. She couldn't figure out what foot to put her weight on. I know you from somewhere . . . I do theatre and have a friend at TEU de Dret. That's it, he said, snapping his fingers. I knew you were a theatre person. Oh, it's just a hobby . . . Blanca had arrived, and the film was about to start. Who's this? I don't know, Natàlia replied. Says he knows me . . . When they were leaving, Natàlia scanned the room for him, but the crowds of people pushed her out. Oh well, she thought.

She was already in her Roman dress, with her hair in an updo. I always look such a mess, she told herself. Someone touched her from behind and said, Got you! Emilio's eyes twinkled. Aren't you a social butterfly! Did you think you'd get away from me, babe? Emilio—quite the coincidence—was on makeup duty. He was friends with the director of TEU de Dret, who had asked him to do the girls' makeup. Even though he was drowning in work, there was nothing he wouldn't do for a friend. The name's Emilio, he said, without missing a beat, and all of us here are reds, got it? He has the name of a radio-drama hero, Natàlia thought to herself. Emilio, who loved theatre, had said to his friend, Sure, why not? I'll set aside the million other urgent projects I'm juggling and do your girls' makeup. And there he was, about to do hers. Natàlia hadn't said a word while he chatted, opened a wicker suitcase, and took out several tubes. A friend who's a professional actor loaned it to me. This guy from Madrid who came here with Tamayo. You know, I lived in Madrid a long time. I'm going to make you look older, since you're playing the servant. Natàlia, who people said moved gracefully onstage—though her voice was dreadful—played the crotchety servant in Plautus's *The Pot of Gold*. Emilio slathered his fingers in a gray paste and applied it to her face. He started at her forehead, smearing streaks on both sides with his thumbs—What're you up to later?—and then went from the top of her nose down to the corners of her mouth, where he accentuated her smile lines. The director walked past—Hey, don't mess around, he said. We're on soon. Emilio started at her top lip, contouring her mouth and running his fingers down to the tip of her chin. Oh look, a chin dimple. Do you want to do something together? His hands were now coated in a brown paste, and he rubbed the stuff onto her neck. You have a lovely neck . . . Like a swan's. With his fingertips, he traced the outline of her eyebrows down to her eyelids—now close your eyes and you, watch out, or I'll get the girl dirty—and daubed makeup onto her eyelids. Now his fingers were back on her forehead and moving toward her ears. The director passed them—Easy on the wrinkles!

Emilio and Natàlia went out several times. He'd pick her up at the French Institute and they would stroll through the Gothic Quarter holding hands. This neighborhood is one of the most beautiful things about Barcelona and yet, look around, there's never anyone here. They often stopped at a bar on Carrer de Banys Nous where grizzled card sharks and students drank wine and ate olives around barrels that doubled as tables. Natàlia liked the smell of the place—the fried sardines and barrels of wine. You like your wine, huh? Emilio asked, and she felt herself blush. They usually ordered tapas—sardines, chorizo, Sevillian olives—and red wine with soda water. Emilio explained that wine with soda water was a "workers' beverage." She nearly always paid. Emilio talked her through everything that had happened in the country since Franco's victory, how hundreds of men had disappeared from towns and villages in Andalusia for no other reason than the callouses on their hands. "Things are going to change," Emilio concluded, and there wasn't much else Natàlia could say except her father used to be red and was now kind of Catholic and very authoritarian. There's just so much fear, Emilio continued. Two or three times, Emilio took her to the house of some friends of his who put on popular theatre in working-class neighborhoods, a couple weighed down by children and aspirations. The woman was slender and perpetually worried her husband was going to fall into another depression. "There's no place in this country for geniuses like me," he lamented. One afternoon when the couple was out, she and Emilio fooled around on their bed. He got on top of her and unbuttoned her blouse, then pressed her nipple like a doorbell. One hand ran down her body while the other stroked her neck—for some reason, Natàlia felt as if he were still doing her makeup—then slid up her skirt. She heard a *click* and her right suspender came loose, another *click* and off went the left one. Suspenders are so sexy, he said while his hand continued to explore her inner thigh. He moved to the back of her leg and, with two more clicks, released the rest of the straps holding up her stockings. Emilio's hand ventured beneath her underwear, stroking her—Time to wake up your clitoris, babe—and her ears burned while her heart felt as though it might explode. But they never completely undressed, and the game always ended abruptly, either because they heard a key turning in the lock or because she drew back and clamped her legs tight. What're you so scared of, Natàlia?

Emilio also took Natàlia to the university several times, where he pointed out his friends: This one's a left-wing Falangist; this one's a xino. What does that mean? she asked. A xino is a communist. With Emilio, Natàlia attended a lot of theatre in working-class neighborhoods. People applauded like crazy. These are the masses—do you see how rich their lives are? She said yes, and yet she could make out the reek of sweaty wood— *The smell of poverty*. Emilio was always busy. I've got so many meetings to go to, he said, I feel like I'm running around like a chicken with its head cut off. One day he confessed to being a communist. When Emilio said, "I'm a communist," Natàlia's first thought was that maybe she'd gone too far. Does that scare you, babe? It's not so much that she was scared. The realization that she was dating a communist had a strange effect on Natàlia: it hollowed out a pit in her stomach. Since Emilio was from Andalusia, he didn't say "sóc comunista" in Catalan but *soy un comunista* in Spanish, *you know, a red.* Aunt Patrícia said communists were evil, that they burned churches and murdered priests. As far as Natàlia's father was concerned, reds were never up to any good, and he didn't want to hear mention of them. Maybe if he'd gone to the Universitat de Barcelona, she said to Emilio, he'd understand things better. Maybe, Emilio responded. She knew Emilio was nothing like her friends, yet she was attracted to him. Who knows, maybe it was an animal attraction, but that didn't change the fact that her ears burned hotter every time they met and that she longed for their friends' bed. One time she even guided his hand to her vulva. You're going to get hooked, Emilio said to her. She sought his fingers, wanted them inside her, and circled his tongue in her mouth with her own. Natàlia started missing class, then her work at an office that employed her part-time. You've been coming home later and later every day, Joan Miralpeix shouted. But Natàlia ignored her father, locked herself in her bedroom, and studied herself in the mirror. She smiled and thought: If only you knew I'm dating a communist! My father is a coward, Natàlia told Emilio. He's terrified of politics and only cares about money. He's been a despot ever since Mom had her stroke.

One day Emilio told her his friends had given him the key to a house in Llavaneres: We could spend the weekend there. But what would I tell my family? You're still scared! he said. Natàlia told her father she was going to Calella with Blanca. You're so selfish you can't even spare a Sunday to look after your mother, Joan Miralpeix screamed. Do Sílvia and Lluís ever take care of her? They're married; they have Màrius to look after. I guess I'll have to get married if I want to go out on Sundays.

The house in Llavaneres was a small, two-story chalet surrounded by pine trees, right between the village and the beach. It was a bright spring night and the moon spilled toward the water. There was the scent of new leaves and the crunch of pine-cones. They sat outside for a while. If they pricked their ears, they could hear the waves. Emilio held her tight and said, It's over, babe. There are more than sixty thousand workers on strike in Asturias alone, and more in León and Bilbao. They're calling for strikes all over the peninsula. I'm convinced we'll manage to shut down the university. Emilio had been in prison in Madrid. Aren't you scared? You're in so deep . . . Why would I be scared? Emilio got up and then went inside for a bottle of wine. He filled two glasses. I'm not scared of prison or being beaten up. I think I could take it. Emilio downed the wine in one gulp. What really scares me is getting old. Emilio drifted off for a moment. I like living, I like eating, I like drinking and making love . . . He nibbled her ear, and she pushed him away. Don't be a dog . . . I'm terrified of death, Natàlia said, and I never want to die. I never want to get old, Emilio replied. Or I might have to follow the same path as Paul Lafargue. Who's Paul Lafargue? Emilio smiled. You've got a hell of a lot to learn, babe. Lafargue was Marx's son-in-law, a man who loved life so much that he ended it the moment he began to feel old. That's so brave, Natàlia said. His wife Laura, Marx's daughter, was just as brave as he was. They both injected themselves with cyanide in their seventies. When was that? Before the First World War. Lafargue left a note that said something like: "Healthy in body and mind, I've decided to put an end to my life before the cruelty of old age robs me of the pleasures and joys of existence, and strips me of my physical and intellectual faculties." Lafargue ended his note with "long live communism and international socialism." It was a different time, Natàlia said. Emilio smiled. I don't see why wanting pleasure and change should belong to a different time! Natàlia wasn't sure what to say next.

Emilio had brought olives, longaniza, fries, and a bit of bread.

They ate in silence. The moon had disappeared behind a cloud. Emilio was so close, Natàlia could feel his breath. You're in deep with all this, aren't you? Emilio stroked her back. "In deep" is such a petit-bourgeois term. I don't get in deep with things, babe. If anything, they get in deep with me. To fill the silence, Natàlia asked: Do you really believe things can change? Emilio wrinkled his nose. Come on! What do you think? If I didn't . . . He let out a breath of wine. Kiss me, he said. Natàlia leaned in and kissed him on the lips. I love that you're a terrible kisser, Emilio teased. She pulled away, lips salty from the fries. Emilio grabbed her wrist. Come here, he said and kissed her with tongue. His tongue was very damp, *like a freshwater fish's,* Natàlia thought. Emilio unzipped her trousers. Tonight, all our clothes are coming off.

In those days Natàlia kept having the same dream. In the dream she was the hero of a heartrending scene—it felt like watching a movie in Technicolor—and that same hero's lover. The hero was handsome and brave and fought against all kinds of bad people crowded in a corner. These people were ugly and unkempt; they had bright red, demonic faces, crow-like claws, and teeth the color of lemons. After a series of clear, sharp scenes, Natàlia turned into the lover, a majestic woman shrouded in mist. The bad people chased after the hero, who ran into the city's sewage system—Natàlia could hear the splish-splash of dirty water, though in reality it was just a leaky pipe in the lightwell—and into a dark tunnel, dark like a breath of shadow. For a while the only sound was dripping water and the hero's footsteps sloshing. And then finally the hero found the lover shrouded in mist and embraced her. Natàlia the hero and Natàlia the lover waded into the gloom. With every new dream, the images grew darker. Hero and lover vanished into a region of endless shadows until suddenly, there was no sound—not the splish-splash of water or the echo of their footsteps; nothing at all, only darkness, which was as black as the throat of night . . ! Without warning, a spotlight lit up a corner of the ceiling, where an enormous spider was hanging by a thread. The giant spider wanted to embrace Natàlia the lover, who was alone once more. Its long, hairy legs groped around the room in search of Natàlia, who was now framed by the spotlight. It wanted to squeeze her, and she couldn't escape it. Natàlia woke herself up several times, arms flailing at nothing. Then someone would switch on the light. It was usually Encarna, asking: Natàlia, have you lost your mind?

It wasn't easy making love in Barcelona. Emilio lived in student housing, as did most of his friends. If only we had a car . . . Emilio said. But they didn't, so they often found themselves wandering the streets of Barcelona with no idea where to go. Natàlia refused to go to a *meublé*, her love was not *meublé*. You're so old-fashioned, Emilio said. What difference does it make? It'll be the same, whether we make love in a forest or next to a bidet in a motel room. One night they walked down a narrow alley near Santa Maria del Mar and stopped in a doorway, where Emilio pulled up her skirt. Their love was fugitive, rushed, eyes askance and ears alert to every noise. Their two bodies pressed together as their hands—hidden and scared to death—groped each other's bodies. Don't be naïve, Natàlia's theatre friend said to her once. Emilio doesn't deserve you. It's true she'd been warned. Are you the one going out with Emilio? people asked, then stared at her like a strange bird. Emilio never lasts long with one girl, you'll see. He's the most notorious *xino* at the university . . . Emilio has no scruples when it comes to these sorts of things, added the wife of the friend who put on popular theatre in working-class neighborhoods. Emilio's family is filthy rich—they own half of Almeria. He stands to inherit the whole lot, if he doesn't fall out with his grandmother, that is . . . The director of the TEU had also tried to "warn" her. You can't trust him. His parents send money from home, lots of it. He's a *señorito*. He's only mixed up in politics because it's a game to him. Natàlia thought people were just jealous. Emilio's too old to still be in school, the friend's wife added. He enrolled in three degrees and dropped out of every last one. Of course they were jealous: Emilio was rich and handsome, a communist who loved life. Besides, every time they made love in a rush on their married friends' bed, he touched her more and more passionately. He looked at her with his bright eyes and said, I need you, Natàlia.

One Friday Natàlia decided she wanted to go to the university with Emilio. It's too dangerous, he said. Things have been strained since they started arresting students yesterday. Why can't I come? Natàlia asked. I support the strike in Asturias, don't I? Aren't you always accusing me of being scared? After a night of bad dreams where the spider had squeezed her harder than ever, Natàlia woke determined to join Emilio at the protest. Emilio sensed a hint of pride in Natàlia, seemingly a first for her. To begin with, he said, you aren't a student—Listen, I'm twenty-four years old. Besides, don't you think the strike in Asturias affects me too? Natàlia repeated. Second, you've never been political, he continued. I have to start somewhere, don't I? Did Paul Lafargue stop Laura from going with him? Emilio smiled. You got me there, babe. And I used to think you were so docile ... Around quarter past five, they went down to the university bar. There was the clatter of glasses and Coke and beer bottles; cigarette smoke fogged up the banter and atmosphere. Emilio spotted a friend. The protest starts at six, in the courtyard. He showed him a leaflet they had recently printed. Look over there, the friend said, pointing at a man in gray leaning against the wall near the public bathrooms. Pigs? Emilio asked. Yeah, they're everywhere. Heads are going to get knocked, the friend observed. Emilio turned to Natàlia. Why don't you wait for me at the bar on Banys Nous? I'm not a child, Natàlia said, gazing all around her as if at a movie. Nerves were frayed and a faint sound of running was coming from the corridor outside the bar. Waiters served tables with worried expressions, the smoke thickening. People chattered nonstop while their eyes followed the older men pacing thuggishly around. Emilio and Natàlia walked over to the courtyard, where at least a hundred students were walking about and sitting down, elbow to elbow. Upstairs, leaning over the banisters of the cloisters, a handful of men observed the scene. There was a tight cluster of students in a corner of the courtyard. Pamphlets briefly fluttered above them, and while some lifted their arms to snatch them out of the air, others bent over to collect the ones already on the ground. Someone began singing "Asturias, patria querida" . . . The men upstairs watched impassively. Emilio's friend said, They look like they could crack any second. Someone unfolded a placard with the word *Asturias*. The students huddled around the sign and made their way to the gardens. Only the wicket door was open. Some students forced open the larger gate to let the others in. They hung the placard at the entrance that led to Plaça de la Universitat. Natàlia saw an army of gray uniforms in front of her, and jeeps idling on street corners like tanks ready to roll into battle. The square was enveloped in a strange silence, broken only by the students' yelling and chanting. Passersby in the area slowed to a stop, looking like background actors in a silent film. I heard there are horses in Plaça Castella, said Emilio's friend, whose name was Joan. The students poured back into the courtyard. A smaller group made its way to the hall. Natàlia gripped Emilio's hand. The people at the head started swearing at the police. A squad of regimented gray uniforms slowly advanced toward the large gate that opened to the street. A man in dark clothes walked downstairs from the second floor, followed by a few custodians. It's Linés—son of a bitch! Emilio shouted. Natàlia asked, Who's Linés? The dean's spy. Linés signaled at the police officers waiting at the gate and a horde of gray uniforms flooded the hall. She didn't feel like she was watching a film anymore—now, she was in the thick of it. For a second, Emilio's hand slipped out of hers and she had to grope for it among the whistles and truncheons. When she found it again, his sweat-slicked hand tugged her toward a corner of the hall, far from the gray uniforms. Run, run, run, Emilio shouted. But she couldn't, she was being tossed this way and that, as if by the ocean. Whirlpools of frantic people spun her around, and all she could see were mops of hair, screwed-up faces, terrified eyes, hands grabbing on to whatever was in front of them, bodies shooting away and then hurtling back, all punctuated by yelling and swearing and girls crying. A student fainted next to her. Natàlia tried to reach her, but the waves dragged her under again. She was back in choppy seas, a shipwreck, while the others were animals chained to a waterwheel. The blows continued. A few people tried to break through the door to the courtyard outside the Literature department but found they were blocked in, there was no way out. They formed a tight circle and scrambled toward the last remaining exit, but several gray uniforms had stationed themselves on the other side and sent the group careening back like a spinning top. The police swung at them furiously, again and again, always at the front line. Their pupils were red, their faces ashen—maybe from the reflection of their uniforms—and they had bulging eyes, clenched teeth, and vacant expressions. They beat people at random, like rabid animals or dogs unleashed after years of living in cages. The tight circle of students went round and round for no reason but to avoid being at the head of the group, within swinging distance of the truncheons. It was as if the men wielding them had no idea what they were hitting, set on the pure, unthinking destruction of beings that held no substance to them. Students fell to the ground and the clubs rained down on their inert bodies. There was the sound of glass shattering: a boy with a bloodied hand had managed to break a door window, and a line of students was trying to push through. A student staggered past, face covered in blood . . . Emilio finally pulled Natàlia through the glass door, along with

Joan and another girl. They stumbled into the garden separating the departments' various courtyards. This way! Joan shouted. They rushed into a dim church. A few nuns were deep in prayer and looked up at them with surprise. The four sat in the front row and waited a long while. Once the sound of struggle retreated from the courtyard, they got up and left.

They must have sat in the church for an hour or so. Outside, night had fallen. The university was silent, but it was a prowling silence. Natàlia felt as if she'd just emerged from combat. Howls sounded in the distance. They walked through the Literature department. The police were still arresting students, though they ignored their small group. The jeeps were packed with detainees peering out from the dark. They walked to the Canaletes fountain. The sons of bitches had water cannons and horses, Joan said. There'll be a general strike tomorrow, Emilio added, teeth clenched. No there won't, just you wait. It was quiet where they were now, even though it felt as if thousands of sentries were posted around them. Twenty or so students were gathered at the fountain. They've rounded up so many people, said a cross-eyed young man. It was awful, whispered one of the girls. Natàlia looked at her for the first time. Until then, she hadn't said a word. The girl was very slim, about eighteen years old, with large, wide eyes that seemed to take up most of her face. One of the students started singing "Asturias, patria querida" . . . At first it was just a hum, quiet and sorrowful as a prayer. The students huddled closer together and the song gradually took shape—the girls' voices, of which there were few, and the boys' husky timbre. As they walked up La Rambla, the students' singing grew louder. People stared at them with a mix of apprehension and awe. Someone applauded. As they gained confidence, so did their voices. *Asturias, patria querida,* they all chanted, even Natàlia. *Asturias, patria querida,* and La Rambla filled with the anthem, which grew louder and stronger. It was a joyful tune, and Natàlia sang like she never had before. *Asturias,* she intoned, as if Asturias were her, or Emilio, or the crushed students. Asturias wasn't just Asturias anymore: this was why she cried out, as if unburdening herself of the heavy silences at home; she cried out without shame to clear it all away. The students were doing more than just sing now, more than just shout. They were howling. *Asturias, patria querida, Asturias, patria querida,* they wailed like a storm-tossed sea. When Natàlia shouted, it wasn't against the gray mass who had beaten them, nor against the jeeps and the water cannons, and it wasn't against the uncaged dogs that had charged at them so unthinkingly; Natàlia shouted against her past, against her father's wrath, against what she had been. And she wasn't scared. All of a sudden, someone cried out, Police! and everyone scattered. Emilio gripped her hand and dragged her into a narrow alley. Joan and the slender girl were close behind them. They ran for a while, then stopped beside a dark doorway. They were panting. Emilio leaned against the wall with his eyes closed. The city plunged into darkness, the evening sun leaving orange streaks on the rooftops.

It all happened so fast, she figured they had been there all along. They came down the opposite end of the street. Maybe they'd cut through an alley, straight from La Rambla. The blond man's features were common, and he wore glasses and a cheviot sports jacket. The other man had brown hair and the face of a sad dog, large jowls accentuating saggy cheeks and deep-set eyes that seemed to stare pitifully at everything around him. They weren't so much walking as strolling, their hands tucked in their pockets. What are you doing here? the blond one asked. We're taking a walk. Or is that a crime now? Lay off it, we know who you are. Hand over your IDs. The one with the common face stepped behind them. Well, well, Joan Oranich and Emilio Sandoval, quite the pair. The man in the cheviot sports jacket took the girls' purses and emptied them out. The officer with the sad eyes said nothing. He looks like a good person, Natàlia thought. Do you know what your classmates got up to at the university?

the blond man asked. They hid behind some trees and threw stones at the police under the cover of dark. The slender girl smiled. The one with the sad eyes lunged at her, knocking her onto the ground. Stop laughing, you tramp! You whore! he shouted, pounding her slender body with his fists. Natàlia felt her underwear dampen and a warm liquid trickle down her inner thigh. *I'm pissing myself.* The others remained still, though Joan made a slight movement forward. Stay right where you are! the blond one yelled, pointing the gun at him. The girl whimpered on the ground. More police officers in civilian clothes, two of them very young, slouched down the street. They collected their IDs, then made the four of them walk in front. The girl limped ahead, cradling her lower belly and weeping. Emilio's face was pale as a clouded sky and Joan pursed his lips with a vacant look in his eyes. We just stood there, Natàlia thought. We just stood there and let them hit her. They stepped onto a wider street, a crossing, where they were approached by men in gray uniforms. Take them to the others. Don't let them out of your sight, said the man like a sad dog. Men and women had poured out of residential buildings and bars to watch the scene unfold. Natàlia felt herself blush with shame. She was scared someone would recognize her. The men forced them into a jeep. Emilio sat beside her, stroking her hand. You know nothing, he told her. The jeeps were at Plaça de Castella. Shortly after, they were driven to the center. It was pitch-black now and the city lights flickered as the vehicle lurched forward. Outside, life went on as if it were any other day. You know nothing, Emilio repeated. The jeep parked outside the police station, and they were ordered to get out. They sent the slender girl, who was still weeping, into another room. The light in the station gave everyone an olive-green complexion. The walls were lemon yellow and caked with years of filth. Everything looked faded. Natàlia was taken to a small room that was cluttered with files and right beside the entrance. Inside were two worn-down tables that reeked of sweat. Heat pipes cut through the middle of the room. On one of the walls, which was full of cracks, was a board covered in pictures: "Dangerous Anarchist Network." A large, pale green portrait of Franco presided over the office. A man with greasy hair and dead eyes was busy at his typewriter, and didn't look up when she walked in. A pair of young police officers entered the room. "Women look prettier in skirts," one of them said in Spanish. "Trousers make you look butch." And the man at the typewriter with greasy hair called out, "Leave the girl alone, she's ugly." A lot of time passed. The clack-clack of the typewriter infiltrated her body. Eventually a fat man with a red face and dark bags under his eyes walked in smoking a cigar. Natàlia looked up at his neck. *What a tiny neck,* she thought. *It was pretty stupid of you to get mixed up with Sandoval,* he said in Spanish. The man with the cigar and the tiny neck told the man with the greasy hair to take down her details. *We'll be informing your family,* the man with the cigar said before leaving. Then came the fingerprints and the mugshots.

She went downstairs to the cell block, where she was met by an older, pot-bellied man in gray. *Well, you're a bit wet behind the ears,* he said. He took her into an empty cell; the one next to hers was crowded with students peering through the bars. Now that she saw the gray, damp, flaking walls, the clammy floor, the stone bench, and the small window that looked out at nothing, yet let in a faint light, Natàlia finally understood what had happened. *They've taken me in but I'm not in trouble.* Though she was afraid, the fear she was experiencing now was different from when she had wet herself—*Why did we just stand there? Why did we let him hit that girl?* It was a deeper fear, a cold, tormenting fear that punished her, body and mind. *What am I doing here?* Outside, there was the drip-drip of a tap, or maybe a faulty pipe, and inside, the slow footsteps of the fat policeman. Every so often she heard the sound of a lock clicking and, upstairs, someone shouting in Spanish—*door!* Then the policeman's slow, tired footsteps would quicken, followed by a firm, confident pace and then another kind of stride—the stride of cold fear, she thought. Time ticked on and the hours wasted away, punctuated by the treading of police officers and new prisoners. Natàlia tried to come up with an explanation for what was happening, but the cold stone bench chilled her spine, her hands felt numb, and her body was stiff. She tried walking around yet immediately came up against the door or small window. She tried counting the guard's footsteps, guessing the number of bars in the cell door, imagining her body was wounded and her brain empty like her mother's, or that she had died. But it was as if time had stopped. She thought of what Emilio had said to her. "We protested because they're torturing miners and because an officer of the Civil Guard whipped a girl with his belt." That's right, she was locked up because she objected to miners being tortured and girls being whipped. *You're being ridiculous,* she thought to herself. *It doesn't change anything, whether you're in here or out there.* Natàlia closed her eyes and saw a courtroom. She was the judge, and the officers she had met that short evening were all on trial. They stood in line, ramrod straight: the blond man, the officer who looked like a sad dog, the man with the greasy hair, the three young guys, the driver, and the officer with the cigar. There was also the gray uniform with the large belly, but Natàlia shooed him out of her fantasy. The ruling was not subject to appeal: They were all sentenced to a slow death by strangulation. The men begged for mercy. Maybe she'd pardon the one with the greasy hair who had called her ugly, and the three young guys. But the blond man, the officer who looked like a sad dog, and the man with the cigar—not a chance. The face of the officer who looked like a sad dog got redder and redder as she tightened the wire and watched it cut into his neck. She startled awake when her head pitched forward, and the back of her neck tensed. It was even quieter now—only distant sounds, like the footsteps upstairs or the fat policeman's heaving breath. Natàlia had been in her cell for two hours or so, and she couldn't—she didn't want to—be alone any longer. She banged on the bars and yelled *I need the bathroom!* in Spanish. A young policeman with a trimmed mustache strode over. *Hey,* he called out to the fat old policeman. *Her highness says she needs to piss!* She peed hovering over the toilet seat, which was smeared in shit and grime. The thought of pulling her wet underwear back on made her sick, so she took them off. As she walked back into her cell, the fat policeman said, *Why don't you try and get some sleep?* And she asked, *Where?* The fat policeman gave it some thought. *Wait there.* He came back a few minutes later with two plastic mats. *They can take more, they're men.*

She tried to sleep but her body felt deadened. The silence came in bursts, broken only by a sporadic flurry of noise. The leaky pipe, someone using the bathroom, the police officers pacing around upstairs . . . But then she started hearing the word *door!* called out more and more often, followed by a few names, the iron doors being opened, and unfamiliar people walking upstairs. *Door, door!* hammered at her ears. Every time she heard it, she gripped the metal bars and checked if they were calling for Emilio. A long, long time passed and some of the people who were called up came back down. One of them had blood all over his face while another was missing fistfuls of hair. Later on, Natàlia saw two men in gray uniforms carry a man down the steps. She heard someone whisper, *They tore out his beard, the monsters!* Followed by more silence. She didn't see Emilio until the following morning. First, his shoulder as he went upstairs. Then, after a while—and it was such a long while—Emilio returned. He winked at her when he walked past her cell. *They didn't do anything to him, they didn't touch him!* Then another man appeared with blood gushing from his nose, struggling to hold himself upright. Emilio and the other guy were lugged down the corridor. All Natàlia heard was the sound of feet dragging. Suddenly a voice rang out, *Compañeros, stay strong! Better dead than a rat.* Was it Emilio? The voice was drowned out by the clanging of bars. She heard boots stomping, followed by bodies rushing downstairs. *You idiots want to go back up?* A few minutes passed and Natàlia heard someone whistling in the dark. It's Emilio, she told herself. Emilio whistling "Le temps des cerises." Natàlia closed her eyes.

Moi qui ne crains pas les peines cruelles
Je ne vivrai point sans souffrir un jour
Quand vous en serez au temps des cerises
Vous aurez aussi des chagrins d'amour . . .

She fell back asleep. It was late morning before the fat policeman opened her cell door. *Someone sent you a package.* Encarna, a godsend. She had sent a thermos of coffee, a packet of Maria cookies, and a box of Madame X sanitary pads, *just in case,* she told the officers, misty-eyed. The warmth of the coffee brought Natàlia back to life. She didn't feel like eating the cookies, so she left them on the bench. *You've got company,* said an officer. Not the fat policeman but the one with the trimmed mustache. *They've cleaned out a bar.* Four women walked downstairs, two of them crying. Natàlia was joined in her cell by one of the criers—a tall redhead—and the woman consoling her—a short, busty brunette with a large mole on her left cheek. What about my son? the brunette asked. I need to get him to school. The redhead sniveled and blew her nose a couple of times. Good thing they put the madam in another cell, she said, or else I'd stab her eyes out, the scheming whore! The redhead's nose was pink from all her nose blowing. Unsure what to do, Natàlia offered the women biscuits. The brunette said no, thank you; the crier took her up on the offer and proceeded to eat them, one by one, for a long time. Then they let in another brunette. Decked in large imitation jewelry, she was wearing a pink nylon robe, her dark hair in a high bun, and holding a toothbrush. *This is a mistake,* she said in Spanish with a sigh. *My husband's going to be so upset.* The redhead stopped blowing her nose. Oh, have I got a mistake for you, she said. I'm just the cleaning woman—and she can vouch for me! She's right, the other brunette confirmed. I'm a hooker, she just cleans the bar. Don't believe me? Just look at these hands. You think I could make a living with these hands? the redhead asked. She held them up for everyone to see. Her hands were chapped, the color of bull's blood. Every morning I'm at the bar with bleach and a cleaning rag, scrubbing things down. What man would ever want me? She blew her nose again. There, there, the brunette said. The woman with the imitation earrings sighed. What a world! She looked at Natàlia. What're you in for? I'm a student, she lied. The world's gone to shit, said the woman with large earrings. She was awash in cheap perfume, and her jewelry clinked when she moved. Natàlia heard her name, Natàlia Miralpeix, with an accent on the *i*. She got up and walked to the metal bars. Break a leg, said the woman with the earrings.

The officer leaned back in his wooden chair as he looked her up and down. *I won't take a statement from you. But let this be the last time I catch you in here,* he said in Spanish. Next to him, a reedy officer with olive skin was cleaning his pistol, scrupulously taking apart his firearm and placing each component on the table. Natàlia got another noseful of sweaty wood. The officer from the evening before, the one with the cigar, strode in. *You have Mr. Claret to thank for your release. Oh! The other girl's out too. My colleagues were feeling a bit nervous, I'm sure you understand. You threw rocks at them, after all. The girl's doing fine, the doctor saw her. I hope we can agree that nothing happened here.* The officer with the cigar stared at her and asked, *Do you understand?* Natàlia said yes. All she could think about was getting out. She walked down that corridor of lemon-yellow walls and rickety benches. For a long time, whenever she thought about the police station, her mind would be filled with lemon-yellow walls, tables that reeked of sweat, and ice-cold benches. She saw the woman with the jangling earrings in an office. *So I've got sticky fingers. What's it to you?* she heard her say.

Emilio was sent to prison. Every other day for a month, Natàlia left a small package at the counter of cell block four, where they kept the political prisoners. She soon learned how to put together the packages: heavy-duty paper and a small card with the prisoner's name and cell block number. Encarna grumbled but still cooked thick, juicy potato-and-onion tortillas without prompting. Natàlia couldn't help feeling superior to the gypsies, who were always arguing and shouting. *Who've you got inside?* they asked in Spanish. *My boyfriend,* she said. *It's political.* The slender girl who took a thrashing from the police had managed to get in to visit Emilio's friend, Joan Oranich. She had to walk with crutches on account of the beating, and Natàlia was sure her eyes were even wider than before. The girl with the crutches and the wide eyes pretended she and Joan Oranich were engaged. Why don't you give it a shot? Just say you're Emilio's fiancée. Natàlia rang the warden's office. *You're not anything of his. But let me see what we can do.* You could sign a document stating you're engaged and scheduled to be married soon, her lawyer advised. Then they might let you see him. A few days later, the warden told her, *I'm sorry. Sandoval says he's never been engaged in his life.* The lawyer called Natàlia in to his office. Emilio asked me to give this to you. She walked outside gripping a letter in her hand. It wasn't so much a letter as a tiny, crumpled scrap of paper. She waited a while before reading it. She was scared. Emilio had written, in pencil, "things look different when you're inside . . . it's a whole other world, you wouldn't understand. I think it's best we not see each other anymore . . ."

The night before their arrest, Emilio and Natàlia had gone to L'Arc del Teatre to drink anis de cazalla, then to a grimy, dilapidated bar. The band was playing a slow tune and red lampshades formed small glades of light in the darkness. The tables were tiny and stained and arranged in a circle to give people room to dance. An enormous hooker dressed head-to-toe in white clung to a skeletal man in a lilac shirt. She calmly swayed her hips, as if dancing in a ritual. In a corner, next to a light, two mute prostitutes communicated in gestures. They were fighting over an elderly Black man who had massive, dark bags under his eyes. They looked like they were about to claw each other's eyes out. The Black man, wearing a gray felt hat, contemplated them with dispassion. The clingy sweat of the bodies and the grime on the tables and chairs made Natàlia feel dizzy, so she and Emilio left not long after. Outside, seeing how pale she looked, Emilio said, You're never going to get used to the misery, are you? An old hooker with sagging breasts stood on a corner hollering at passersby in what felt like a litany. She cried hoarsely, every now and then letting out a chilling scream. An old man with a limp rummaged through the rubbish as a drunkard sobbed, telling a story to himself. Before meeting Emilio, Natàlia never went to that part of the Raval after dark. She pressed into him now, just as Natàlia the lover had sought shelter in the arms of Natàlia the hero. Do you think this will ever end? she asked, and Emilio said nothing. You know, Natàlia continued, when you talk about our recent history, and everything that's happened because of Franco and his supporters, I don't always follow. But then, when I see this—Natàlia looked around her—when I see all these people and how hopeless they are, I finally understand. Do you think it will ever end? she asked again. Emilio said nothing. Instead, he started whistling a low tune. What are you whistling? she asked. A song. By a poet of the Paris Commune. His name was J. B. Clément, and he was waiting for the time of cherries:

> *Quand vous en serez au temps des cerises*
> *Si vous n'aimez pas les chagrins d'amour*
> *Evitez les belles*
> *Moi qui ne crains pas les peines cruelles*
> *Je ne vivrai point sans souffrir un jour*
> *Quand vous en serez au temps des cerises*
> *Vous aurez aussi des chagrins d'amour.*

He wrote this song during the Paris Commune, when people were rising up against a fiercely oppressive regime. He knew the conflict would be followed by terrible repression—seventy thousand workers were killed and the survivors sentenced to build the Sacré Coeur—and he dreamed of the time of cherries, the springtime of joy. The poet knew the time of cherries would come with its own share of heartache, Emilio continued, but he wished for it anyway. As do I. I can't wait for the cherries to bloom. And then Emilio gave Natàlia a look she would never forget.

She found Emilio's friend in one of the corridors of Hospital Clínic. He was a medical student with brown hair, square shoulders, and childlike eyes. He remembered her from the time they met at the bar on Carrer de Banys Nous. You're asking a lot, he said. A lot. Don't you know any gynecologists? The ones I know who'd have done it in theory are too scared to do it in practice. In a way, he added, I get it: They'd be putting their careers on the line, they could lose their licenses. When Natàlia realized her period was late, she didn't think much of it—*it's because of everything they put me through at the police station, all the stress and Emilio being in prison.* Her father said nothing to her the afternoon she came home. The two met at lunch—Judit had eaten earlier, with the help of a carer. Father and daughter ate together in silence, the only sound the clinking of spoons against their plates. Encarna sighed as she served them their food, glancing at Mr. Miralpeix out of the corner of her eye. In the kitchen, the other housemaid was washing Judit's dishes. Natàlia and her father looked at each other sidelong a couple of times. For months they had only spoken when strictly necessary. Joan Miralpeix had always been reserved and had only become more so since Judit's stroke. Natàlia didn't feel at ease in her own home, yet she could think of nothing else to do than to watch the days pass her by. "We don't have anything to say to each other." Natàlia judged her father harshly, and there was a time when she was sure she hated him. "All he cares about is money and respectability. He's a coward," Natàlia told Emilio. Natàlia's father finished his dessert of poached pears and asked for coffee—strong, as usual—which Encarna served in the sitting room with the display case where they kept Judit's trinkets. Mr. Miralpeix opened that day's issue of *La Vanguardia*. Natàlia got up and went to the medicine cabinet for an aspirin. It took her a while to find the bottle among all of her mother's medications. Natàlia felt under the weather after her night at the police station. The last time Natàlia and her father had a real fight was the summer before, when she announced she couldn't stay home to look after her mother because she was going to travel around Andalusia for three months. Since then, their relationship had turned cold, transactional. Every morning Natàlia would go into Judit's room and give her a kiss. "I won't throw away my life to tend to a vegetable," she had shouted that day. Joan Miralpeix went from pink to bright red. You ingrate! he yelled. Don't you love your mother? Of course I love her, Natàlia said. Was she supposed to waste away while telling her family I love you, I love you not? Her father looked at her, and the bags under his eyes were even more pronounced. He pressed his top teeth into his bottom lip. Then he slapped her. You have no morals, Joan Miralpeix screamed. By the time Natàlia came home from Andalusia, they weren't speaking. But she'd done it: she had "a life of her own" now. You remind me of Kati, Patrícia told her, weeping. You're going to end up just like her. Kati was an old friend of Patrícia and Judit, a snob and hopeless romantic who practiced free love, spent all her time with painters and thespians—bon vivants, Patrícia called them—and went "red as a radish" during the war. She fell head over heels for a man in the International Brigade—"a foreigner," Patrícia noted—who died on the front, then killed herself by drinking hydrochloric acid—it burned a hole in her stomach—the same day the Nationalists took Barcelona and people like Patrícia, Sixta, and Sixta's husband shouted, "They're here! Our people are here!"

You always do exactly what you want, Encarna said. But she didn't know what she wanted, only that she didn't want what was right in front of her. "A father who is filthy rich, smug with 'spirituality,' and clears his conscience with visits to the monks of Montserrat. And a mother with one foot in the grave who was never all there to begin with." Natàlia signed up for various classes and took on odd jobs, "anything to get out of the house." The roof isn't going to cave in on you, Encarna teased. Her friends were all getting married and glowing with joy: new flat, young husband, and before you knew it, a toddler with snot hanging from his nose. You're not married because men find you unpleasant, Encarna said again. Maybe she's right, Natàlia thought. Maybe I'm not married because I don't know how to get men to like me ... She tried her hand at several jobs. She worked at a ceramics studio—that was her last one—went to the Trade Fair three years in a row, studied languages, learned to play the guitar, attended classes on upholstery and industrial design, worked at a prêt-à-porter shop, learned to machine-knit sweaters, took cooking lessons, worked part-time at an office, filing news articles ... She wanted to do everything, to learn it all— and yet, "You do none of it well," Harmonia observed more than once. Even though she didn't need much, her father continued to fund her, albeit one peseta at a time. "I don't appreciate the way you live your life. You're unfocused," Joan Miralpeix said. "My father is the picture of equanimity and mental well-being," Natàlia told Emilio. Of course, her father knew what he wanted. He had a communist past, a fact she had gleaned from key words and loose conversations. But there was nothing left of that time, only a few Catalan books that pre-dated the war and were shelved in the library. A monk in Montserrat had brought him into the fold. Up until then, he had been somewhat aloof in matters of religion. He kept a copy of the Bible on his nightstand and sent his two children to denominational schools: the girl to Jesús Maria and the boy to the Jesuits. What other choice did he

have? A faint ember of Catalan nationalism continued to smol-
der inside him, and he still felt moved whenever he listened to
"La Santa Espina" on the gramophone. Natàlia occasionally
heard her father mention the Catalan independentist leaders,
Lluís Companys and Francesc Macià, though, "At the end of the
day," he remarked, "they were wrong." Once the war was over,
Joan Miralpeix told himself it was time to live—"I just want to be
left alone." Natàlia explained to Emilio how her father made his
fortune: The houses he built in Verneda and Trinitat had stair-
wells so narrow that when a tenant died, the body couldn't be
carried out in a coffin. Don't you think you're being a bit hard on
your dad? Emilio asked. You're not saying I should suck up to
him for his money, are you? Babe, it takes skill . . .

Natàlia's father went to architecture school a little late in life,
around twenty-five, and completed his degree before the start of
the war. After the war, he became one of the first architects to
design residential buildings for low-income workers. "I'd rather
not be an architect at all than have to construct eyesores," his son
Lluís said, "even if they're meant for workers." And Joan Miralpeix retorted, "But I get them out of the slums . . ." Lluís smiled.
Don't be so naïve, he said. Lluís was not a fan of his father's work:
cramped spaces, colorful façades, narrow balconies, diminutive
exits, cheap tiles, poor finishes, functional design, Formica counters, wallpaper, shoddy plumbing . . . "It's what the market wants.
What would you have me do?" Mr. Miralpeix would say. Natàlia's
father had gone into business with Joan Claret, Sílvia's father, in
the 1960s. Together they founded the development company responsible for throwing up hotel chains all along the Costa Brava.
A year later, they expanded the business and opened a branch in
Lloret de Mar—That's where the tragedy at the hotel happened,
Natàlia told Emilio.

Joan Miralpeix finished reading *La Vanguardia,* yawned, and
got up from his seat. It was time for his nap. I need some cash,

Natàlia said. Joan Miralpeix had finally been given an opening to vent: Can you believe the nerve on her? he said as if addressing a front-row audience. Here we go again, Encarna mumbled in the kitchen, where she was drying the dishes. My daughter gets herself arrested, Natàlia's father continued. She spends the night at the police station, says nothing about how she wound up there, and on top of that, she has the gall to ask me for money! Did you even bother asking? Or picking me up from the station? Natàlia snapped back. I called Claret and had him collect you. I hope you have the courtesy to thank him. I don't owe that crook a damn thing! Joan Miralpeix pressed his top teeth into his bottom lip, a tic of his when he was angry. Well, if it isn't Mother Teresa! You go out every night, at all hours, so that your own mother has to be looked after by a carer, and then you have the gall to talk to me about morals! If it wasn't for Claret, you'd be in prison right now. You have no idea what kinds of people are in there . . . For a moment Joan Miralpeix's voice softened. We haven't had a moment's peace in this house since Mrs. Miralpeix fell ill, Encarna remarked to the other housemaid. Oh yes I do, Natàlia replied. I met them yesterday. You don't care what I went through at the police station, or what I saw at the university. The university? Natàlia's father asked. What were *you* doing at the university? You have no business being there. The students are always making trouble. And why not? People are on strike right now in Asturias, or haven't you heard? Don't you read the news? Of course I read the news. But the strikes will end and, besides, they aren't going on here. If you'd seen what I've seen . . . Oh, don't start, Dad! I'm so tired of your memories. To be fair, Encarna continued, there wasn't much peace before the missus fell ill either . . . Sometimes I get the sense there's a devil in this house . . . Well, you won't get another peseta out of me, Mr. Miralpeix said with some difficulty. When you're twenty-five, you can do whatever you please. Until then . . . Joan Miralpeix ended every argument with the same words. Goodness, a devil? the other housemaid asked. You mustn't say things like that, Miss Encarna . . . Natàlia's father yawned again and went off to have his nap.

Natàlia flung the napkin on the table. She felt nauseous, and her lower back was throbbing. She threw up every last bit of her lunch. Encarna heard her heaving and went to the bathroom. What is it, sweetie? But Natàlia told her to leave her alone. Fine, then! Encarna walked out and closed the door in a huff. Natàlia brushed her teeth to wash out the sick taste in her mouth, then lay down in bed. *It's the fault of those bastards at the police station, and everything they put me through.* She had the sudden urge to cry, and burst into tears. She cried for all of it: the officer with the sad-dog face whom she'd mistaken for a good person, Emilio, who was still at the station, the cleaning lady who was confused for a hooker, and most of all, for herself. "What am I to do now?" She blew her nose. Encarna was outside Natàlia's bedroom door when she heard her whimper. She walked in and sat beside her. There, there. Get out, get out, Natàlia screamed, then immediately threw her arms around the housemaid, weeping. No, don't leave, Encarna, sweet Encarna! I don't know what I'm saying. There, there, Encarna said. You'll feel a whole lot better once you get some sleep. Encarna rocked Natàlia in her arms like a baby.

It was dark by the time Natàlia woke up. The flat was perfectly quiet. She slipped into her mother's bedroom, where Judit was asleep in the shadows. Our Lady of Sorrows gazed out from the display case with her pathetic cheeks, waxen face, open mouth, teary eyes, and open hands. Two electric tea lights flickered red on either side of her.

The test explained the nausea and the bitter taste in her throat. It had been two months since her last period. At first she had chalked it up to nerves. By the third month, she decided to visit the gynecologist. He's the most progressive gyno in Barcelona. Wait until you see his office, Blanca told her. The office was in Bonanova, on a steep hill crowded with single-family homes. The gynecologist's practice was located in the only tower block on the street, and it had a glass entrance, fig trees and bright green subtropical plants, as well as vines tangling over the whole front. A doorman dressed in white-and-blue-checkered overalls opened the door for them. There was soft background music, a cobalt-blue carpet, an ochre-velvet sofa, polished glass lamp-shades, and quiet, weightless elevators. The office was on the second floor and attached to the gynecologist's home. A thin nurse greeted them at the entrance. She had long golden hair and lips so pale and pink they were almost white. Dressed in an apple-green lab coat and light stockings, she ushered them into a waiting room with parquet wood floors, leather armchairs, a Japanese lamp, and prints of a Picasso and a Miró. In the room sat two nervy women, probably a mother and her daughter. Natàlia glanced at the woman who looked like the mother and whose plunging neckline revealed a generous cleavage. It's boiling in here, said Blanca. I don't get why they don't just turn on the air-conditioning, said the older woman. She was cradling a crocodile-skin handbag that matched her shoes and had on several gold bracelets strung with heavy coins. The daughter was broad-shouldered and wore her bleached-blond hair in an impressive backcomb. The mother didn't say a single word to her daughter, and instead simply fanned herself with a back issue of *Elle*. The nurse called in the mother and daughter, and Natàlia and Blanca gave them a once-over while pretending to leaf through a copy of *Triunfo*. Natàlia noticed that the daughter's behind was even flatter than her mother's.

It was finally their turn. Natàlia had spent the entire wait on edge. Relax, Blanca said to her. This doctor is open-minded, I promise. But Natàlia had never been to a gynecologist in her life. She had only been examined once, by Judit's midwife, and that was eleven years ago, at the time of her first period. The gynecologist looked surprisingly young; he was trim, wholesome—you could tell he worked out—and tanned, even though summer had only just begun. He motioned at Natàlia to sit down, then looked over her test results. What can I say? Natàlia and Blanca sat there in silence. The test is a clear positive. Which one of you is Natàlia Miralpeix? Her, Blanca said. The gynecologist called the thin woman over. Please start a file, nurse. The gynecologist's eyes were as blue as the sea. He looks good in that white coat, especially with his tan, Natàlia thought to herself. Age? When was your first period? Have you ever had surgery? For appendicitis, for example. Any infectious diseases? Family . . . ? Natàlia was starting to feel antsy, but the doctor carried on. Have you only ever had intercourse with the same man? How long ago was the last time? Did you use anything? Natàlia didn't understand. She looked at Blanca. Surely, it must have occurred to the two of you to use some form of protection. No, nothing . . . The nurse wrote it all down. The gynecologist thanked her and said she could go. We came here, Blanca said, because we want to know if there's anything that can be done about it . . . Slow down, one thing at a time. The gynecologist breathed softly. It never crosses your minds you could get pregnant, does it? You never think these things through beforehand . . . OK, what should we be doing? Blanca asked. You should be educating yourselves, seeking advice, coming to see me or any other doctor. Instead you fly by the seat of your pants! Natàlia wanted to know more about specific methods. *Coitus interruptus, Ogino,* washing after intercourse . . . The doctor saw her look of disappointment. Yes, fine, I'm aware these methods aren't always effective, and I never recommend them to my patients. But we've started receiving diaphragms from America and Britain, he said, and I can help you get one. One of my friends got pregnant while using a diaphragm. The gynecologist gave her a blank look. I'm sure your girlfriend, he said, wasn't using it properly. Listen, he continued, this country isn't getting any better. You know why? We lack maturity. People insist on behaving like idiots, women in particular. Just now a mother waltzed in here with her daughter and a fistful of money. I had to examine the daughter from behind to keep up the appearance she's still a virgin. After screwing her way around God's green earth, the girl has finally come to her senses and is getting married to a business magnate twenty years her senior. Her mother would hit the ceiling if she knew her "little girl" wasn't a virgin. And her husband will get quite the surprise himself once he realizes. What am I supposed to do with patients like that? Well, Natàlia said, the reason I'm here . . . The gynecologist got up and rang the bell. A tall brunette with short hair came in. She was wearing the same apple-green coat as her thin blond counterpart. Prep her for examination, the gynecologist instructed. The nurse blinked, then smiled at Natàlia. Follow me, she said and ushered them into the room next door. Please get undressed. Natàlia found herself behind a grass-colored folding screen. *It matches the nurse's uniform.* There was a large, frameless mirror. *Now what?* She called out to Blanca. Do I take everything off? Blanca smiled. No, just your underwear. Why didn't you say so? Natàlia asked. I'd have worn a skirt. Natàlia took off her trousers and underwear, then looked at herself in the mirror. She felt ridiculous with her vulva hanging out and a thicket of chestnut hair between her legs. *I'd rather die than walk out like this,* she thought. Blanca, she called out. I'm too embarrassed . . . Blanca went to fetch the brunette. She says she's embarrassed. Smiling, the nurse gave Natàlia a pink cotton sheet and instructed her to wrap it around her waist. Natàlia did as she was told and stepped out from behind the screen. The sheet fell to halfway down her calves, showing her socks. Should I put my shoes back on? No, said the brunette. Natàlia padded across the room. A glass-doored cabinet stacked with metal tools stood flush against the wall. In a corner of the room, beside the large windows, was a small sink, and in the middle, a long narrow table with a pair of steel stirrups. The stirrups faced up on either side of the table, which was covered in a sky-blue sheet. Up here, the brunette said, helping Natàlia onto the stool at the bottom end of the table. Natàlia sat back. Scoot a little closer to the edge, the nurse instructed. She removed the pink sheet and draped another sky-blue sheet over Natàlia's lower abdomen. Now put one leg on either side of the table and lie back. Should I take off my socks? Natàlia asked. The nurse said there was no need. Natàlia lay down and stared up at the ceiling. She couldn't figure out what to do with her hands. Her legs were open, and her feet were dangling from the table in their white socks. The gynecologist came in, lifted the blue sheet, and began pressing down on her lower abdomen. Does this hurt? Natàlia said no. What about this? No. And this? Ow! The doctor put on a rubber finger given to him by the brunette nurse, then slathered it with gel and started feeling inside Natàlia. He did this while looking away from her, at the wall. The patient's uterus appears to be enlarged. He took off the rubber finger and said something to the brunette, who walked up to the glass cabinet and grabbed an instrument resembling a pair of large metal tongs with a ball screw. He inserted the tool into Natàlia's vagina and tightened the screw. *I'm going to tear.* The doctor examined her in silence. He called over the brunette. See that? Yes, the brunette said. They spent a long time peering into Natàlia. Your uterus is prolapsed. Is that bad? Natàlia asked, but the doctor mustn't have heard since he proceeded with the examination. Look at the state of it, the doctor said to the brunette. Goodness! Trich? she asked, and he replied, By the looks of it. The doctor fetched a small glass rectangle from the cabinet and used it to scrape around inside Natàlia's vagina. Then he examined the rectangle under a microscope. He called over the brunette. Look, they're moving. The doctor went back to Natàlia. Didn't you have any itching? I did ... Well, it looks like you have trichomoniasis. What does that mean? she asked. It means your sweetheart gave you parasites. The doctor went back to her side and pressed again on her lower abdomen. Does it hurt here? A little ... I'm going to write you a prescription for an oral antibiotic. He washed his hands, then turned to the nurse: A question, to wrap up. How many months along is the patient? Hmmm ... The nurse hesitated. Come on, weren't you listening? I was, I was, replied the brunette nurse. I believe the patient has missed three cycles. Is that right? Precisely, said the doctor. You're an exceptional student. He grabbed Natàlia's file and went back to his office. Natàlia was still on the exam table, staring at the ceiling with her legs in stirrups, unsure of what to do with her hands. Oh, pardon me, said the brunette. I forgot all about you.

No, said the gynecologist. I'm sorry but there's nothing I can do. There must be something, someone you know who could—Listen, the two people I used to know are now in prison. The doctor looked at Natàlia. Your best course of action is to have the child. No, especially not now, Natàlia said under her breath. Suit yourself. The doctor slid her file into a white envelope. The words *Natàlia Miralpeix* had been scrawled at the top by the very thin nurse. The doctor saw the two women glancing at each other. Don't worry, everything we do here is confidential. My nurses are the picture of discretion. He wrote a prescription for antibiotics to treat Natàlia's parasites and then saw her and Blanca to the door. Natàlia could smell the doctor's cologne. *It's the same scent Lluís wears.* The thin nurse was waiting at the exit. That'll be seven hundred pesetas, she said.

Your best bet, said Emilio's friend the medical student, is to speak with a sex worker. They know more about these things than anyone. Natàlia was tired—she'd been to three addresses, *Dr. Martínez is away on travel,* said the first, the second didn't let her upstairs, and the third didn't exist—so awfully tired she'd decided that very morning to have the baby. But then a dizzy spell and bile reflux steeled her resolve to end things once and for all. All she wanted was to get the taste of hair out of her throat. That night she met Emilio's friend at a bar on Carrer Urgell. This is the place, he said. Inside: a counter, red mood lighting, and background music. A waitress who looked around thirty and had long mascaraed eyelashes, pink cheeks, and dyed amber hair gave them the address. At first she'd eyed them with distrust, but then Emilio's friend mentioned a medical student she had helped a couple of months ago. You *nice* girls always come to us for help. After, it's like you wouldn't know us from Eve. Natàlia sat down, her complexion sallow. Between the morning sickness and the bitter taste in her mouth—I just can't take it anymore, she said. Maybe if I'd never got Emilio's letter or if he wasn't in prison . . . She'd heard Emilio was getting hit with serious charges. The woman, whose amber hair was lacquered and very teased, turned to another waitress chatting animatedly with a client. What should I do, give her Casilda's address . . . ? The waitress, who had a masculine face and dark-green eye makeup, shrugged and said, Suit yourself.

The place was easy to find. Around the corner from Carrer d'Aragó, right where the hooker with the amber hair said it would be. A faded sign hung outside: *Casilda Cabrils, Midwife.* Casilda was a heavy-set woman with sagging breasts and sweaty underarms. Even though it was hot out by then, she wore a white long-sleeved robe. Angeleta sent me . . . The door was ajar and Casilda opened it all the way to let in Blanca and Natàlia. There was no one around. Come in, she said. They stepped into a dusky room with shuttered windows. Half the wallpaper had been stripped. There was a glass cabinet similar to the one in the gynecologist's office, except smaller and gray. A white towel was draped over half of the worn-leather exam table. The midwife asked Natàlia to lie down, then plugged in a cervical catheter. To help you dilate. Come back tomorrow. The next day, a man met her at the door. He was tall, slender, and bundled up like a mummy: he wore a helmet pulled down low over his forehead and a handkerchief up to his eyes. His gaze was empty—it was as if he were peering through a crack and his body were the wall. *He has the eyes of a crow.* The man with crow's eyes dug around inside Natàlia for a while, using a tool that resembled a deep, inverted spoon. As he dug inside her, Natàlia felt a pain in her chest. What's wrong with her? asked Blanca, who hadn't been allowed in and was waiting outside. Nothing, she's just nervous, the midwife said. A cold sweat that started at Natàlia's spine wrapped itself around her, followed by a surge of heat and the feeling that her heart was about to explode. Give her some Coramine, said the man with crow's eyes as he continued to dig around. There was nothing left inside her. She was an empty echo chamber. Finally, the crow stuffed a cotton pad in her with his claws, then another, and another. One blood-drenched pad after the other fell to the floor. When he was done, Casilda walked her to the door and gave her a box of sulphonamides. That'll be four thousand pesetas, she said.

Back at home, Natàlia's fever spiked and the room clogged with dancing shadows. A spider lowered itself toward her from the ceiling, in a spotlight, growing larger and larger, legs shuddering, until it reached and embraced her, squeezing her tight, its hairy, viscous legs branching into thousands upon thousands more that fumbled around for her body, then plunged into her. Natàlia's temperature rose, and she felt as if all her insides were shredding, unraveling. She felt a warm, hard body between her thighs and then several others, which slid down her legs as the spider kissed her and kissed her again without stopping, every single one of its legs kissed and stroked her—forehead and cheeks, chest and neck, legs and lower belly, her whole body bound together by thousands of hairy legs pinning her in place. At long last, the spider let go and Natàlia plummeted into a deep, dark, eternal well—a deep, black, bottomless well. Down and down Natàlia tumbled as she searched frantically for some limb to hold on to—where were they?—until she saw the spider's legs at the mouth of the well, their hairy tips peeking over the lip. Natàlia stretched out her arms—if only she could reach them—but only fell deeper and deeper with every passing moment, deeper into the gloom . . . Natàlia woke drenched in sweat.

The sheets were soiled. She stripped them off the bed, then soaked them in bleach in the sink. Her temperature was even higher now. She called Sílvia. Come over, right away. I don't feel well. I don't feel well at all, she muttered.

Sílvia arrived at the flat. What's wrong? she asked with a candid look on her face. What have you done? Natàlia regretted calling her the moment she walked in. Promise you won't tell my brother? Tell him what? Sílvia asked. Swear you won't tell him? Natàlia pressed. I swear. If you tell, Natàlia said, then you aren't really interested in helping. Of course I am! Sílvia shouted. I had an abortion, and I don't feel well. I have this horrific pain in my belly, and I keep losing huge clots of blood. Heavens, Sílvia said, bringing her hand to her mouth. Natàlia gave her the gynecologist's phone number, and Sílvia called him. "He says we're to go to this office, if we can manage." Thankfully it was Thursday, and Encarna was out. The carer was in Judit's room with the manicurist, who was doing Mrs. Miralpeix's hands and feet. Natàlia got dressed and splashed perfume on her hands and neck. You won't tell anyone, will you? Natàlia asked again.

The brunette nurse was already waiting when they arrived. She took them to a room attached to the doctor's flat and furnished with a sofa and white pinewood table. Natàlia lay down. Sílvia was jittery and could not stay still. Back in a minute, she said. The gynecologist wasn't long. The first thing he did was press down on Natàlia's belly. She felt a searing pain, like a drill boring into her body. The doctor kept pressing down on her as clots of blood gushed down her legs. That monster left half the fetus inside you, he said. Then he turned to Sílvia, who had just come back: Are you family? Sílvia said yes, her eyes fogged up. We're going to have to intervene. I'll take her to my clinic. Don't worry, I'll say it's a miscarriage. Natàlia turned to Sílvia. Remember, not a word to anyone at home. But Sílvia was so terrified she had already told Lluís.

PART FOUR
QUIETNESS

And quietness, grown sick of rest, would purge
By any desperate change.

WILLIAM SHAKESPEARE, *Antony and Cleopatra*

Joan Miralpeix began to climb the stairs—he felt so very tired. Whenever things went awry, Joan Miralpeix turned to sleep. He'd done so even as a little boy. He'd doze off, then wake up feeling infinitely better. When Natàlia left home, he took a long nap. She wasn't even twenty-five yet, a minor. But who was he to track her down and force her to come back? When Encarna said, Natàlia left, her clothes are all gone, he felt empty inside. What should he do? Lluís telephoned. Don't worry, she'll be home before you know it. It's not like she has a lot of options, anyway: a girl on her own, with no money or support . . . But Natàlia didn't come back, she didn't even write . . . Joan Miralpeix would doze off, and the headache would lift. He was only on the first landing and yet already panting. He knew he hadn't done right by his daughter when she was arrested, *I didn't want to say anything, it dredged up too many memories.* Encarna had opened the door for him in a fluster: The police telephoned. They have Natàlia . . . He knew straight away that it was "political." But he refused to go back there, he had buried it all deep down. Then came Natàlia—selfish Natàlia who hadn't a clue what she wanted nor any time for her own mother—stirring up the scent of the past. Don't kid yourself, Lluís told him. Natàlia didn't leave because of the arrest or because you didn't visit her at the clinic. All right, he said to his son. Then was it because of the hotel in Lloret? Lluís smiled. You're so naïve.

Joan Claret had connections in Madrid and so the whole ordeal was swept under the rug. You got yourself caught up in the dumbest way imaginable, Lluís told his father. Joan was frightened of his son—he had cold eyes. Joan had never fought with him. The two were wary of each other; they may have spied, stalked, and sniffed one another like dogs, but they never argued. It was different with Natàlia: Was it because she was more like him? Because she went after everything he had given up? Natàlia had her grandfather's temper, and the same deep gaze as Judit. Joan Miralpeix felt tired as he lumbered up the steps. He stopped on the second landing. "You should've spoken to her." Those were Father Jesús Maria Farriols's exact words to him the day he went to Montserrat for help: "You're proud and your pride is hurting you." But that wasn't quite it. He wasn't proud, he just wanted to rest . . .

It was the start of a bleak time for him, and Joan did his best to forget the person he had once been. Had it been possible, Joan and Judit would have altered their faces, hands, feet, and arms. Joan had only kept his language because it was too late to do anything about that. He sent postcards from the front that said: "Judit, my love, how I miss you . . ." But things began to fall apart at the Betanzos concentration camp, when he was made to write in a language that wasn't his own: *"Dear Judit, I heard what happened to Esteban in Gualba. Commie nonsense! Fortunately, they won't be around to make trouble much longer . . ."* They had to leave behind certain attitudes and behaviors, which had brought them so much misfortune. They needed to recast their thinking, change their way of talking, dress how *they* wanted, shut themselves up at home, sleep, fall into a long, deep slumber. They had to stay off the streets because the streets were *theirs*—the only possible revenge: making money—to greet people as they were told, and go to church—"naturally, there's no doubt at all that God exists." They had to take Communion and never laugh in the open—nor cry, for that matter—and burn the books *they* didn't like. They had to accept their language was worthless, buy things from the

German department stores, keep the house neat and tidy, go to the cinema, raise their right hands, and pretend not to hear questions like "Did you hear how many people were shot at Camp de la Bóta?" Joan Miralpeix was ever so tired when he came home from that dirty war. Lluís, who had wanted to be a professor, died, and they executed Antoni, who believed in the Republic until his very last. Joan Miralpeix learned early on that his friends from L'Ateneu Enciclopèdic Popular, Francesc and Emili—and Xavier—had managed to cross the border. Joan had the fewest charges against him and so chose to stay, a decision that cost him three years at a concentration camp—years he would never forget. And what about the others? He envied them for a while, during which he lived in the darkest fear. Later he found out Xavier had escaped Argelès-sur-Mer and moved to Mexico, where he made his fortune. Emili stayed in France and died in a German air raid right over Pont d'Orléans. Francesc died at an extermination camp, and those who saw him in his final days still remember his shell-shocked eyes and starved face: He'd gone mad and so the Nazis had him killed. He, Joan Miralpeix, had outsmarted them all—he'd saved his neck. Now all he wanted was to sleep like he had when he was a little boy and his father caught him with his head in the clouds and tugged his ears until they went the shade of red wine. I don't like daydreamers, Miralpeix Sr. used to say.

Joan Miralpeix and his friends ... After leaving L'Ateneu Enciclopèdic Popular, they would go out for an aperitif and talk and talk. Now and then—like the time after a Pau Casals concert—they would stay up into the small hours of the morning, discussing art, literature, politics, and, of course, their hopes and dreams for a different world. If only we could fill Barcelona with harmonious lines, and reconcile art and technique, said Joan Miralpeix, who had connections to the GATEPAC architects. Francesc was always butting heads with Emili, whose taste in literature differed from his own. Emili was partial to the avant-garde, to revolutionary fervor, and the eradication of the ego, while Francesc preferred the literary realism of Dos Passos and Hemingway. We need to return literature to everyday life, Francesc said. Just look at Hemingway's prose—he writes like he's talking to his mother. Emili laughed, Which is exactly why everyone thinks he's a terrible writer. So what? Francesc shot back. He writes that way so people will understand him better. Don't you see? Emili cut him off. You're an idealist. The people want flourishes; Hemingway's writing is too unrefined. Have you read *Point Counter Point*? Joan Miralpeix interrupted. Do you know what struck me about it? The way Huxley tries to reconcile physical and spiritual pleasure . . . It can't be done, Francesc quickly countered. Why not? Emili asked. British writers have been obsessing over the issue for generations. Haven't you read any D. H. Lawrence? Loving mind and body, melding them—it's extraordinary! Emili said, his eyes closed. In *Point Counter Point*, Joan Miralpeix continued, Mark Rampion talks about the barbarity of the soul and intellect . . . He says that Christianity made us barbarians of the soul . . . Isn't that a bit cynical? Francesc asked. And off they went again. The problem is you keep dreaming of a humanity that doesn't exist, Emili said. In that respect, you're a lot like Joan . . . Joan Miralpeix wasn't listening. Hey! That one was for you—you're always away with the fairies! Xavier walked up to them, All right, enough with the nonsense. Guess what I just heard: Madame Rita, the one who charges three pesetas, has some new merchandise. Steel yourselves, my friends. Rumor is there's a new French girl with a hole finer than a silk stocking! Everyone laughed except Joan Miralpeix, who pressed his top teeth into his bottom lip. Of course, you couldn't care less about these things. You have Judit . . .

There was a time when he rushed up the stairs. Once in a while, just to prove he could, he took them two at a time. *And look at you now,* he thought, *a clown. Heaving, clinging to the guardrail so you won't fall.* A hammer struck at his temples and a heavy slab pressed down on his chest. He felt like he was suffocating. He ought to take a deep breath—inhale, then slowly exhale . . . There, he felt better now. He, Joan Miralpeix, who'd been quite handsome back in the day. You look kind of Celtic, Emili said to him once. And maybe he did, one of his grandmothers was born in Galicia—what a long time ago, that was—before finding her way to the masia in Gualba. The father of the heir of Casamitjana had married a Galician. That was why Uncle Pepe looked so different from everyone else—"You have Galician blood," Miralpeix Sr. told him once with disdain. Joan Miralpeix was tall and blond with blue eyes. Liars have blue eyes, Judit would tease while touching him. He'd always had pale, swollen bags under his eyes, but now they were black and sunken, and looked like deep pits in a sea of wrinkles. You Miralpeixes and your under-eye circles, he heard all the time in Gualba. They make you seem exhausted. Ever since Mrs. Judit's stroke, Mr. Miralpeix has become a husk of himself, Encarna would say. A husk . . . She was right. He was hollowed out. His hairline receded in peaks and whenever he drank or grew overexcited, his skin glistened like that of a freshly skinned rabbit. He was a good dresser, Mr. Miralpeix, that much was true. A bit fuddy-duddy though, Sílvia noted, and she said this because Mr. Miralpeix still went around in gloves, a waistcoat, and a hat. He liked dark suits and roomy sports jackets that cinched at the waist; full-lined suits were a personal favorite, something Ribatallada, his longtime tailor, knew full well. When it came to his taste for fine clothes, Joan Miralpeix was like his uncle Joan Antoni on his mother's side, the man who taught him to love his country and introduced him to Marcel Proust . . . One day, Joan Antoni knocked on the door of the damp, run-down attic where he lived on Rue Montgolfier and said, Come on, stop messing around. Don't you see you're going cold and hungry? then treated him to dinner at La Coupole. That dinner—*Belle-vue de foie-gras, filet à la godard, légumes à la toulousaine, dindonneau à la broche, biscuit glacé, fromages, champagne frappé*—brought him back to life. As he bit into the turkey, his uncle said, I'm taking you with me to Barcelona. You should know I understand where you're coming from. You're a man of the world, you don't want to go back to the house in the country. But there must be something you'd like to study. And then Joan Miralpeix told his uncle he wanted to be an architect.

The following day he went for a stroll along the Seine. It was an evening of light rain—Paris rain. The docks were damp, and he walked as far as the tip of Île Saint-Louis. The water formed small eddies as it flowed. Joan Miralpeix looked up at the Paris sky, a vast sky that died on the horizon. A wiry old woman came up to him. Her legs were stiff like planks and her buck teeth nicotine-yellow. Between breaths of alcohol, the old woman explained to Joan Miralpeix that she wrote poetry, though not the kind of poetry people considered literature. The poetry she wrote was meant to be read in *intimité*. She showed him some of her poems. I dedicated this one to my cigarette smoke, she said. Don't you find that cigarette smoke awakens the imagination? Joan smiled. Ah, Paris . . . How much for the poem? he asked the woman, who replied, *Ce que vous voudrez* . . . He handed her five centimes. Is that enough? The old woman said yes, then added that she didn't like money, she only wanted it *pour vivre*. A boat lit up with lanterns glided down the river. There was the sound of violins. For a moment, Joan and the old woman were illuminated by its glow. There were people dining on the boat, and small, round candles shimmering on their tables. The woman left, feet dragging behind her. Under the Paris drizzle, Joan Miralpeix said goodbye to the city where he had discovered art.

He never saw Miralpeix Sr. again. A year or so after returning from Paris, Joan Miralpeix met a young woman with curly brown hair, emerald eyes, pale, translucent skin, and a neck like a swan's. She was the daughter of a Jewish man from France who settled in Barcelona after the First World War. The name of the young woman, who did not have a mother, was Judit Fléchier, and she had trained as a solo pianist. Those in the know said she played like an angel. But after being bedridden from the age of fifteen to seventeen, Judit had been made to give it up. The doctor said she would always suffer from poor circulation—this explained her pallor—and that even the softest touch would leave crimson marks on her white skin. Her father, who had moved to Barcelona in search of a fortune he could not find in his own war-torn country, died of typhus, leaving Judit a rather meager income. By the age of eighteen, Judit was fully independent and worked as a piano teacher at a few select houses. One of her students was Engràcia, the plump, cheerful daughter of Joan Antoni Farré, a well-known lawyer in Barcelona, and Joan Miralpeix's cousin. The first time Joan saw Judit he thought, *She's a Modigliani*, on account of her long neck, big eyes, and sallow gaze. Her eyes were restless and seemed always to be peering into the distance, as if looking to another world for help. She had a pathetic, helpless face, with cheeks the color of prune flesh, a yellowish shade that barely stood out from her wan complexion. *She's deathly pale*. Judit wore her hair short and up in the shape of a ring, which drew attention to her swanlike neck—a silken neck, Joan thought—and her breasts were small as clementines.

The first time Joan Miralpeix saw Judit, he stood frozen in front of her. What are you doing, dummy? his cousin said. This is the new piano teacher, Miss Judit Fléchier. Joan Miralpeix turned to the new piano teacher. A pleasure to meet you, he said and then couldn't think of what to do, whether to stay or leave. Engràcia started playing the first notes of a Chopin nocturne and Judit's hands—my God, such pale hands—adjusted Engràcia's warm, chubby fingers. For the sake of filling the silence, Joan said, All right . . . I suppose . . . I'll be on my way, then. Judit looked at him for a moment with something like melancholy, which was actually just her lazy eye. As he closed the door behind him, he heard Engràcia whispering and Judit tittering like a bird.

Joan was panting again by the time he reached the third landing and needed a rest. All because the landlady, an old stick-in-the-mud, refused to install an elevator. Yet Joan Miralpeix couldn't bring himself to leave the flat on Carrer del Bruc. Maybe it was because he could still see a faint spark in Judit's eyes, particularly when she sat in the conservatory gazing out at the inner courtyard. Back then, the inner courtyards of L'Eixample felt like islands of calm. What would her emerald eyes do if all they could see from the roof terrace in Bonanova were balconies? He rested his gloved hand on the guardrail. Now that his heart had quieted down, he felt he could breathe more easily. He heard the door of their flat open—it was Encarna, polishing the peephole and golden doorknob with Netol.

Joan fell more and more in love with Judit every day. *She's just like a Modigliani; she loves life and wants to hold it in her eyes.* They bumped into one another periodically on the stairwell of his uncle's place on Carrer Llúria with Carrer Diputació, and she greeted him in her French lilt. But Judit never smiled, she just kept climbing the stairs while Joan watched her until she was only a shadow and a rustle of footsteps on the landing. The scent of hollyhock filled his nose when she walked past him. One day Joan decided to wait until his cousin had finished her lesson. Bonbon? Engràcia asked. It's Judit's birthday. They offered him one that was chocolate on the outside and filled with a treacly sweet liqueur that flooded his mouth and dribbled down his throat. His breath grew sweet, and he had the urge to kiss Judit on both dimples, leaving a sugary mark. How old are you? he asked. You oughtn't ask a woman her age, Engràcia scowled with her moon face and apple cheeks. Was it possible she was in love with Joan Miralpeix? But Joan stared deep into Judit's eyes, and she tittered like a bird while taking a bite of a *marron glacé*. I don't mind. I just turned twenty. Isn't that awfully old?

He followed her out and walked behind her for a while. As they neared the intersection of Carrer Claris and Carrer Casp— she saw him out of the corner of her eye and slowed her pace—he caught up with her. May I walk with you? They strolled all the way to La Rambla, where Joan gave her a bouquet of roses. I'd like to get you a birthday present . . . Pick a color. Judit didn't give it much thought. The red ones, she said, and Joan Miralpeix bought her a spray of bright red rosebuds. She closed her eyes and sniffed them. I'm happy, she said. It wasn't long before Joan learned that when Judit was happy, she made it clear. Likewise, when she was sad. They stopped in front of a restaurant called Nuria and walked in. Joan greeted three women at a nearby table. Friends of my sister Patrícia, he said. The one who's always laughing is Kati. Kati had painted eyebrows and wore a knitted jumper and pleated skirt. She smiled at Judit while saying something to the very elegant woman beside her. That's the eldest of the three, Joan Miralpeix said. Her name is Mundeta. Isn't that a funny name? Judit ordered red currant syrup and he asked for a dry sherry. Judit looked outside and watched people strolling by.

Although her emerald eyes absorbed everything, she didn't give a single smile. Neither spoke much, but they sat there together a long time. She traced the gray and black veins in the marble with her finger. As they got up from the table to leave, Judit said, Oh look, the rosebuds have bloomed! then tittered like a bird.

One day Joan Miralpeix convinced his uncle to let him use the Hispano. He intercepted Judit on the ground floor of the Farrés' building and said, I'm taking my uncle's car out for a spin. Care to join me? Judit hesitated. It's dreary out, and it'll be dark soon ... But then she changed her mind and said yes without smiling. They went to Garraf first, a village desolate under a gray light and the quarry dust caked on its gardens and homes, but where the little houses looked like palaces. Judit and Joan laughed as they strolled by these small residences designed to look like stately homes, their tiny gardens crowded with statues. In the tiniest of spaces there might be a cherub or a reclining Aphrodite, as well as a water fountain and a stone bench. Everything was compact and crammed between the bougainvillea arbor and the pots of geraniums or hydrangeas. The statues had probably been white once, but they were filthy with quarry dust now—it was a day of high winds. This place looks like somewhere Snow White and the seven dwarves might live, Judit said. I could murder the architects responsible for these monstrosities. In architecture, it's the poetry of space that matters, he added. Later they went to Sitges, where they walked along the narrow streets and admired the vast doorways and pompier-style balconies of the town's elegant homes. It was very quiet. Judit and Joan made their way down the promenade to the murky sea, its waves fading into the clouds darkening on the horizon. A black cat followed them indifferently, and Judit thought it a bad omen. It was a drab, wet evening, an overcast evening of heavy seas. The water kissed their feet, and Judit bent over to wet her arms. They kicked off their shoes and ran as the waves grew tall and white with sea foam. Judit, who never smiled, let out the occasional birdlike titter, which faded into the roaring sea as though into a conch. They sat on the damp sand and Judit found a starfish. It's missing an arm, she said and frowned. Then she hunted around for shells. Joan sat, watching her. Find me some seashells, she commanded, I want to make a necklace. And Joan Miralpeix, who didn't care for the sea or the sand—it got into his shoes—spent an hour and change looking for seashells for the girl who tittered like a bird. He found one the color of stars and another the shade of sleet. You know, Judit said, I'm going to see everything one day, I'm going to travel to the end of the world. Suddenly the sky opened and fat raindrops drummed holes in the beach. The levant wind blew the sand up in a single sheet, and the waves grew tall and rough. As they ran for shelter from the storm, the rainwater battered Judit's clementine breasts, which showed through her shirt. They took cover in the Cau Ferrat Museum, where Joan told Judit everything he knew about Santiago Rusiñol, one of the leaders of the Catalan modernist movement. The bad weather finally cleared, the storm clouds thinned out, and the sky was streaked in ash gray and white. They went to a hotel near Cau Ferrat, a hotel with a carpeted lobby and a stately marble staircase with columned banisters on either side. They were both dripping wet, soaked to the bone. Why don't we get a room to dry off? Judit suggested. And they did, they requested a room and a couple of towels. The hotel looked out at the sea, and there was a view of the storm from the balcony. Now the clouds blackened as if it were nightfall, and a narrow sliver of blue sky lined the horizon. It wasn't raining, though drops fell from the balcony. Judit left the door open when she went into the bathroom and Joan saw her shadow and heard her singing under her breath. He toweled off in the bedroom.

Once his hair was dry, he sat on the edge of the bed, unsure of what to do.

Judit walked out of the bathroom naked. Her body was white as snowdrift. As she switched off the small light over the night-stand with the green lampshade, Joan's entire body broke into a sweat. He had the sudden urge to sleep. He wondered what to do, how he had got there. He wanted to leave. Judit opened the window, and air gusted into the bedroom. It was as if the wind were trying to steal the organdie curtains, which flapped about like the wings of seagulls. Are there ghosts? Judit asked, tittering like a bird. Leave, that's what he ought to do. But he was a statue cemented in place. He could smell her near him, the scent of her skin, the hollyhock perfume. One minute her skin was cold as snow, the next it was hot as embers. Kiss me, Judit said. All he could make out was her silhouette and the sound of his heartbeat in the silence between each crashing wave. Whose heart was beating harder? He had to tell her, he needed to explain he'd never managed before. The prostitutes he used to go to would either laugh or act maternal toward him. I don't know, Judit, I don't know if I can. And Judit, who burned like hot coal, reached for his lips, his tongue, all of him. Judit was not Judit, not the snow girl with translucent skin, nor the girl with the sallow gaze. He stroked her shoulder, then traced it with his finger. Why was he stopping? He set his palms back down on the bed. Judit, I don't know if I can . . .

There was a long silence. Let's see what we can do, Judit said. Hours passed. Now and then he had the urge to flee and pushed her away. But she kept coming back. She kissed his lips and mouth, their tongues entwined, his ear, the dimple behind his ear, her tongue inside his lips, her tongue on his teeth—it felt wonderful, and the hollyhock lulled his senses. Though he still had the impulse to run, she clung to him and held him close. She bit the nape of his neck and rubbed her breasts along his body, her touch shooting through his spine. He closed his eyes and felt her tenderly caress his sex. At first she kissed his penis so softly it was as if a light breeze had swept past him, and then there was a damp touch, the tip of her tongue. They tried four times. He was erect and she held him, guided him toward her. I can't, I can't, but his voice was subsumed by kisses and tears. She came back to him again and again.

He was still afraid and wanted to break free. But then Judit would say, eyes ablaze: Again. Finally, hardened by her kisses and her touch, he penetrated her, pushed himself deep inside her. He cried out and she tittered like a bird. Then came the gasps and the sweet exhaustion. They lay in an embrace, almost drifting off. See? And he said: I love you. In response, she asked: Shall I tell you a secret? I don't like roses, they bloom too fast. I prefer red carnations.

They made love several times that evening and with such intensity that by night they were breathless, so they called down for two glasses of dessert wine with sugar and an egg yolk.

On Christmas Eve Judit used to haul several potfuls of broth into the conservatory. They were too large for the refrigerator, and instead of lids she covered them with kitchen towels to regulate their temperature. Judit's broth was fatty; left to cool, a thin skin grew over the noodles. Holidays at the Miralpeixes' flat were well attended. There was the five of them—Pere, the youngest, hadn't died yet—Patrícia and Esteve—the family went to the Miràngelses' for the Feast of St. Stephen—Uncle Joan Antoni, the poor fossil, doddery Aunt Engràcia, and her daughter, Engràcia Jr. Engràcia Jr. was forty and unwed. "No one will marry her because her underarms are always sweaty," her mother admonished. Every Christmas Judit played the piano while Natàlia turned the pages, Esteve read a poem, Engràcia sang *"A Aragó hi ha una dama / més bonica que un sol d'or..."* while her mother nodded off beside the brasero, and Patrícia sang cuplés while tipsy on champagne. They all sat around the table and admired the *fiambres* prepared by Judit and Patrícia, the truffle-stuffed turkey, and monkfish in green sauce made to look like lobster. On the table set with Lagartera linen and fine crystal, Judit hid a present for every guest. By meal's end their cheeks were flushed and their heads warm and drowsy. On Christmas Eve Joan Miralpeix would read Natàlia and Lluís a story in Catalan from *Págines Viscudes* by Josep Maria Folch i Torres, while Pere entertained himself with the cardboard horse. To get you used to the language, Joan told his children, and Natàlia or Lluís would ask: What does *paó* mean? Meanwhile Encarna raked the charcoal in the brasero with a poker to keep it from going out. On those evenings Joan Miralpeix was more cheerful than usual and spoke to his children about all manner of things. We're a small country, he said. You must learn to love it, no matter how difficult things get. Encarna, who was only twenty-five years old at the time, would have prepared the brasero by lighting a few wood chips and covering them in charcoal or olive pomace. No scratching, Judit warned Natàlia, whose hands were covered in chilblains. Christmases in those days were freezing cold and they were fortunate to have a brasero. Joan Miralpeix would finish reading the story and turn off the light, as the children had to go to sleep before the grown-ups left for Midnight Mass. Judit prepared the Christmas *fiambres* herself—the store-bought ones weren't nearly as delicious. Those were difficult times and only rich people like them could afford to eat *fiambres*—though homemade, of course. A few days before Christmas, Patrícia and Judit would set to work in the kitchen, where no one was allowed in but the maids. Once the *fiambres* were ready, they displayed them on the table like artifacts in a museum and called the family over to admire them: pork loin stuffed with pig's ears, minced veal and pork mixed with truffles; duck neck stuffed with minced beef, truffles, and hard-boiled eggs; and cold beef stuffed with cooked ham and bacon, roasted a few days earlier. They would set them on silver platters covered in starched towels. And the family would exclaim, What a banquet! In the kitchen, Encarna was plucking the quills and feathers from the turkey they'd had butchered at the shop because it broke her heart to kill animals.

Everyone in the neighborhood said Judit was a bit much, yet every time she walked past the men turned to watch her. She wasn't pretty, but she had a certain quality that set her out from the other women of L'Eixample. In fact, Mr. and Mrs. Miralpeix together made quite the impression. She in her astrakhan coat, or a *renard argenté* wrapped around her neck, her *mouton doré* and boater hat with its upturned brim, her dark-colored sheer stockings and gloves . . . He in his hat and gloves, his waistcoat and tailored suit. People stared at them when they went out together. Although Judit wasn't a snob, she didn't have any friends. She tolerated Patrícia and greeted her neighbors from a cold distance. "She's proud," they declared, because she never smiled.

Judit only ever had one friend: Kati. They met in 1931. The first time Judit saw her, she told Joan that Kati was a rather strange girl. She was much more unruly than Judit—she laughed for no reason and liked to be the center of attention. Kati has no tact, Patrícia Miralpeix often said. Maybe so, maybe Judit's sister-in-law was right: Kati was always sticking her nose in, she knew everything and kept track of every detail. I like Kati because Kati likes life, Judit told Joan Miralpeix. Joan was delighted that Judit and Kati were friends, different though they were. Judit was reclusive; she liked the quiet, taking long walks on her own, and whiling away the time. Unlike Kati, a whirlwind who couldn't sit still. Maybe, Joan thought, it was Kati's lust for life that so captivated Judit. Kati was brave. She drove cars, went skiing, rode motorcycles—she adored high speeds. Kati dressed as the mood struck her, while Judit preferred dark shades and white, the color of snow, as well as fine clothing. Kati wore trousers and smoked like a chimney. Patrícia told Judit that Kati refused to wear a bandeau bra because she believed women ought to dress and feel free. When it became fashionable to do your eyebrows in almost hairless, pencil-thin lines, Kati had them waxed and would later have to paint them on. It makes her look exasperated, Mundeta Ventura observed. Kati looked a bit like Coco Chanel: they had the same thin lips, pressed into a determined, energetic line; the same gaze, somewhere between sad and defiant; and eyes that were incredibly dark and tired-looking. Kati admired Coco Chanel. I'm in love with her, she said in front of Joan Miralpeix and laughed. One day Joan saw Kati and Judit strolling round Patrícia's garden. Kati picked up a rose from the ground and gave it to Judit. Their hands lingered together. Then they let go and held each other's gaze for a moment or so. Kati walked quickly, torso erect, shoulders back, eyes forward, while Judit stopped every few seconds. Kati would call back to her from up ahead. Joan watched them for a long time. Kati wants to conquer Barcelona just like Chanel conquered Paris in the final days of the *belle époque,* Judit said, with only a pair of dresses. But Barcelona isn't Paris, Joan replied. Kati and Chanel are a lot alike, Judit continued. One of them went to a convent and the other to a finishing school for girls, but they're both orphans. As soon as Kati was fifteen, her relatives started fighting to have her stay with them. It turned out Kati was rich, very rich, her father having left her half of Valldoreix and a portion of Sant Cugat in his will. Kati decided her life belonged to her and only her and that she ought to make the most of it. The only person who stood up for her was Judit. She treats men like puppets, Joan said. Well, isn't that what they are? Kati asked with her dark eyes. Kati is frivolous, Joan told Judit. Her great-aunts in Terrassa were scandalized by her. They'd like me to be proper, a nice little girl, but they don't love me, Kati explained to the Miralpeixes. Kati is independent because she doesn't need men for their money, Judit remarked, and then she and her emerald eyes grew sad. Kati often said that money was freedom. Is she right, do you think? Judit asked Joan. Maybe she says that, he answered, because she doesn't have someone who loves her the way I love you . . . And Judit tittered like a bird. Don't be silly! she said. One day Judit told Joan: Kati says she doesn't want to die ugly. That's why she has so many lotions and dresses, Judit added. She wants everyone to know she exists. What Kati wants is to conquer the world with her manly ways, said Sixta, who could not stand her.

But then came the war—that dirty war, as Joan Miralpeix put it—that unsettled people's minds and rattled their souls. For Kati the war was a shared adventure, that of the many working together to build a brand-new world. Her transformation was drastic: she donated all her properties for use at children's summer camps and joined the Aliança de la Dona Jove, dragging Judit with her to their meetings for young female Marxists and Republicans. Don't you see? Everything is changing, she said with excitement. Kati had always been an avid reader, and now she devoured any Soviet book she could get her hands on. You know, she told Judit, I think I've found my calling. At night, Judit filled Joan in on all the ways in which Kati was changing. She did this in writing, since Joan had been among the first volunteers to march to the front. You miss him, don't you? Kati asked, and her eyes grew darker still. Kati and I, Judit wrote to Joan, are raising funds for Komsomol. Any day now, I'll be there on the front with you. Don't come, Joan replied. You couldn't bear all the death and misery . . . You know, Judit wrote, some of Kati's old friends are saying she isn't fun anymore, that she's lost her sense of humor. They're wrong . . . And do you know why? Joan answered. Because Kati is truly independent now. You're right, Judit wrote. We're learning so much from this war! I'm not the same person I was before, either. I see the children coming from Madrid and the Basque Country, and they're mere chicks, but with death and bombs seared onto their eyes. Our lives won't ever be the same if we win the war, Judit wrote to Joan, I'm sure of it. I'm going to go back to work. Kati says . . . And Joan smiled because all her letters were riddled with Kati says this and Kati says that. One day Joan got a letter from Judit that went: Guess what? Kati's in love, and this time it's serious.

Kati's beloved was in the International Brigades, an Irishman as blond as an angel, with dreamy eyes and full lips. He had rosy cheeks, a delicate jawline, velvety skin, and according to Kati, the chin of a prince. Called Patrick O'Brian, he changed names when his comrades in the International Brigades left because he wanted to stay and fight. He was one of the last to die in the Battle of the Ebro. And Kati, who loved life so deeply, killed herself the day the Nationalists descended on Tibidabo. Judit was terrified and shuttered herself at home. I'm not like her, she said to Joan when he returned from the concentration camp.

It was for this reason that Judit, who'd been brought up by her father, a French Jew with scant faith in Jehovah, endured everything that followed: She was not as brave as Kati. She converted to Catholicism and married through the Church. She and Joan baptized all three of their children, for how else would they get into religious school? True, she wasn't like Kati, which was why she attended Mass with Joan and the children and meekly returned home when she was turned away from the church for not wearing stockings. Joan Miralpeix went to Montserrat to seek advice from the monks because he didn't know how to behave. Joan and Judit closed in on themselves, souls folded into one another. Judit missed Kati and decided she wanted trinkets, a menagerie of objects that she began to worship like small gods. She fetched Our Lady of Sorrows from Gualba and placed the Virgin with the pathetic, waxen face beside her bed with two electric tea lights on either side. We'll fill the house with trinkets! she told Joan. And Judit, who never smiled, made sure the house was overrun with porcelain cherubs, holy cards, pictures, plastic flowers, quirky antiques—such as an owl that doubled as a doorbell—silver combs, a small blue carved-wooden box by Adolf Fargnoli where she kept the orange blossoms worn by all the family's brides, paper hand fans . . . I want there to be trinkets in our home, she said, and Joan would declare, The lady of the house would like trinkets! then go out and buy them for her himself. He got her a hunting horn and a hand fan made of peacock feathers, a medieval-looking dagger, and a Roman oil lamp. He got her leather coins and Renaissance plates, cheap imitation brooches and a Rococo mirror. After the war, Judit scattered these objects all over the flat. Now we can have different ambiances, she said. We can have the fan room, the doll room, the little-box room . . . She arranged three silk Japanese-motif folding screens in the sitting room, the largest in the flat, and every other room had a display case filled with her trinkets. This was why they could now say their home had several different ambiances. The dolls were the most important of all her trinkets. Judit spent several years acquiring them. There were dolls of all sizes, with and without clothing, and made of rubber, celluloid, or porcelain. In the end she hid them in her bedroom: Japanese, Hawaiian, and Chinese dolls; dolls in silk, tulle, organdie, and poplin; dolls with ringlets, braids, and Pamela bonnets. Judit stabbed holes in their eyes and tore off their hands. The more she made them suffer, the more she loved them. There was one doll with empty eye sockets, a chubby little girl that Judit enjoyed nuzzling after she fell ill. She would sit the doll in her lap and together the two of them would gaze at the courtyard from the conservatory. There were also dolls with glorious bodies, queenly bodies, and twiglike legs. Judit used to make crinolines for them and cover their little bodies in satin. Look, the boy dolls don't have penises, she'd say with her birdlike titter.

Those were cold, sorrowful days. Silent days of no rest, and there was very little Judit could find joy in. This was why she and Joan were happy when Christmas came around. Joan in particular smiled when he saw Judit arrive home tired after turning the city upside down and still no idea what to cook. She went to the Boqueria and to the best charcuterie shops in Barcelona; she bought the latest dairy products from the Mantequerías Leonesas and ordered wafers and nougat straight from Prats-Fatjó. Christmas came around and Judit made her *fiambres* and large pots of broth, then laid the table with the help of Encarna and Maria, the housemaid who got sick and died an old woman at Hospital de Sant Josep. They laid the table like a ritual, stretching the Lagartera tablecloths tight like bedsheets, which Judit smoothed with her hands, and setting out the silverware, including the utensils for fish, meat, dessert, and coffee, the crystal wine glasses, the porcelain dinner service with an illustration of a deer, the silver fruit bowl, bouquets of strawberry-tree branches and mistletoe, and ceramic red carnations from Judit's collection of trinkets.

When Judit and Joan got home from Midnight Mass, she would survey her domain: the broth cooling in the conservatory, the neatly tied *fiambres* in the casserole, the part-roasted turkey, the fire in the brasero slowly dying down . . . Then she would walk to Natàlia's bedroom and give her a kiss, to Pere's and give him a kiss—poor thing, she'd whisper, because her son had Down syndrome—to Lluís's, another kiss, and go into the fan room to examine her trinkets. It's so quiet, she would say.

Miralpeix Sr. had white hair and white whiskers. He sat at the head of the table and began to say grace while a pair of elderly, unwed aunts lowered their heads and whispered the Lord's Prayer. Joan Miralpeix was daydreaming, as always, and his father smacked him on the head. The family prayed under their breaths. Bless us, O Lord, and these your gifts, which we are about to receive from your bounty. Through Christ, our Lord. Amen. The housemaid served the escudella, and they all ate without speaking. Miralpeix Sr. was sullen and the two stale, decrepit aunts, of indefinite age and uncertain expression, whom Miralpeix Sr. maintained in exchange for them teaching Patrícia and Paquita how to be ladies, sighed while slurping the stew. The loudest slurper at the table, though, was Miralpeix Sr., whose every spoonful was an entire symphony. On Sundays the table-cloths were a brilliant shade of white and a chicken was slaughtered for the groundskeeper to roast. An uncle, a chaplain of the Barcelona curia, with trembling hands and innocent eyes, sometimes joined them in Gualba on Sundays. They also had the occasional visit from Miralpeix Sr.'s younger brother, Uncle Pepe, who was quick to laugh and liked to eat and drink. I'd sell my soul for a drop of ratafia, he'd say and burst out laughing. But then Miralpeix Sr. would throw him a chilling look and lunch would proceed with its usual gravity. This uncle didn't visit often, and the others whispered that he was a lost soul bound to meet a bad end, like all no-good men. And so he did: a few years later, Joan Miralpeix and his uncle Joan Antoni, on his mother's side, visited Uncle Pepe at the infectious diseases hospital. They found Pepe on his deathbed, face and hands covered in lesions from syphilis, contracted heaven knows where.

Grandfather Miralpeix had been a lifelong Carlist, much like his father before him, and died at the age of ninety. Miralpeix Sr. had to wait until he was sixty-seven to be the man of the house. His wife died when Paquita was born. In town, people said she was a victim of her husband—and when people call women victims, what they mean is that they are a fool or a saint. Every Sunday the parish priest stopped at Casamitjana for a glass of dessert wine, and the two aunts laid out starched tablecloths, then sat by the fire, hands folded and legs crossed. The parish priest was advising Miralpeix Sr., the new heir of Casamitjana, on parish affairs. Around Easter the parish church sent the Sacred Heart with a candle from house to house. Casamitjana was the first to receive the Sacred Heart, after the parish church.

Always with your head in the clouds, his father would say, and give Joan a hard smack. It was because of this that one night, when Joan heard a noise upstairs—a squeaking, and a long, drawn-out sigh—he was determined to track it down. He pricked his ears up and followed the murmur to his father's bedroom door. Yes, that was where the noise—and a low whimper—was coming from, he was sure of it. He asked himself what he ought to do: Should I take a peek, or should I leave? He felt a tingle in his stomach—but he was already at the keyhole and loved snooping, so he peered in. What he saw was so unusual that he couldn't make sense of it at first. Why was Remei tied to the headboard? And why did it look as if his father were riding her like a horse and scratching her back at the same time? The squeaking came from the bed—maybe the springs were worn. On the headboard was a wrought-iron Sacred Heart that moved back and forth at shorter and shorter intervals, as though being rocked. This to-and-fro had something to do with his father and the way he scratched Remei's back, as well as her whimpering. Why were they naked and why was he saying, hush, hush, my little mule? Why did Remei let out a small cry, a cross between tears and laughter that reminded him of the sound their spotted hen made whenever the rooster pestered her? The next day he asked Cinta, What was Remei doing tied up in my father's room? Why was my father scratching her back? And Cinta said, What a colorful imagination you have! But then Cinta must have told Remei and Remei must have said something to Miralpeix Sr., or how else could Joan explain the thrashing he got from his father that starlit night, when he was whipped around like a bell clapper and hurled to the floor? By the time he was done beating his son, Miralpeix Sr. had a limp hand, and Joan's tongue was like a rag from clamping his mouth shut and clenching his teeth, his lips bruised and his eyes bulging. Yet he didn't lose a drop of blood or shed a single tear. He went to Gorg Negre to gather wool— that's right, to wool-gather. He stayed there from evening until the dead of night, staring up at the stars, trying to count them and then starting all over again whenever he lost count. There was one star in particular that twinkled—was it Venus? And he told himself: That's where my mother is . . . The star blinked open and shut like an eye, its eyelids silver. Then he reached Gorg Negre, which was as black as a lie and dark as a well—*I'll swim all the way to Mallorca.* Uncle Pepe told him once, This will take you straight to Mallorca. He could hear the roar of water falling from the top of the Montseny mountains, and the torrents reminded him of his mother's tears—*Why aren't you here?*—which mixed not only with Remei's whimpering but with Ramon Berenguer's cries of pain too. For according to Uncle Pepe, in 1082 the Towhead was murdered in that area by his own twin brother, who wanted to be Count of Barcelona. Back then people killed for power, Uncle Pepe said. An awful thing, power . . . Do people not kill for power anymore? Joan Miralpeix asked his uncle. Nowadays, he said, there is more than one way to become

powerful. Ramon Berenguer's body plummeted down the water-
fall and Gorg Negre swallowed it up into whirls of darkness and
disquiet.

Ten uneventful years passed. Joan Miralpeix waited to come
of age and run away from the masia, his only company the voices
of Gorg Negre and the star with silver eyelids. Before Paris, he
spent three months in Barcelona. Joan Miralpeix didn't believe
in love; he thought women were basically small animals. This
was why he went to see that little whore Elvira from Rita's. I
want this one, he said when he stepped into the room and saw
her in front of him. He wanted Elvira because she had a mop of
hair as black as the waters of Gorg Negre. But it was hopeless,
she wouldn't take it—no is no—and, sure enough, neither could
he. Elvira said, Who do you think you are? Hearing the woman
shriek, Madame Rita came to their room and asked, What's
going on? But as soon as she heard, Madame Rita said: The customer is always right. Go on, hop to it. Elvira, who was from the
countryside, went up to the lacquered imitation Japanese wardrobe, the kind with three doors, and pulled out a porró of wine.
She was so nervous she drank straight from the bottle. Let's see
if she could stomach this odd young man tying her up, scratching her back, and calling her his mule, his little mule. Hey, listen!
I may be a floozy but I'm no mule. Where do you get off? But the
man wasn't listening, it was like he thought the whole thing was
like shooting fish in a barrel . . . And it was hopeless, Joan Miralpeix just couldn't do it. He tried the cheaper whores at Sagristà's,
the ones who went for three pesetas. He picked an older woman
with a wizened face caked in clumps of makeup. He picked her
because she had the same eyes as Remei, the eyes of a stunned
animal, and the whore said, You're only doing this to me because
I'm old and poor, or else you wouldn't dare. I used to be the
queen of this brothel. I had tits like a pair of fresh apples. Joan
immediately untied her. He couldn't stand to see her cry—the

only thing worse than a whore was an old whore . . . And he couldn't do it then either.

Joan couldn't do it because he believed he'd fall in love with a woman who was like the star with silver eyelids, a woman with wings, like his mother, a shadow of love. Other women, every last one of them, were mules. When he met Judit, he thought she was pure soul, a breath of spirit. Love was one thing and sex another, intercourse was sad and dirty, and rife with squeaks and whimpers. When Joan met Judit, he couldn't believe his luck. Where had she come from with her snow-white skin and Modigliani eyes? Seeing her, he instantly thought to himself: I must tell her I love her. What he failed to realize was that he only had this urge because he was reading *The Red and the Black,* where Julien Sorel was gripped by a similar passion for Madame de Rênal. But it was Judit who loved Joan like fire and not like an outstretched wing. She was sex and soul wrapped in one, his only breath of life after the war . . . It was for this reason that Joan Miralpeix couldn't bear to see the dead look in Judit's emerald eyes as they gazed at the courtyards of L'Eixample without seeing them.

After Judit had a stroke, Joan made regular trips to Montserrat to speak with Jesús Maria Farriols. In the monastery he found peace unlike anything he'd experienced outside. At night he strolled round the garden, among the shadows and mist of the mountains, and thought of Gorg Negre, so dark and wet, of the voices sinking in the whirlpools and the murdered count's howling, of his mother's words and the star with silver eyelids, of Remei whimpering like a frightened animal. The gurgle of water carried the hue and cry of the dead . . . Now, in the silence of the monastery, the mountains that rose up like apparitions reminded him of the plaintive sobs of the men and women who had died with their sorrows inside them, like the casualties of the war, the casualties of cold and fear . . . The mist shrouding the mountains of Montserrat, which stood like frayed, restive ghosts, must have also been descending over Gorg Negre. Like the mountains, he too could not find rest. He wanted to sleep, that was all, to sleep and forget the money he had made, to forget, above all, what had happened at the hotel in Lloret. Do you love anyone? Father Jesús Maria Farriols asked him. He wasn't sure he did, love anyone that is, only that he wanted there to be life again in her emerald eyes.

After the incident at the hotel in Lloret, Joan Miralpeix withdrew further into himself. The only thing he did of his own accord was to sit beside Judit in the evenings and stroke her unmoving hand. The problem, Father Jesús Maria said, is that you haven't let God fully into your heart. Maybe he was right, maybe he hadn't. The Benedictine continued, You've burrowed deep within yourself and know not how to get out. Joan Miralpeix stared at the priest and saw a glistening black eagle enveloping him in its wings and lulling him to sleep. As Father Jesús Maria laced his limp fingers together, his features altered: His ashen face morphed into that of an imperious raptor fanning out its black, lightning-bolt feathers. The eagle pursed its pale, frigid lips. The problem, Joan Miralpeix thought, wriggling free of its wings, is that your lips have never known a woman . . . The mountain peaks teemed with winged spirits, the same kind he had seen in Judit. He couldn't find rest in the monastery, perhaps because of how deeply he had loved their short life together, which started that one damp and dreary evening in Sitges, so very long ago. Do you read the Bible? the monk asked. Of course he did. He'd been reading the Bible ever since the world had been sullied with capital, after the war ended and a new era began when everything they touched turned to rot. Everything but Judit's body, which was made of snow but burned like embers . . . Before the war, Uncle Joan Antoni had given his nephew some books he'd bought during his brief visit to Paris. They were by a French author named Marcel Proust. It was Proust who taught Joan to love things not for what they were but for what they meant, but then things stopped meaning what they were, and all Joan Miralpeix wanted was to sleep. This was why he started making money, because making money was a kind of sleeping. But then Natàlia grew up and called him a coward, while Lluís called him naïve. Only in the Bible did Jesus Christ say to him: I do not hate you . . .

He reached his floor in the building. Encarna, no longer polishing the golden details, was waiting for him. Hurry, Mr. Miralpeix. Your wife is dying.

PART FIVE
GUARDIAN ANGELS NAPPING

*The new generations are born with good sense
and, cheated of their instinct for drama,
a thousand guardian angels are napping.*

JOSEP CARNER, "Rural Night"

There was nothing in the world Sílvia liked more than eating sweets. Whenever she went on a new diet, it took all her strength not to walk into the patisserie. The fragrance of burnt sugar, the smell of sweet milk and pastry, delicate puffs spilling over with whipped cream, *marrons glacés*, cake rolls dusted with confectioners' sugar, Sarah Bernhardt cookies, coconut and custard cake, trifles, and borregos de Cardedeu, with their hint of cumin . . . All Sílvia ate that Friday morning was a pot of yogurt. After wrapping the tape measure around her waist, she'd felt desperate. Five whole centimeters! Lluís didn't hear her because he was immersed in a sports-car catalogue sent by the Automobile Club. A single pot of yogurt—she was famished. That's why she let herself be seduced by the smell of pastries on her way to the gym. She ordered a hot cocoa and an ensaïmada, though not one filled with candied spaghetti squash—crazy as she was about squash-filled ensaïmadas. A regular ensaïmada would soak up the chocolate just fine.

As she walked into the changing room, she spotted her friend Merche, who was getting undressed. We had dinner at Scala last night, Merche said. What about the kids? asked Sílvia. I found this sitter. She's a perfect angel, charges fifty pesetas an hour and even puts the kids down. We drank buckets of champagne. Ramon was a riot, he had me in stitches. Dolors came over to them. Girl, you and your parties. Ramon insists on going out at least once a week, Merche said. Almost always on Thursdays, now that we're out of town on weekends. Lluís would happily eat out any day of the week, Sílvia lied. He doesn't really care when. I always overindulge when we go out, Merche continued, and then wind up bloated. Tell me about it, said Sílvia. You know Lluís thinks I'm overweight? You're not so bad. Dolors ran her hand along Sílvia's waistline and pinched her love handles. So maybe you have a little padding around the middle. And this ass! said Sílvia, turning her backside to the mirror. Just look at it! Have you seen mine? Merche asked. Though Ramon likes it when I have some meat on me. You know how it is, Dolors said, they want something to hold on to. Meanwhile, we're here starving ourselves. All three women laughed, causing Teresa to turn to them. What's so funny? Oh, nothing, men. Ugh, do not talk to me about men. Why, what's the problem? Mine. He wants to do it all the time. The man won't leave me alone. What a dog! the three women exclaimed. Teresa went on, He got it into his head that we should have another baby. Uh-uh, not a chance, Dolors said, fool me once . . . What are you doing about it? Sílvia asked. The pill. The pill makes me put on weight, said Merche. It gives me a belly. And heartburn, Teresa added. I heard you can get breast lumps too. Oh, hosh-posh! Dolors exclaimed. You're all just old-fashioned, it's utterly harmless. I was using a diaphragm for a while, Teresa said. It's a pain, Sílvia cut in, having to guess when you're going to do it and remembering to use the gel. Definitely, Teresa continued. It was awful. I mean, what if you forget? One time, my diaphragm slipped, which is how I got my darling son. I wouldn't mind having another baby, Sílvia said, seeing as Lluís won't let me work. But it's hopeless. Besides, Màrius is all grown up now . . . Carme came over to them. Do you girls want to try this new lotion? They say it melts away your fat. Honey, there's nothing I haven't tried, said Dolors. Lately all I seem to do is throw money at new fads. I slept in rubber trousers all summer to try to slim down, but all they did was make me sweat—I'm still a cow. What did your husband think? Teresa asked. I wore them in Pineda, he doesn't sleep there most nights. My husband, said Teresa, doesn't want me using anything. No creams, no rollers, nothing—he's a total bore. Sure you don't want any? Carme insisted. It's done wonders for me. After showering, I scrub my belly and thighs with a sponge, then rub cream all over my body with my hands flat like this—up and down, up and down. If your palms aren't perfectly dry by the time you're finished, you've done it wrong. Do you think I've put on a lot of weight? Sílvia asked Carme. She gave her a clinical look. What can I say, sweetheart? You've always been a bit full-figured. Sílvia frowned. You should've seen my silhouette when I was a dancer. Thin as a bamboo stalk. Time flies, honey . . . Sílvia and Merche didn't have calisthenics that day, so they started toward the sauna. Remember, girls, Tupperware party at Sílvia's tomorrow, Merche reminded the others. Sílvia felt put out. Do you think Carme is a bit jealous? What makes you say that? Merche asked. That thing she said to me. What? About me being a bit full-figured. Oh, don't mind her, said Merche. She's just bitter. Her husband cheats on her every chance he gets, the poor thing . . . The two women were wrapped in a pair of white towels that just about covered their bodies. They flipped the sauna's hourglass, unwound their towels, and lay back on the wood benches. *At least my breasts are still youthful,* Sílvia thought, glancing at Merche, who had four children and a flabby chest. Look at my belly, Merche said. I've got stretch marks all over. My skin just gave in after the third pregnancy. Ramon says I look like a model, but I tell him to cut the jokes—I have eyes, you know? You should get a massage, Sílvia suggested. Might help strengthen your skin. The only thing that will fix this is surgery. Merche ran her sweaty hand over her flaccid, stretch-marked belly. Sweat dripped down the grooves of her body and thinned out near her behind, where it turned into small, wispy rivers flowing down to her calves and ankles. But, Merche went on, who's going to remind Ramon that we still have to pay off the house in Pineda. The other day I got this fabulous massage, it did away with a good chunk of my cellulite, said Sílvia. Swear to God, I went from a size forty-six to a forty-two. You're so lucky, Merche lamented. I doubt I'll ever be any smaller than a forty-six. But it's just your belly, Sílvia said. Merche was seated. Sílvia looked over at her creased torso, where small folds of skin ran all the way down her belly. She looks like an accordion, Sílvia thought. The two women wore their hair wrapped in towels, a few errant strands plastered to their sweaty faces. Their bodies were encased in a thin layer of liquid, which formed a damp coating on their skin. The wood benches were hot to the touch and the air pressed into their chests. They sat in silence for a while, thumbing through magazines hardened by the dry heat. They flipped the hourglass three times before reaching their limit—they were suffocating—and leaving the sauna for a cold shower. They were both bathed in sweat, and it felt glorious to spin in front of the sprays of cold water jetting out from various points in the shower. Sílvia was happy after her steam, happy to feel the spritz of cool water on her skin. The women dried themselves on a pair of plush towels, then went back to the sauna and lay down on the benches. You know, Sílvia said, Lluís and I went to Perpignan to watch *Last Tango in Paris,* dubbed into Spanish . . . Merche's eyes twinkled. Oh, yes, tell me everything. I hear it's filthy. Sílvia shrugged. What can I say? I thought it was trash. Two strangers meet up in this empty flat—an old, musty place. He, Marlon Brando, doesn't want to tell her his name, and he doesn't want to know hers either. All right, but what do they do? Everything, Sílvia answered, in every way imaginable. Standing, on the floor, in the front, from behind. One time, she touches herself because he isn't paying attention to her. Goodness! Merche said. That does sound intense. Shush, said Sílvia. Now where was I? So she tells him that she is Little Red Riding Hood, *I'm a Red Riding Hood,* she says to him, *and you're the wolf.* Then she says, *What strong arms you have.* And Brando goes, *The better to squeeze you.* Then the girl says,

What long nails you have. The better to hold your ass, Brando replies.
What a lot of fur you have! And he goes, *The better to let your crabs hide
in,* and the girl touches all the different parts of his body. *What a
long tongue you have! The better to stick in your rear.* That's vile, Merche said. And they get up to all this in the flat? That's right! And
what else? Merche asked. Well, he tells her that *slaves used to be
branded on the ass,* and she confesses to feeling as if she'd been
branded by him, *I'm not free,* she says . . . And it's true, she isn't,
because she goes back to that flat every chance she gets. The girl
has these enormous, heavy breasts. Look at mine, Merche gazed
down at her chest. They're like eggplants. Sure, but the actress is
still young. She also has full lips and dark, baggy eyes, as though
she's done a lot of drugs . . . Do they meet for the first time at the
flat? Merche asked. No. They meet, or rather see each other, in a
restroom. A restroom? Merche almost screeched. The movie
sounds like pure filth! Both of them look dirty, like vagrants. Except *he's* Marlon Brando, Merche pointed out. But he's not the
Marlon Brando we know. He's . . . how can I put it? Old, burned-
out. He must be in his fifties now, right? Yes, but the thing is that
in his other films, he was acting, he was making movies. In this
one it feels like he's just playing a part, like he's playing himself.
Himself? Merche asked. Exactly, and even though the film is awfully crass, I felt sorry for him. What sorts of dirty things do they
do, though? All sorts. For example? Merche insisted. Is the butter
scene as vile as everyone says? Definitely . . . What does he do?
So it's breakfast and he's eating bread with butter. She gets to the
flat and starts sulking because she thinks he doesn't love her—
even though, at the end of the film, you find out it's the other way
around, he's the one who loves her, and she's so scared of Brando
she kills him—anyway, as I was saying, she's sulking because she
decides she simply needs to know his name and apparently, this
incenses him, so he throws her on the floor and starts roughing
her up; he treats her like an animal, a slave, just like he said he
would at the start. Merche's eyes filled with tears. He gets on top

of her and takes her from behind. From behind? Merche asked. From behind, but since he can't get it in, he smears butter on her ass like it's a canapé ... And the girl cries and screams—it isn't what she was expecting—but he's become this animal, he isn't listening, and he forces himself into her. How awful! Merche said. I know, Sílvia went on. And the girl, who started the whole thing as a joke, bawls her eyes out ...

Sílvia went to Perpignan—the City of Sin, as it was known in the Spanish press—on a cloudy Sunday. The evening before they'd stopped at the casino in Le Boulou to *flâner,* as Lluís put it. They lost six thousand pesetas to baccarat. "I'm not the kind of man to just give up," Sílvia's husband said, and he went back again and again until he lost half the money he'd brought with him. "We had a good time though, didn't we?" Perpignan seemed like a small, quiet city to Sílvia—she might have called it pale white—with a melancholy park of poplar trees that encouraged dreaming, and what looked like a cardboard castle. In Perpignan, Sílvia bought perfume and cheese and Lluís bought the latest issues of *Lui, Playboy,* and *L'Express.* Sílvia wore a pair of coral trousers that were a tight fit—they were a size too small—and a silver blouse that occasionally showed her belly button. Lluís dropped her off at the hotel and went to buy a copy of *L'Indépendant* so he could see what films were on at the cinema. Sílvia thought she would hop in the shower. When she undid her zipper, she took a deep breath and gradually let the air out of her lungs. After showering, she daubed cucumber milk on her face and then another lotion, Desert Flower, made of lanolin, all over her body. She examined herself in the mirror. Her waistline was a little slimmer. The last diet she tried had been more effective than the others, though now her chest had started to sag like autumn leaves. She took a couple more bottles and carefully applied the contents to each breast, avoiding the nipples—*Look, still pink.* The first bottle was filled with oil and the second held a creamier substance meant to help firm up the chest. She rubbed each breast in a circular motion, first in one direction, then the other—*I'd die if I had a chest like Merche's.* As she rubbed her breasts with the palms of her hand, she could tell they were still fairly pert. The chill of the liquid dripped through her fingers as it was absorbed into her skin. *I don't understand why Lluís won't let me go braless,* she thought with a sigh. She leaned into the mirror and studied her lips, wetting them with her tongue and moving them around a little, *I have to buy some cocoa butter—my lips are dry.* Lluís came back with *L'Indépendant.* Are you still in the bathroom? Hurry, I need to go. What films are they showing? At half ten, we'll watch *Tango.* At two, *Shock Treatment;* I heard Delon gets naked. At four, *La masseuse perverse.* At seven, *Caresses intimes,* and at nine, *Anomalies sexuelles.* A hell of a lineup! Lluís remarked. Sílvia padded out of the bathroom. She was wearing a pink dressing gown. What does *masseuse* mean? Don't you think it's a bit much? I'd like to watch at least one normal movie . . . Come on, Lluís said as he walked into the bathroom, don't be such a prude . . .

The day after Natàlia had lunch with her brother, she and Síl-via met at Bar Samoa. Just black tea with lemon for me, Síl-via said, I swear it's serious this time. The two of them sat outside, next to the window. Sílvia chatted nonstop, as usual, while eye-ing the passersby and the patrons sitting inside the bar on a kind of raised platform. Sílvia couldn't help commenting on every-thing she saw in front of her, and this was one of the busiest street corners of Passeig de Gràcia. All of a sudden Sílvia grew serious and asked Natàlia why she was back. I don't know, Natàlia answered. Sílvia barely waited for her to respond before saying, See, things are the same here as they've always been. Màrius is all grown up, I'm getting on, time takes its toll . . . You mean *we're* getting on, Natàlia amended. Well, yes, but it'll be different for me, Sílvia said, I'm going to get old without realizing, without having lived. It feels like only yesterday that I was a little girl. I wonder what happened. You know, Natàlia, and I'm saying this to you because I trust you, but sometimes I feel like Lluís is turn-ing into my dad. I don't know if that makes sense . . . What I mean is, I don't see Lluís as my husband so much as my father. Do you understand what I'm saying? I feel like he's always about to tell me off for misbehaving, especially when we make love . . . Sílvia changed the subject and Natàlia thought to herself, Same old Sílvia, always bouncing around. You're strong, you've always done whatever you want, Sílvia said. Are you sure about that? Natàlia asked. Looks can be deceiving . . . The thing is, Lluís was never in love with me and now it's too late for me to change. Say, Natàlia, why did you leave? Jimmy had also asked her why she'd decided to come back. The truth was, she didn't have an answer for either of them. Don't you know? Oh, of course! The abortion. Sílvia looked pensive. I was so scared . . . That's why you called Lluís, isn't it? What else was I to do? Sílvia asked. I needed money for the clinic. There are some things women just can't do on their own, without men. *Especially* when there's money involved. You're not wrong, Natàlia said. But you told Lluís, and you must've known he would tell Dad. How could I have? How was I supposed to guess your father would want to cut ties with you and hand you over to the police? But he didn't, Natàlia said, because of the incident in Lloret. Natàlia smiled. The same "honorable" man who wanted to turn me in to get back at me let five people burn to a crisp in a hotel! You know, she said, it made me laugh, reading about it at the clinic. I was so disgusted by my father, I didn't think twice about running away. The truth is I'm still disgusted, that's why I haven't gone to Gualba to visit. Lluís says you left so you wouldn't have to take care of your mother, Sílvia said. Is that true? There's some truth to it, Natàlia conceded. I didn't want to be holed up in the flat for the sake of a woman who was effectively dead . . . Didn't you feel sorry for her? Listen. Natàlia was beginning to get irritated. I've spent the past twelve years trying to teach myself everything all over again, even compassion, love, pleasure. I was a kid when I ran away, or at least that's how it felt. I had to unlearn all the values I'd had drilled into me since I was little. So don't you start on me now. I'm sorry, I didn't mean anything by it, Sílvia said. Why did you have an abortion? Why do you think? Do you really believe I was in any condition to have a child? You know, Sílvia said, I'm just dying to have another baby. Màrius is all grown up, he doesn't tell me about his life or give me kisses anymore. Natàlia went back to the previous subject. How come you didn't help me on your own, like I asked, when I had the abortion? I told you, I was scared. Damned fear, Natàlia thought. Those cold, miserable days . . . Sílvia had moved on to another topic. Passeig de Gràcia had turned ash gray, and a gust stirred the plane trees' naked branches. Sílvia sucked on the half-moon slice of lemon from her drink and wiped her lips with a Kleenex. They say spring is supposed to come late this year. Don't you think Barcelona looks particularly sad right now? Sílvia asked Natàlia as she picked at the lemon rind. Of course, you're so well traveled, you must think everything I say is ridiculous. I've only been to Paris and London. You know which city I know best? Perpignan. We go there a lot; we were just there watching *Last Tango in Paris* . . . Have you seen it? Natàlia shook her head. She didn't know how or why, but a thought drifted across Sílvia's mind like a storm cloud. You know, when I saw what Marlon Brando did to that girl—something everyone thinks is filthy, the same thing Lluís has been doing to me since we got married—I was shocked. Lluís only likes to have sex with me from behind, and I thought it was the same in all marriages. But when I saw it on the movie screen, from a distance, I felt sick to my stomach . . . Sílvia's eyes welled up. That must be why I don't get pregnant. I should take a lover, shouldn't I?

Aunt Patrícia had the runs on account of the Jumilla wine and so couldn't attend Encarna's wedding. Lluís and Sílvia had committed to a dinner honoring the president of the Tennis Club—an important relationship for Lluís to cultivate. Natàlia and Màrius were the only Miralpeixes to attend Encarna's marriage service.

Encarna's feet hadn't touched the ground—she'd been in a frenzy all Saturday morning because the salesgirls at Pronovia still hadn't finished her dress. On top of everything, she'd decided to go back to the salon for a manicure. Her nails were a disaster from all the dishes she washed and the bleach she scrubbed with, and she wanted to have them painted green, like Liza Minnelli in *Cabaret*. Isn't it a bit much? the manicurist asked, and Encarna was affronted. Who did she think she was? As soon as she was married, Encarna thought, she would never set foot there again. And so she told the girl that she wanted her nails done green, like Liza Minnelli in *Cabaret,* and that was that. When she got home, she found her dress wrapped in tissue paper and held up with pins. The seams had been let out a fair bit and a strip of lace—a gift from Patrícia—sewn to the front. Encarna had purchased a girdle with hook-and-eye clasps that fastened at the thighs. The other kind, made of Spandex, was always rolling up and giving her a hideous lump round her middle. Back at the flat, Encarna made Mrs. Miràngels some chamomile tea. The poor thing had drunk too much the evening before and had a terrible stomachache. I feel wretched, Encarna! I was so looking forward to your wedding. Encarna comforted her a little while, then went on her way, she had such a lot to get done before the ceremony. She filled Mrs. Miràngels's bathtub with piping-hot water, added a pinch of green bath salts and a generous splash of pink Moana. The suds drifted up in a cottony cloud. Encarna was happy—like in the movies, she thought. She lowered a white, bunioned foot into the suds only to immediately pull it out again as the water was scalding. She tried again, little by little. She poked her nails into the suds, then plunged in her fingers. Still too hot. She turned on the cold water and swished the liquid around with her hands. Finally, Encarna got in and lay all the way back with only her head and feet sticking out. She extended one of her legs, which was short and plump, and realized she hadn't waxed, nor would she have time to. She had a mountain of things that needed doing. Encarna felt content in the water. She raised one leg, then the other, both covered in varicose veins, with fleshy calves and bulging knees. She touched her breasts. Her nipples were dark, almost black, small pimples clustered all around them. Will Jaume still want me after he sees me naked? Encarna thought back to when she was young, when she had small, firm breasts like new apples and nipples so pale rose they were nearly white . . . Pedro, who'd gone to Germany never to be heard from again, used to twist her breasts like he was unscrewing a lightbulb. Jaume had been courting her for ten years, yet Encarna couldn't make her mind up. At first she hadn't wanted to abandon Mrs. Miralpeix—she felt so sorry for her, except then Mr. Miralpeix went and lost his marbles and started behaving in such an odd way . . . But Jaume was a good man—fifty years old, a widower from his first marriage, no children. Woman, you're a fool, Rosalia said to her. Don't you want a family of your own? Encarna didn't know what to do. On the one hand, she needed a place of her own to live, or she might end up at an old folks' home; on the other, she'd spent her whole life taking care of everybody but herself. What difference did it make now? In the end she decided to write a letter to Elena Francis, the agony aunt. She listened to her show every evening while doing the ironing under a twenty-five-watt bulb because Mrs. Miràngels couldn't spare the money. She mulled over her letter a long time. "Dear Mrs. Francis," it started. Should she get right to the point? No, what if she offended her . . . "Congratulations on a very enjoyable radio show." Encarna deliberated for a moment, then decided she wasn't quite satisfied with the word *enjoyable*. She settled on *fantastic* instead. The letter continued. "I've been dating a man for ten years . . ." She ought to mention her age . . . "I'm fifty years old and have been dating a man for ten years . . ." No, she couldn't bring herself to send it. Mrs. Francis might laugh at her. On second thought, there was no one else in the world she could turn to . . . "Only you can help me." Encarna reflected again. Should she mention what she did for work? "I'm a housemaid." No, no, no. Her being a housemaid was beside the point; also, someone might identify her. "I earn a good living." Quite truthfully, she hadn't been given a raise since Mr. Miralpeix had cracked up and didn't have the heart to ask poor Mrs. Patrícia. "I earn a good living, am well-mannered, fulfill my duties . . ." It was time to introduce Jaume. "The man I'm seeing is fifty years old. He is serious and polite . . . I used to think he loved me, but lately, when we get together, he is sullen and jittery. We met at my sister Rosalia's bar and, frankly, I'm tired of working every day of the week . . ." She posted the letter. Fifteen days passed and nothing. Mrs. Francis had forgotten all about her. Encarna put it out of her mind and told herself the show was a scam. Then one evening she heard her letter on the radio followed by a reply from Elena Francis to "Shy Woman in Madrid." The letter read: "Dear Mrs. Francis, First of all, congratulations on a fantastic radio show. I'm fifty years old and have been dating a man for ten years. Only you can help me. I earn a good living . . ." Encarna puffed out her chest and went on folding the towels. She felt happy—it gave her a thrill to hear herself being talked about on the radio. She listened to the response: "Dear friend, A decade-long relationship in one's fifties weighs a lot on a man. This is something women don't often get to see for themselves. Long courtships are hard for men. Buck up, dear, and stop acting like a child. Show your sweetheart some compassion and marry him as God intended, THE SOONER THE BETTER. Yours truly . . ." The words *the sooner the better,* which Encarna felt had been written in capital letters, rang through her far beyond the final notes of the jingle. Encarna's chest contracted again. It sounded like she ought to marry Jaume . . .

By the time Natàlia and Màrius reached the church, Encarna was married. It was ten past six. It would seem that the pastor was exceptionally prompt: the wedding had lasted exactly ten minutes. Natàlia and Màrius had to wait quite a while to see Encarna, though, as she and Jaume needed to be photographed with all their relatives. Encarna and Jaume with Rosalia and her husband and small children; Encarna and Jaume with Encarna's godson; Encarna and Jaume with Jaume's goddaughter; Encarna and Jaume with Jaume's elderly uncle; Encarna and Jaume with Encarna's niece and Encarna's niece's husband; Encarna and Jaume with a pair of married friends they had known all their lives; Encarna and Jaume with Jaume's little brother and his little brother's wife; Encarna and Jaume with two of Encarna's cousins; Encarna and Jaume with a neighbor of Rosalia's who was like a mother to her . . . The last photo was of Encarna and Jaume with Natàlia and Màrius. Jaume seemed dazed, Encarna looked stiff in her Sissi-style wedding dress, and Màrius couldn't figure out how to hold his face and so turned his right cheek to hide his pimple. Encarna was deeply offended when she found out Sílvia and Lluís wouldn't be at her wedding. "I cared for Mr. Lluís like my own son, and this is what I get in return . . ." she said earlier that morning to Patrícia, who hugged her tearily after realizing she wouldn't be able to attend. "I wish you all the happiness in the world," Patrícia said as she squeezed her tight. Encarna had to blow her nose to keep from weeping like a baby.

The reception was held at Rosalia's bar. The newlyweds seated themselves rather solemnly at the head of the table. Jaume was a lean man with short hair and a shiny forehead and wore a generously cut gray suit that was somewhat showy. He was a timid fellow with pale eyes and sweaty lips that gleamed when he smiled. Encarna looked smug in her mousseline dress with its puffed sleeves and lace neckline. A bit immodest for someone so long in the tooth, don't you think? Natàlia heard someone next to her say. Encarna had on a thick layer of foundation and bright-red blush on her cheeks. Her top and bottom eyelids were painted in white eye shadow that faded into blue and looked a tad bruise-like. Her eyelashes were double-mascaraed, and a few had clumped into a thick curtain. Encarna had done her own red lipstick in the shape of a heart. She looks like a clown, said the same voice as before. Rosalia and her husband served the first course, and their niece served the second. I hear she sank nearly all her savings into that dress. Natàlia turned around to see who was speaking: a fat woman with a manly face was chatting with a short woman with gaunt features. It doesn't suit her, said the woman with the gaunt features. A bit much, isn't it? added the woman with the manly face. They passed around pa amb tomà-quet and beef, as well as large pieces of chicken, steaming-hot potatoes, bowls of olives and tomatoes, and jugs of sangria. At first anyone who happened to come in was treated to drinks. After a while, the shutters were pulled down, as more and more people kept wandering in. Everyone there was Andalusian, with the exception of Jaume and his uncle, who were from Murcia but spoke Catalan, a couple from Aragon, and Natàlia and Màrius. Encarna's sister Rosalia was a short, fat woman with a moon face, turned-up nose, and small, ferret-like eyes that sparkled with life. Her chest was fuller than Encarna's and she wore a dress that showed off her glorious cleavage. She liked telling people she was a straight talker, and always insisted on having the last word. Rosalia sat all the guests around the table. Her husband was short and scrawny. His hands trembled and his speech was slurred from when he had fallen off scaffolding and crushed his brain. He sat in a corner of the room with a cigarette hanging from his half-open mouth. The man's breath stinks, the woman with the gaunt features said about Rosalia's husband. When things became rowdier, Rosalia's husband got right in the middle, did a couple of flamenco steps, clapped his hands, and yelled *olé!* then sat back down in silence. Rosalia, who was already pickled, yelled, Get over here, hubby! The fat woman with the manly face said, Sure she calls him over now, but later the tramp will treat him like a ninny! And Rosalia's husband fluttered over to her like a nestling.

Not all the guests fit around the table, so they placed another one right next to it. Both were covered in white polyester table-cloths with a scalloped, perlé finish. Jugs of sangria passed from hand to hand, and as people got more and more raucous, En-carna wrinkled her nose and furrowed her brow. One of the clasps on her girdle had come undone and was digging into her skin. Jaume whispered something in her ear, and she said no. Jaume was sweating, hair plastered to the nape of his neck. He looked a bit like a lost dog amid all that commotion. Someone started yelling in Spanish, *To the newlyweds!* A guy three sheets to the wind shouted, *Kiss, kiss, kiss!* and then again, *To the newlyweds!* Everyone laughed. Someone at the head of the table called back, *To marriage!* A chubby woman from Aragon with blue eye shadow started singing jotas while shimmying her body. A young man pulled Jaume up from his seat, held out his necktie and snipped it with a pair of kitchen scissors. *Careful where you wave those things!* Rosalia yelled in Spanish. *He's got work to do tonight!* added the woman with the manly face. Someone took a photo of the neck-tie being lopped off. Màrius covered the pimple on his cheek. Did you see? asked the woman with the gaunt features. Encarna had her nails done just like the woman in *Cabaret*. Natàlia went up to Màrius. Are you bored senseless? No, he said. This is a living document. Natàlia smiled and thought, *He still sees life as a "living document."* A short, ugly man played the guitar for the woman singing jotas. Màrius closed his eyes. What are you thinking about? Natàlia asked. Nothing . . . Maybe he was thinking about Rimbaud or Everett Millais's *Ophelia.* She disliked the damp smell of poverty. Natàlia thought back to when she and Emilio used to watch the popular theatre shows his friend put on in working-class neighborhoods—there was the same whiff of misery, the reek of hot air, condensation seeping through the walls, the waft of cheap wine and garlicky breath . . . *The poor always smell the same,* Natàlia thought. One night she'd admitted to Emilio: I'll never get used to it. And she was right, she never did. Everyone she met abroad was rootless like her—lost souls fleeing crumbling cities, people who wouldn't accept or delve into the smell of poverty, but instead caught a whiff of it from behind disinfected glass while brandishing theories about what might save the children of the poor from that centuries-old stink. A twelve-year-old girl with crossed eyes, possibly the daughter of the Aragonese woman who was singing and the man pounding the guitar, danced in the middle of the room. Someone took a picture. The girl, whose breasts were as small as olives, shook her ass like she was thirty years old. *It's unbelievable, I've been back less than a week and all my years abroad are already a blur. It's as if nothing has changed.* Just look at him staring at her, the no-good bastard! said the woman with the gaunt features, glaring at a fat, ginger man whose face was cratered by smallpox and who couldn't take his eyes off the woman from Aragon. The man was smoking a cigar, which he occasionally slipped behind his ear, smiling like an idiot. The woman from Aragon disappeared, only to reappear soon after in her husband's pajamas with a stocking over her face, a Cordobés hat, and a matador's cape. The Aragonese woman was making a fuss and messing around with everyone. Her husband paused his guitar playing to clap along. Someone took a picture of the Aragonese woman with a stocking over her face alongside her clapping husband. A man with milky skin and an aquiline nose clapped. Next to him, Rosalia smoked a cigarette with a fake ivory mouthpiece while pulling faces, mostly with her lips and tongue. Look, said the woman with the manly face, she thinks she's one of those women from *Un, dos, tres* . . . What's *Un, dos, tres?* Natàlia asked. A game show on TV, Màrius replied. Encarna's sister got up from her seat and scrambled onto her chair. She hitched her skirt. Ugh, how cheap, said the woman with the gaunt features. Skirt hitched up, Rosalia joggled her flabby thighs and shook her ass like a ship in a storm on the high seas. Someone took a photo. A man in a beret with tomato-red skin, gray whiskers, and pinched lips shouted out coarse encouragements in Spanish. Encarna was pale and woozy; the clasp digging into her thigh hurt like the devil. The guy who was three sheets to the wind hadn't stopped shouting in Spanish, *To the newlyweds!* as the others shouted back, *Kiss, kiss, kiss!* Another man with frizzy blond sideburns played the guitar and sang serranas while his wife stared at him like a lost puppy, surrounded by their children. She looked like a child herself. At the other end of the room, a man with small, wide-set eyes and a flat nose was belting out a soleá. Rosalia went over to Natàlia. You see the man over there singing soleares? One day his wife comes home and says, I'm off to the dry cleaner to starch the bedspread. Except she gives him the slip, and he never sees her or the bedspread again. The tart left him with two little ones to bring up. That was fifteen years ago. The man with the wide-set eyes was singing songs deriding women. The woman from Aragon shook her backside and the ginger man with the cratered face winked at her. From time to time, her husband let out a cry that was like the howl of a caged animal—though judging by the expression on his face, his was a happy cry—then huddled in a corner with Rosalia's husband, who had started drooling. Nearly everyone was clapping now, even the wife of the man singing serranas and surrounded by children, though she did so with a sad air. At first the bride and groom didn't play along, but the crowd wouldn't stop hollering *Kiss, kiss, kiss!* so eventually Jaume pulled Encarna toward him and gave her a hard, determined kiss. The woman from Aragon waggled a banana and everyone laughed. But the newlyweds embraced for a long time, so long the guests stopped joking and started watching them in silence. Some took a photo of the bride and groom kissing, and another of the guests watching. The man with the cratered face, the woman from Aragon, her husband, the man with the wide-set eyes, the woman with the sad air, the one with the manly face, the man with pinched lips, the one with the milky skin, Rosalia's husband, the girl with breasts as small as olives, the woman with gaunt features, the guy who was three sheets to the wind, the man singing serranas, the children, Rosalia, Rosalia's niece, all of them gazed with respect and gravitas at the bride and groom as they kissed. Natàlia and Màrius also watched the bride and groom kiss while at the same time watching the guests who were watching the bride and groom.

Once they finished, everyone applauded, and the revelry resumed. Rosalia beckoned to her niece, and the two retreated to the kitchen, resurfacing a while later with a present for the newlyweds: an uncooked sausage with an egg on either end. The whole bar began shouting, and the sounds of applause mixed with *ooooooohs,* which mixed with stomping feet and clapping hands, with children squalling, the guitar pounding, the jars and glasses clinking, and the sound of one man singing serranas and another soleares. Rosalia placed a small cup of coffee on her chest, jiggled her breasts, and said, Look, look, it's not falling. Jaume smiled faintly at the sight of the sausage and eggs, and Encarna pretended to be embarrassed. The last picture taken was of the bride and groom kissing again while in front of them the Aragonese woman's lover waved a sausage.

At first everything in Sílvia and Lluís's new flat was just lovely. A couple of decorators who had worked with Lluís before designed all the furniture in the sitting room and had lengthy discussions on how to fill the space. Every object was carefully considered, and Sílvia had a hard time persuading them to let her keep the collection of small owls she'd started at the flat in Guinardó. Lluís hung up Cubist paintings, decking the walls in geometric lines and frosty tones. Only the library was kept in a traditional style. The lamps, tables, and shelves were all designer. Lluís was one of the first people to use light tones and display Arte Povera—so-called "poor" art—in the maisonette on Carrer de Calvet, before sofas were displaced by cube poufs and built-in shelves supplanted the pinewood bookcases that once furnished so many of the flats of Barcelona's illustrious bourgeoisie. Later, when things broke down, Sílvia commissioned new ones from Vinçon. The glass lighters chipped, and Sílvia bought more. The imported Japanese curtains frayed, and Sílvia bent over backward to find an identical pair. Lluís wanted his home to be kept just so. In his words: the flat ought to look like it's about to be photographed for a design magazine. And so he smugly showed off the new metal-tube shelves that took the place of his father's stodgy walnut bookcase. But there were things Lluís didn't notice: tiny chinks in the crystal, nicked corners, gaps along the bottom of the walls, leaky pipes, moth holes in the velvet upholstery, beaten-up mats, tattered bedspreads.

Sílvia covered up the holes and tears, the loose seams and chipped crystal—not so much fixing everything as making sure Lluís would not see it. Only two things mattered to Sílvia: the kitchen and her body. Sílvia had gradually let herself go, so she was even more determined to keep their house, that stronghold of lost love, presentable. All I want, she said, is for there to be peace at home. Lluís worked long hours, he wasn't cut out to fix up the house himself. Sílvia knew this perfectly well.

Every Saturday after lunch, Sílvia went out of her way to tidy the house even more thoroughly than usual. She made sure the crystal was spotless and the corduroy poufs well-positioned in the sitting room, that there wasn't a single speck of dust on the shelves or any old papers in the magazine holder. She also cleaned the ashtrays and starched the rug under Judit's piano. Saturday was when her old school friends came to visit and all four of them—she, Teresa, Dolors, and Merche—went to the gym together. It thrilled Sílvia to see her friends admiring the flat. Everything's so modern! Teresa would say. Original too, Dolors added, running her fingers along one of the curtains in the maisonette, or across the tablecloth. It was an obsession of hers, being able to recognize fabric by touch. No, don't tell me, she'd cry out. Hemp! It isn't? Then it must be linen, she'd conclude triumphantly, only for someone to correct her: satin. Merche would walk into the kitchen and breathe in the smell of food. Sílvia, you angel! Are you baking us a cake? And all four women would crowd in front of the oven. What a treat! Teresa would exclaim with glee.

On the Saturday of Encarna's wedding, her girlfriends were coming over with their husbands. Lluís was close with Tomàs Renau and especially Ramon, Merche's husband. Barcelona was up against Bilbao, so they'd agreed to meet at the Miralpeixes' before heading out to watch soccer. The women, meanwhile, would have a Tupperware party—Merche had convinced her husband to let her run them. You could host! Merche had said to

Sílvia. Your house is so cozy. All you have to do is throw together some snacks, and if the girls buy a container or two, Tupperware will send you a gift. Sílvia agreed. But when she told Lluís about it, he said, What an asinine idea. You women will do anything for a kick. But there was soccer on that day, and Ramon and his friends were coming over, so in the end he conceded: Suit yourself.

The first to arrive were Dolors and her husband Albert Mateu, a manager at La Roca. Sílvia showed Dolors a piece of lingerie she'd bought on sale. Dolors touched it, feeling the fabric beneath her hand and stroking it with her fingers, then concluded: Very nice. And I got it for a song, Sílvia said, all smug and satisfied. Sílvia dragged Dolors into the kitchen to smell the custard pastissets baking in the oven. I just love the scent of burnt sugar, Dolores sighed. Meanwhile, Lluís was showing Mateu the latest sports-car catalog. So, what do you think of the Jensen-Healey? Mateu didn't miss a beat: Powerful motor, spot-on suspension, good cylinder capacity—an excellent purchase, my man! Then he patted Lluís on the back. My dad, Mateu continued, had a Jensen 541 with a fiberglass body—an extravagance at the time. What Mateu failed to mention, and Lluís never forgot, was that his father had been a chauffeur and that the Jensen 541 didn't belong to him but to a famous business magnate in Barcelona. Mateu was very proud he had made it this far—a manager at La Roca with a house in Pineda and a Seat 341—surely no one could tell he was the son of a chauffeur? British cars are terrific, Lluís said. Jensen was the first company to produce a vehicle that could go up to 180 kilometers an hour—a tremendous feat. Guess what Albert got me for our anniversary, Dolors asked Sílvia. What? A cruise around the Greek islands. Isn't it a dream? How marvelous, Sílvia said. You'll get to see Greece. The doorbell rang. It was Merche, her husband Ramon, and Teresa, who'd come on her own. Tomàs is in Malaga; it sounds like they might send him there as the director of La Caixa, you know.

The men sprawled in the office in leather armchairs, drinking coffee and Torres 10 brandy. They smoked cigars while discussing the energy crisis and the Middle East's bid to enter the world of capital. How are we supposed to manage without oil? They'd better not tell me to tighten my belt. Don't worry, Mateu reassured them, we've got plenty of reserves. There's oil from Venezuela, Lluís said. Sure, Mateu replied, except it's nationalized. Don't you think Russia is behind all this? I bet they made a deal with the Arabs just to mess around the Americans, Ramon said. It's certainly possible . . . Merche unwrapped the Tupperware and set it all out on the glass table in the sitting room. The women were drinking black tea with lemon, with the exception of Dolors, who liked hers with skimmed milk. Tea or coffee? Sílvia had asked the men. Coffee, Lluís said. And a drink too! the others protested. Why not a cigar, while we're at it? Lluís suggested, taking a box of Montecristos from the walnut desk drawer. As Sílvia served her girlfriends tea, she whispered, As soon as they leave, I'll bring out the pastissets. They all laughed, delighted to be her accomplice. What's so funny? Ramon asked from the office, whose door had been left open. Nothing, just girl stuff . . . Merche had removed the last of the plastic containers from her leather suitcase, which had purple marbling. What a pretty suitcase, Sílvia said. I bought it in Italy, Merche replied. And it isn't a knockoff, you know! Real leather. I saw one just like it at Loewe, Teresa added. Sure, those aren't authentic, though; I saw them in the shop window as well.

Now look, Merche said, Tupperware containers come in a bunch of sizes . . . But Rexac is constantly offside, Mateu complained. He's a lump, Ramon noted. No, he isn't. The issue is he's chicken. The guy's got a good pair of legs on him too, Lluís added. Me, I'm partial to El Cholo. You mean Sotil? That's right. You know, I hear he used to live in one of those flats in Pedrables that's worth millions and that he and his family ate on the floor. I don't get it, Ramon said. When he could've been living like a king . . . Merche held up a container. This big one here is good for vegetables or salad. Or a kilo of meat! Dolors teased. They don't look so different from the ones at the grocery store. True, but food stays a lot fresher in these than it does in any container you'll find at the market. A week, fifteen days, you name it. All you have to do is put the seal on tight and push down on this little flap sticking out from the lid, then lift the seal a teensy bit on one side and let the air out. See? Like this, right on the middle of the lid. With no air inside, the food stays fresher. But meat spoils after two weeks, Dolors insisted. Honey, you are dumb as a box of rocks. Didn't you hear what I just said? Teresa was seated on a leather barstool, arms crossed at her chest and legs tucked beneath her. Dolors was lying on a rug on the floor, smoking one cigarette after another. Sílvia had remembered to put the biggest ashtray next to her. Dolors was wearing a leather, antelope-skin miniskirt and matching grayish boots. She had a very thin black line penciled over her eyes and light-green eye shadow. Merche was the dressiest of the four friends, and wore fake eyelashes, which she fluttered with a mix of innocence and guile. She was awfully proud of her husband. The man's a genius, she asserted, and he did it all on his own. The four women had succeeded in getting their respective husbands to become friends with each other, which is how they themselves had managed to stay friends since convent school. Lluís designed the Mateus' and Renaus' houses in Pineda, and Tomàs helped them get a loan at the bank.

Albert Mateu wore a beige sweater, and corduroy trousers that were a shade darker, and Lluís a checkered pullover like the ones popular in the 1950s. The women would go out shopping together for their husbands and, while they were at it, catch up over tea. Teresa, who sat closest to the men, eavesdropped on their conversation and giggled at Ramon's wisecracks. Merche continued, There are smaller ones too, perfect for storing grated cheese. Dolors whispered to Sílvia, It's always best to keep the men where you can see them, not out and about. The two women laughed and stared at Teresa, who was listening to Merche go on about how to prevent aioli from separating. Store the meat in the freezer and I swear it keeps longer than fifteen days, Merche said with her eyes on Dolors, who barked with laughter. You mean, *they're* better when we can see them. Sílvia winked at Teresa and Dolors. The two of you are shameless! I'm quite happy with my husband away, said Teresa, who had heard everything. Sure you are, Sílvia replied. Will you please all listen to me, yelled Merche, who was beginning to feel put out. Oh, honey, we're sorry, the three women said and turned their attention to the containers. These round ones are for broth. But all you girls do is complain, Teresa said, her cotton-white skin a touch loose and hands as translucent as a lampshade. What matters is that your man sticks with you, she said, misty-eyed. It's not like you see much of your own husbands. The veins in Merche's neck were beginning to pop. The three of you are going to drive me up a wall, she said. Tupperware is better than tin foil. More practical, cheaper in the long run. Plus, it can hold liquid and all the rest. See them? Please, said Sílvia. They're never home. Meanwhile, we're whisking the children all over the city, Teresa added. Sílvia turned to Dolors: You wouldn't have a recipe for stuffed cabbage, would you? Why do you ask? My sister-in-law's back, I want to make it for her one day. That minx is home, is she? Teresa asked. She's not a minx, she's just different, Sílvia said. Merche turned to Teresa. My ears are still ringing from my kids shrieking in them. All I do all day long is wipe snot and clean up pee. Don't you have a sitter? Teresa asked. Of course I do, but I'm their mother . . . If I were you, I'd put them in daycare. But Ramon won't allow it. He says children need to be with their mothers. I agree, Teresa said. I for one would like to work, Sílvia told Dolors. Merche heard her and jumped in. You should do Tupperware demonstrations like me. They're a hoot, there's free food, and you get to spend time with your girlfriends. Merche addressed everyone, Now, if you could all please let me know what you're planning to buy, or *I* won't get my commission and poor Sílvia won't get her gift. Dolors picked out two of each—she figured she could give a set to her mother, who was becoming more sophisticated by the day—and Teresa four small ones. What a cheapskate, Merche said under her breath. Well, my husband won't hear a word about me working. Neither will mine, Teresa added. He hasn't exactly said no. He just passively resists. You know, Merche said, the last time I got pregnant was when I saw Humphrey Bogart in *Casablanca* on TV. That part where he goes, *Here's looking at you, kid* . . . Don't you think my Ramon looks a bit like Humphrey Bogart? Especially when he half smiles with his left side. If you say so, Sílvia teased, and they all burst out laughing.

The men left to watch the match. Mateu lingered at the door, then turned to Teresa and said, You're looking better every day. Obvious, isn't it? That her husband's not around, Dolors whispered to Sílvia. Sílvia slowly shut the door and then waited a minute until she heard the hum of the elevator. She called out, They're gone! The others responded, Hurrah! Bring out the pastissets, Dolors commanded. Sílvia went to the kitchen, where she arranged the custard-filled pastries on an oval platter. Merche scowled, Aren't you wicked, depriving the poor men of dessert. Don't be a hypocrite, Teresa replied. Dolors asked, Should I grab the sherry? The cognac too, Sílvia suggested. We're going to let loose today, Merche exclaimed and then let out an electric shriek. Woo! Teresa joined in, clapping. The four women sat around the glass table, then dug in. I live for sweets, said Sílvia, her lips smeared in custard. The Tupperware had been set aside, the suitcase was open, and papers were scattered all over the floor. Kneeling, they took one pastisset after another. I absolutely love custard, Dolors fawned with her mouth full. The bottles on the floor got emptier and emptier. Teresa was on her fourth glass of sherry. Greedy, greedy, she chided Sílvia. Says the pot to the kettle, you lush. This sherry is divine. Dolors went, Say *xérès*, like the French. It sounds more elegant that way. Teresa's tongue was thick. If I say *xérès*, does that make this a *fête*? I guess it kind of does, Sílvia reflected. Lluís says we're European. Is that right? Merche giggled. Long live Europe! Sílvia fluttered her arms like she was performing the dying swan. You're all a bunch of snobs, Dolors snapped, her eyes flashing. Merche: Oh dear, I feel a bit woozy. You really can't hold your drink, can you? Dolors teased. The bottle of sherry was half empty; Teresa, Merche, and Dolors were sherry drinkers, while Sílvia preferred cognac. Look, look, watch me gargle, Sílvia cried out. Doesn't that hurt your throat? Teresa asked. I like cognac. Sílvia licked her lips. But remember, according to TV, it's a man's drink, Dolors reminded her. The liquid was disappearing faster and faster from the bottle. Their cheeks were ablaze. I'm burning up! Sílvia yelled, yanking off her turtleneck sweater. Now there's an idea, Dolors said as she undid her blouse and her skirt, stripping down to her tights and bra. Teresa was the last person to undress. What an adorable set, Dolors said, complimenting Sílvia's black-lace bra and underwear. You like it? I've always enjoyed wearing nice underwear. I don't, Teresa said. I mean I don't care, considering what they're for. Let's play a game, Merche suggested. Let's! Teresa clapped. How about charades? Oh, fun! Dolors and Sílvia exclaimed at the same time. Who's up first? Dolors volunteered Sílvia. Why me? Because you're the host . . . And who baked you those pastissets, hmm? You've no shame, Dolors. Now, now, girls, don't fight, Teresa said. We'll count it out. Eeny, meeny, miny, moe . . . Merche's up. That's not fair. Afraid so, love. The numbers don't lie. Merche left the room. She was gone for a while. She sure is taking her sweet time. Don't chew it over so hard, will you? You're not a cow. As they waited for her to finish mulling, the three of them whispered, now and then roaring with laughter. Merche came back, and the three formed a circle around her. She knelt on the floor, looked up, and brought her hands together as if in prayer. An anchorite! Sílvia called out. Merche gestured

to say no. A saint. Merche lowered her head. But what saint?
Merche nodded. She lifted her shoulder and drew a large circle
around her head. An important saint. Merche waved her hand.
Got it, Dolors said. A very saintly saint who prays a lot. Teresa
cut in, St. Maria Goretti! But Merche shook her head. If it isn't
St. Maria Goretti, then maybe it's St. Gemma Galgani. Merche
shook her head again. Oh, oh, I know! Sílvia cried, clapping her
hands. St. Eulalia. Merche said yes, then, Phew! St. Eulalia, Teresa grumbled. What are you complaining about? It was an easy
one ... Your turn, Sílvia, since you got it right. I already thought
of one, so you don't get to talk behind my back. So mistrustful!
Sílvia bent over, as if she had a large humpback. *The Hunchback of
Notre Dame!* Dolors yelled. Sílvia shook her head. It is a hunchback though, right? I suppose it could be a camel ... Sílvia shook
her head again. All right, a hunchback. But who is it? All three
women were deep in thought. Rats, I can't think of anyone. Who
could it be? Teresa asked, and Sílvia laughed. She pointed at her
upper lip and drew prickly hairs with her fingers to show she had
a mustache. A hunchback with whiskers? Sílvia planted herself
in front of Teresa and slapped her on the cheek. Ouch, that hurt!
Sílvia rolled her eyes back and moved her hands around rest-
lessly. What are you doing now? I think she's praying the rosary,
Merche said. Teresa and Dolors both called out at the same
time: Mother Rosario? Sílvia nodded. The sherry and cognac
bottles were now empty. The women's eyes gleamed, growing
wider and wider. Now let's do the time the nuns tried to burn
Sílvia's hands, Dolors proposed. Remember? Merche and Teresa
said, Of course we do. Don't touch me! Sílvia cried out, but the
three women were already on top of her. Sílvia was on the verge
of tears. Leave me alone, please, leave me alone! But Dolors
wasn't listening, and her hands grabbed at Sílvia. Teresa mumbled, Maybe we should stop ... Then Dolors said in Spanish: *I am
Mother Asunción and you are Mother Superior.* She went to Sílvia's
bedroom and came back wearing a blanket over her head. *Sílvia*

Claret, you look filthier by the day. Please inform your mother that if she doesn't wash your uniform tomorrow, we'll have no choice but to burn your hands. And Sílvia went, *No, please. I promise not to do it again. Fine,* Dolors said. *In that case, pray three Hail Marys.* Merche was playing Sílvia's mother, You tell Mother Asunción I'll wash your uniform when I feel like it. Sílvia turned to Dolors, *My mama says she'll wash my uniform when she feels like it.* Dolors's eyes glazed over. *Hmm, I see.* Her mouth widened into a large grimace. *Is that right? Then I guess we shall have to burn your hands.* Merche was in the kitchen, where she made a show of lighting the stove. Teresa and Dolors dragged Sílvia toward her. No, Mamà, please, don't let them do it! Sílvia cried, but the two nuns howled even louder, and the Mother Superior slapped her on the mouth. *Shut up, you insolent child.* Sílvia was sweating and her hair was tousled. She cried, Mamà, Papà! Come back, don't leave me here. *Speak Christian,* Mother Asunción ordered. *You're a naughty, naughty girl!* Sílvia's bra straps had snapped, exposing one of her breasts. *You dirty little Jezebel!* Merche was in the kitchen, shouting, *Let the devil take her!* Mother Asunción covered her eyes and roared, *Holy Mary Mother of God. You're naked. A mortal sin. You'll be going straight to hell!* Their racket filled the sitting room, and as the women dragged Sílvia to the kitchen, the corduroy pouf shifted this way and that. The Mother Superior broke a ceramic ashtray with her foot. Sílvia held on for dear life to the curtains separating the sitting room from the dining room, unraveling the hem. They finally stepped into the kitchen. Merche, now Mother Sagrario, waited for them with the burners on. Just as they were going to place Sílvia's hands on the fire, Dolors morphed into Mother Socorro, who said, *What are you doing to my sweet child? Leave the poor girl alone. It isn't her fault she has a bad mother. What about her grandmother?* Mother Superior asked. *Letting them walk around without sleeves.* Mother Socorro ran her fingers through Sílvia's hair. *But our girl is a perfect angel, isn't she?* She cradled her like a newborn babe. *There, there, my angel, my little angel,* said Mother

Socorro while comforting Sílvia, kissing her on the lips, removing her bra, and caressing her breasts. *What about us?* Mother Sagrario asked. *What if the devil dresses up as a man? What will we do then?* Merche transformed into a devil with horns, a tail, and a bloodcurdling face. She pulled Teresa out for a dance while spitting left and right. *They danced, and the devil dressed as a man stroked her naked back,* Mother Socorro said as the devil unbuttoned the girl's blouse, *and his claws marked her for the rest of time, Amen. My sweet lamb, you must conquer men without them realizing.* Merche kissed Teresa's breasts. *Get away from me, you devil! I want to stay pure. Please don't make me sin.* Teresa folded her hands in front of her chest. But the horned devil had already mounted her—and he was howling, clawing, kissing, and nibbling her body from head to toe. In a corner, Dolors was petting Sílvia. Merche jolted up and said, *Girls, girls! What's going on? You're sinning!* Then she pulled Sílvia and Dolors off one another, and the two yelped in surprise. *Let us now pray for forgiveness: O Lord, Jesus Christ, Redeemer and Savior.* The four women knelt beside the glass table, naked and disheveled, surrounded by leftover pastries and empty bottles. *For every sin we have committed, we shall stick a single needle in the Sacred Heart.* Sílvia stood up and went to the sewing table, where she fetched a blood-red pincushion in the shape of a heart. They each stuck in a needle.

It was a long time before the women snapped out of their alcohol-fueled daze. All four were draped over the corduroy pouf. The first to wake up was Merche, who staggered to the bathroom to get dressed. She was in there for a quarter hour, in silence. Then the whoosh of water out of the toilet tank and the open tap sounded faintly in the sitting room. She left without saying goodbye. In the meantime, Teresa and Dolors helped one another to their feet. They shut themselves in the bathroom after Merche and pulled on their clothes, each assisting the other with her bra. They washed their faces and returned to the sitting room. They gave a feeble goodbye to Sílvia, then groped along the wall to the entryway. Alone in the flat, Sílvia remembered she needed to change for dinner at the Tennis Club. She turned on the shower in the bathroom and let the water trickle over her body, so hot the rising steam almost burned her. She scrubbed herself with a sponge, but it was too soft, so she reached for the pumice stone. She soaped her body, then used the pumice stone on her skin—and so hard, it turned bright red. There, I'm nice and clean now, she muttered to herself.

Natàlia and Màrius left with the party in full swing. Rosalia's husband lowered the shutters behind them, yet they could still hear the commotion as they drew away. Outside, there'd been rain. The streets were wet, the balconies dripped, and the tree trunks were dark. Natàlia and Màrius walked the stretch to the bus stop, Màrius with his hands shoved in his pockets and his shoulders in a slight hunch. Natàlia's arms were crossed beneath her chest. The jacket pocket of her corduroy suit swung back and forth in time with her steps. What did you think of the reception? Natàlia asked, but Màrius said nothing, only the beginning of a smile flitting across his dark face and strawberry lips. They walked a while longer without speaking and Natàlia was reminded of Jimmy's silence when they used to stroll along the banks of the Avon at daybreak, their shoes damp with dew and their faces rosy from the brisk morning weather. It wasn't long before the bus pulled up. Màrius didn't say a word to Natàlia the entire ride, and merely smiled in response when she spoke. Why don't you take me somewhere? she asked. Where do you want to go? I'm not sure . . . Take me to see some music. Even though Màrius didn't reply, Natàlia followed him when they got off the bus. This way, he said, and Natàlia complied. Màrius remained sullen down the steps into the metro and then into the last train car, which was more or less empty at that late hour on a Saturday, out of the station, and onto Plaça de l'Àngel. They walked along Carrer Princesa, which was damp and gloomy, then turned down Carrer Montcada. Isn't the Picasso Museum on this street? Màrius said yes. Carrer Montcada was dark and narrow, pressed between palaces guarding centuries of silence. The patina of history and everyday life had given the buildings a mossy green coating. A black cat slipped through a doorway. They circled the Basilica of Santa Maria del Mar, the only sounds water trickling from the balconies and distant footsteps reverberating in the quiet streets. They walked past a vacant lot that doubled as a parking lot. "Al fossar de les moreres no s'enterra cap traïdor," Natàlia recited. What's that? Màrius asked. Oh nothing, something your grandfather used to read me. *No traitors shall be buried in the Fossar de les Moreres.* Do you know Serafí Pitarra? Màrius said no. The Santa Maria neighborhood hasn't changed, Natàlia thought to herself. Dim streetlights, dank walls, the smell of mildew, silence, the deadened patter of feet, the shadow of the church like a ghost in waiting, enclosed balconies with the occasional wilted geranium, laundry hung to dry on Carrer de Sombrerers. Every now and then a section of ruined wall revealed faded murals or the outline of a staircase. The neighborhood is dramatic, run-down; it's as if the buildings had been decorated only to be moved to a different stage, Natàlia thought. They walked past a church and onto a street that intersected with Montcada. Why did we go the long way around? It's a ritual, Màrius answered. I get this feeling in my stomach when I'm in this neighborhood, like I used to live here a long time ago. Natàlia laughed. Who knows, maybe in a past life . . . Màrius looked at her with Judit's eyes. Don't laugh, I'm sure of it. Years ago, I lived right here in this part of the city. Natàlia said, My father told me once that his mother's parents, meaning your great-great-grandparents, lived in this neighborhood their whole lives . . . See? Màrius looked triumphant. Over the entrance of a building halfway down the street was a large sign with the names of old textile warehouses written in modernist type. We're standing right where our forebears lived, Natàlia said. Our ancestors, who thought they were helping Barcelona become a city of consequence! The two laughed. The old textile-warehouse lobby was now a large, drafty hall with stripped walls. A pair of thick velvet curtains separated two open-plan rooms. The ceiling was carved wood, as were the cornices and molding. A folding screen split the large entrance in two, one side cluttered with modernist mirrors in golden frames. The tiles drew a pale flower garland on the floor, worn down by footsteps and the passage of time. On the other side of the velvet curtains—red like the Union Jack—were the counters of the old thread warehouse, which now served as a bar. There was the sound of a guitar, and Natàlia and Màrius walked inside. Next to the counter, a wood partition wall pointed to the late existence of an office space; now the room served as storage for empty bottles. Natàlia said, Your great-great-grandparents probably had a warehouse like this one . . . The room was crammed with bar tables surrounded by second-hand, worn imitation-leather armchairs. The place was packed, mostly with boys and girls fogging up the room with smoke and listening in silence as a guitarist struck some opening chords. The boys and girls—*and the occasional old hag like me*—were dressed in bright colors, long skirts, suede boots, loud scarves, uncuffed blue jeans with faded back panels, and waistcoats from old three-piece suits . . . Esteve Miràngels's great-great-grandchildren, Natàlia thought. I bet they've never heard of Rusiñol either . . . Natàlia took it all in, just as she had the outburst of youth in England—from the outside. She often had the sense of being late to everything, and she had this same feeling when she walked into that room. One day Sergio, who had tried and failed to convince her to go with him to Latin America and join the guerrilla resistance, told her, You see everything as a performance. Was that why she'd chosen photography? Sometimes Natàlia felt as if she was a lone owl, peering out at history. Things happen right in front of your eyes and you just watch, Sergio said. What she wanted, though, was to capture a precise image, to stop the relentless slippage of time. She wondered if that was why she took photographs: It's a way of rebelling against time. A spectator, that's how she felt in that room of brightly colored boys and girls. It was the same distant feeling she'd had in front of La Modelo prison, when she'd stood shoulder to shoulder with the Roma women who were bringing packages to the prisoners. A pale, frail boy, with shiny black hair like crow's feathers, was playing guitar onstage, tenderly strumming its strings as if making love to a woman. Màrius and Natàlia sat at a table in a dark corner of the room, next to them a lamp with a red, pleated lampshade; Natàlia thought the boy looked unreal, his hands so white and beautiful. She could see the blue veins in his pale neck. Toti Soler, Màrius said. An awesome musician. The waiter was at their table. Natàlia asked for a screwdriver and Màrius ordered a glass of wine. Màrius shut his eyes and nodded along to the music while tapping his thigh. Natàlia gazed at Màrius's strawberry lips and his dark hair. He's handsome . . . she thought. Màrius felt Natàlia looking at him and rested his right cheek on the palm of his hand, right where the whitehead had popped and left a spot of grease. Natàlia offered him a cigarette. Smoke? Màrius shook his head.

A blond kid with pageboy hair in a pair of bleached blue jeans and a Turkish shepherd's coat with sheepskin lining came over to them. He was with a young girl with big eyes, curly hair, and long earrings made of beads and wire. Got any dope? they asked, and Márius said no. They sat next to Natàlia and Màrius. The girl was very young—seventeen, maybe?—and Natàlia saw that her eyebrows were unwaxed. The blond kid who looked like a pageboy was chatting with Màrius in a low voice. First they exchanged a bit of small talk, then they grew animated. The boy on the guitar opened his mouth and bared his teeth. He kind of looks like a vampire when he plays, the girl said to Natàlia, but he's really great.

The kid with pageboy hair turned to Màrius. Why don't you

come by the flat? Màrius looked over at Natàlia. Who's she? My
aunt. For a minute I thought she was Roser Roura. No, no.
They're very different, Màrius replied. My aunt is old. Older
than Roser Roura? No, I mean old as in washed-up. She complained when I made her walk around Santa Maria del Mar to
get here. She doesn't know how nuts you are about this neighborhood, the kid with pageboy hair observed. My dad says my
aunt left home because she's an idealist, but that the truth is she's
failed at everything and hasn't got a clue what she wants. Isn't
that a good thing? the friend asked. Your aunt looks nothing like
our mothers . . . I guess not. But if you met Roser Roura, you'd
think my aunt was ordinary. Roser Roura is different. She seems
young, even if she's forty. She is determined to live life to the
fullest, plus she understands our language and appreciates it.
Meanwhile, my aunt lives in another galaxy. That's not how it
looks to me, said the kid with pageboy hair, glancing over at
Natàlia. She dresses like us. She's attractive. She seems generous . . . Roser Roura is sensational in bed. Her back is like velvet,
and she bends like a crescent moon when we make love, giving
herself to me fully.

Cuando contemplo tu cuerpo extendido
como un río que nunca acaba de pasar . . .

the kid with pageboy hair recited. *When I contemplate your body,*
long like a river that never ceases running. Aleixandre said it himself:
love or destruction. Novalis too, Màrius added, "We touch heaven
when we lay our hand on a human body." Roser Roura is daring.
Are you in love? the kid asked. I don't know, Màrius said, but I do
know I'll never get tired of sleeping with her. One day she woke
up and decided she'd had enough, left her husband. Now she just
lives, without questioning herself. My aunt, on the other hand, is
judgmental about everything . . . They turned to look at her.
Natàlia was chatting with the girl with earrings, whose name was

Lola. Lola had already told Natàlia all there was to know about her life—she was a cheerful, talky girl. They glanced over at the boys. Màrius is unlucky, Lola said. I'm pretty sure he's never had sex, you know? He's like an older brother, an older brother with a good heart.

The kid with the pageboy hair took them to his place on Carrer de Flassaders, a big, unfurnished flat with high ceilings trimmed with cornices and molding. In one of the rooms, which let in a draft of air from the street, there was a gas heater and a mat on the floor. Tucked in a corner, a straw mattress was covered in a Moroccan blanket. A pair of Jimi Hendrix and Janis Joplin posters were fastened to the wall with four drawing pins. They're my dearly departed, said the kid with the pageboy hair, staring at them sorrowfully. They were killed, Lola said to Natàlia. I just know it. They had too much life in them. The squares couldn't stand it. Màrius put on a Frank Zappa album and lay back on the mattress. I heard Zappa took a shit onstage recently, said the kid with pageboy hair. Everyone smiled. Wait, I'm not done. He went on: So what happened is that Zappa had a gross-out contest with the audience, where he challenged them to do something even crazier than him. This guy stood up and said, I'd be willing to shit onstage. Me too, Zappa said. Then why don't you? the other guy asked. I will shit on this stage and eat it . . . And he did. I don't believe it, Lola contested. Your loss, shrugged the kid with pageboy hair, whose name was Antoni. That's cool if he did, though. I bet the audience was shocked, Lola said. If fifty thousand people shit onstage, does the act then become meaningless? Màrius observed from the mattress. Lola turned to Natàlia. Do you live with Màrius? No, I just moved here from England. I live with Màrius's great-aunt. Lola looked straight ahead. England, she said, the country of music and freedom . . . I'd love to go there someday! Why don't you? I can't. My dad won't sign my passport application. Natàlia took a closer look at Lola and realized she was even younger than she'd first thought.

Her complexion was pale, and the white of her skin made her large, hollow eyes look even hollower, as though she were ill. Her features were rough-hewn, unfinished; it was like Lola didn't realize she had the potential to be an incredible beauty. Antoni set a bottle of cognac in between them and passed out some paper cups. Sorry, he said. I only have the bargain stuff. Isn't he decadent? Lola asked. How about some dope? Antoni suggested. Màrius gave Natàlia a quick glance and whispered, Later, just in case ... Zappa was shredding his guitar, making it howl like a dying man. The music faded in and out of the room as air slipped through the rickety shutters and everyone but Màrius huddled close to the gas heater. The light was low, and the reddish flame lit up their faces in the gloom. The room was full of the thick, lumbering smell of gas. Lola was telling Natàlia, My dad thinks family's sacred, you know? They have their thing, I get it. My mom cleans houses and works at a locomotive factory, La Maquinista. My dad cried when I was suspended from school. That's when we found out that his employer had opened a dossier on him too, ages ago. It had scared him so much that he left politics altogether, and my mom had never had any idea ... Màrius said, You're going off on a tangent again, Lola. You'll tell one of your stories any chance you get. Shut up, Lola snapped. Antoni, who was pouring himself glass after glass of cognac, asked, The Rolling Stones or Blood, Sweat & Tears? The Stones, Màrius answered. My mom squeezed my arm so tight it went black and blue, Lola continued. She couldn't stand the sight of my dad crying ... I thought you came from a good home, Natàlia said. Oh no, Màrius is the only person here from a good home. Antoni's dad works a lot. Lola changed the subject. I worship the Rolling Stones. Aren't they amazing? Lola rocked her head and body to the beat of the music. My parents are good people ... But they wouldn't let me go out when I wanted, so I ran away. I was gone for four months. Did the police not look for you? Natàlia asked. They did for about a week. Then they gave up. More and more women are running away every day, haven't you heard? My dad threatened to send me to reform school. I've got a plan, though. Do you want to know what it is? I'm going to get Antoni to marry me so I can be free. Lola clapped along as the Rolling Stones played the song's final notes on their electric guitars. The music was so loud Natàlia could hardly make out a word Lola was saying. Her head felt leaden, weighed down from the cognac and the sangria at Encarna's wedding. The music stopped, and there was the sound of a horn as a ship set sail from the port. Lola continued. You know what I'd like more than anything in the world? Natàlia shook her head. Children. I want seven of them ... Natàlia gazed at Màrius, his face in shadow. He looks sad, she thought to herself. His strawberry lips were closed and his gaze distant. I wonder where he's gone ... Should we leave? Natàlia asked Màrius. Whatever ... Oh no, how sad! Lola exclaimed. Don't you want to get high first? Antoni suggested. Màrius said he didn't want any. They stuck around a bit longer, drinking cognac in silence while listening to the Blood, Sweat & Tears' wailing. Natàlia suddenly perked up. It's funny, she said to Lola. You want children while we did everything not to have them ... Lola looked at Natàlia. That's because you're the pill generation ... I think the most wonderful thing a person can do in life is have children, take care of them, love them with all your heart. I can't wait to be a mom. Antoni and I are going to try, you know. For the moment, I'm staying with my parents because they seemed so sad that I felt guilty leaving them. But I was happy as a clam when I lived with Antoni! He worked on the dock. I stayed in bed until after noon, went grocery shopping, and made lunch. Then we ate at home and lay in each other's arm until sundown, just listening to music. We were an island ... Natàlia thought of Jimmy and the times when he used to come home from university in a rage. He'd say: The problem is the students have everything and are interested in nothing. Jimmy was of the mind that young people were a small society within a larger society, like a

big fish that eats a little fish, and the little one none the wiser ...
Màrius jumped up and said he was leaving. How come? Because,
Lola, I can't listen to any more of this crap. She had tears in her
eyes. Did I say something wrong? she asked, crestfallen. Antoni
turned to Lola. Don't mind him. He just doesn't want to be
around people right now ... As they walked downstairs, Natàlia
heard Antoni ask Lola, Will you stay? and then she heard Lola
say yes.

They left behind Carrer de Flassaders and took another turn
around Santa Maria del Mar. Natàlia thought to herself, The
younger generation seem to love the streets of Barcelona as
much as we did. The same streets she and Emilio hid in whenever they were drawn to each other's bodies with a furtive hun-
ger ... It was getting light. The sky was streaked in white and
gray, save for an orange band over the sea. The balconies had
stopped dripping, and the city was slowly beginning to stir.
Màrius walked at a brisk pace and Natàlia struggled to keep up
with him. Finally, he sat on a bench in Plaça Palau. There were
people waiting for the bus with bundles wrapped in newspaper.
The first rays of sunshine seized the final shadows of night. The
streetlights cast a faint glow. Vans zipped past loaded with car-
tons of vegetables and fruit. Màrius's cheeks were red, and his
eyes glazed as they peered into the middle distance. He looks
like my mother, Natàlia thought. Out of nowhere, Marìus burst
into tears. What's wrong? Why are you crying? she asked. Màrius
turned away. Leave me alone. A tear rolled down his cheek.
Natàlia didn't know what to do. I can leave if you want ... Màrius
was silent. Natàlia moved as if to walk away. No, don't. Stay ...
he said. They sat in silence. Màrius stood up and started walking
toward La Rambla. I came back here because I wanted to understand, Natàlia told herself, and yet nothing makes sense ... Night
receded behind Montjuïc, and the air was crisp. The sounds of
daybreak are different from nightfall, she thought. Purer somehow. Màrius's eyes were bright. Like emeralds, thought Natàlia.

As they crossed Via Laietana, he said, One time, when I mixed tobacco and oil—Oil? Yeah, the stuff you get from hashish resin. Anyway, one time I was high and thought Via Laietana was a tunnel, or like a very large, very endless tube. I slipped and realized it was the 1940s. I was low to the ground and could see pink ankles in sheer stockings . . . Why did you turn Antoni down when he offered you weed? Natàlia asked. I didn't know how you'd react . . . What kind of person do you think I am? I'm not sure. You make me uneasy. You're the same age as my mother, but all she does is complain. She sounds like one of those women on radio serials. And Dad's a phony. Màrius fell quiet. I'm going to escape soon. He turned around. I want to do the same thing you did—get far, far away from here. I don't like this city. Sometimes I feel like it's crumbling, piece by piece . . . Natàlia said, I used to think the city was crumbling too, but then I left and realized we carry the city inside us. Màrius said nothing. Then, his voice steadier, Who was Julián Grimau? Why do you ask? Because of what happened to Puig Antich. There were people handing out leaflets at school that mentioned a man called Grimau. So much has happened, Natàlia thought. Grimau was a communist leader. He was assassinated the same year I left, around springtime. What year was that? Màrius asked. Was it the year it snowed in Barcelona? That's right, the year of the snowfall. And of the floods, she added. You know what? Màrius said. This country makes me sick. I used to feel the same way. But I came back. I won't, Màrius said. See, one day I woke up and realized it wasn't the country so much as the people in my life that disgusted me, Natàlia explained. Myself included. And you know why? Because deep down I was scared that the time of cherries would come. And if you want the time of cherries, then you need to have faith that it will come. The time of cherries? Màrius asked, and Natàlia explained it to him. They chatted for a long time, and as they did, the sounds of the city thickened, and the night fog melted away. Màrius was talking ten to the dozen, as if they were old friends. When they killed Puig Antich, Màrius went on, I felt sick to my stomach. Just as sick as when I found out what they did to Grandpa. Natàlia froze. What about your grandfather? My parents didn't tell you? No ... Grandpa is in a mental asylum. Dad had him committed last year.

Natàlia and Màrius walked and walked until they reached La Rambla. At that time of day, the boulevard was milky-white and the pedestrians moved along it in a slumberous daze. Men and women nodded off on the benches side by side while a street cleaner swept away the night's rubbish. For about half an hour, Natàlia and Màrius sat in silence on a bench damp with dew. So my father is in a mental asylum... But Natàlia's thoughts were clouded and there was no rain to clear the skies...

... Ever since meeting the poets of El Manifiesto, Màrius had been fixated. Sure, he realized one thing has no bearing on the other, but he also knew his friends would all laugh if they found out, Lola most of all... Màrius wanted to have sex. He was tired of touching himself every night beneath the bedsheets, which brought him about as much pleasure as picking his nose as a child. His mother used to chide him, Where's your hankie, you little piglet? then smack him on the back of the head and kiss the spot where she'd hit him. It was always the same with Sílvia Claret: First she slapped him, then she kissed him once and again, right where it hurt, so it wouldn't leave a mark... Hidalgo was the first person he met when El Manifiesto was formed. Tall, slender, with a wry gaze and inquisitive, glacial eyes, the guy could think up a plausible response for anything, and he was so sharp and cultured he knew all Rimbaud's poems by heart... Hidalgo would've laughed at him. Don't tell me you're still a virgin, man. Màrius knows exactly what Hidalgo would do: he would recite Baudelaire, or tell him about Artaud and the destruction of the ego. You're not you, you have no individuality, he'd say ... Then Hidalgo would go off with Roser Roura, and the two would laugh as they vanished down the beach ...

... his was an enormous shame, like a heavy burden he hauled around day and night, always on his own, or like a creeping sensation that tore him up inside, refusing to let up or leave him alone, not even when he listened to Jimi Hendrix—*Why did you have to go and die, man?* ... Màrius wasn't happy anywhere—not with his friends at the old textile-warehouse bar, or with his friends in El Manifiesto, or at home, or at school. That's why he liked riding his motorcycle, doing trials where he plunged into the dark woods and mastered the mountain while jumping, racing, branches parting to let him through. He'd been to Els Tres Dies dels Cingles de Trial in Gorg Negre and watched world champions ride their motorbikes near his grandfather's masia. The motorcycles purred. First there was a brief popping sound, then the crackling of the engine, which hummed nonstop. He wished he had a sixty-five-horsepower Suzuki, so that he could scare away the branches and crunch over the pine needles as the wind cleared his head. Then he'd rattle downhill, bound over a flood of water, zip up the slope, and go round and round the wilderness, snaking through the backwoods. A modern-day knight ... He felt happy when he rode his motorcycle, he really did—happy and capable of love. The trees rustled their leaves while they embraced him, urging him on and on, as if he were about to take flight. Flight ...

Natàlia and Màrius said goodbye near the Canaletes fountain. They looked at each other for a moment. Then Natàlia kissed Màrius like she hadn't kissed anyone in a long time. She vanished up Portal de l'Àngel and Màrius stared after her for a while. He heard birds singing in the plane trees, perched side by side on branches dotted in new buds. Spring is coming, he thought. He sprinted up Carrer de Pelai toward Gran Via. He stepped in a puddle and leaped over the oil rainbows that formed in the wake of rainfall. Happy.

Near Plaça d'Urquinaona, a street cleaner yelled at Natàlia in Spanish, *Hey girl, what are you doing out on your own at this hour?* Natàlia smiled. At least someone out there still found her young. She crept silently into the flat so as not to wake Patrícia. She relieved herself in the bathroom, then looked in the mirror. Her mouth felt dry and she ran her tongue over her lips. She had dark shadows under her eyes and a wan complexion, like she was ill. She undressed in front of the mirror and started touching herself. Soon her lips were moist again, as was the skin around her mouth. Her eyes shone. The pleasure was brief. She picked up the clothes she had left on the floor and went to bed. She turned off the gas, just as Patrícia had instructed her. Someone was already making noise in one of the kitchens that looked out on the lightwell. The steely morning light turned the bedroom gray. *I'll see Lluís on Monday. I want to know what's happened to Dad.* As she began to doze off, she saw dozens of white objects zigzagging toward her. Then came the spider, whose thousands of hairy legs enveloped her in the kingdom of sleep.

PART SIX
ONLY DREAMS

*You will know no quiet
in the warm shadows
of home, only dreams
in the depths of my eyes.*

SALVADOR ESPRIU, *First Story of Esther*

Every morning he would stare at the silk stockings. They were sheer, almost see-through, the color of clementine against his skin. When he woke up and opened his eyes at the first morning light, he didn't reach for the Bible, as he had before. Nor did he reach for the radio, as he would later. The stockings hung on the back of an armchair, toes down—torpid and neglected, lifeless. At first he'd wanted one of those stockings that went up to the waist, the kind that hugged the feet and the ankles, that hugged the knees and legs, the kind that hugged the crotch and thighs, the hips and lower belly. But then it occurred to him that it might be dirty to go around with your lower body covered in a pair of stockings that didn't breathe. Stockings with no exit, stockings that were closed, turned inward. So he bought a loose pair. He could hold them up with a suspender belt—garters were too tight around the thighs. He dithered over the color for a week. Apple? Orange? The color of a rainy sky? The color of night? Of ash? The color of stars? He removed each stocking from its packet, carefully pulled out the cardboard, slipped his hand inside and stretched out his fingers, hand splayed open like a fan—like a palm tree buffeted by hurricane winds, like a starfish—straining the silk. He spent a long while considering the effect of each one. He weighed the pros and cons. Apple, too showy. Orange, the color of sin. Rainy skies, a bit dreary. The color of night, the color of death. Ash, a touch pale. Stars, too artificial. Amber, pretentious. He felt the fabric with both hands.

But first he removed his gloves and asked the salesgirl to show him stockings in pearl gray. He didn't want anything too showy; just a nice, discreet pair. A fine silk stocking. In the end, he chose clementine. An orangey-pink hue, the color of young citrus.

He tried them on that very night. He took off his clothing, one piece at a time. First his trousers, then his shirt and undershirt. He stood in front of the mahogany wardrobe, the one with Judit's trinkets, God rest her soul. He stood in front of the mirror, though not before switching off the electric tea lights and pushing aside Our Lady of Sorrows, who watched him with her waxen cheeks, pathetic face, teary eyes, open hands, and daggered heart. He caressed the stockings, which were ever so fine, like rosebud petals, then nuzzled them and slid his fingers into the toes. They were fit for a princess. Our Lady of Sorrows watched him with her bleeding eyes. He turned her around so that she faced the corner, but the saint refused to leave him alone. Finally, he took her to the trinket room and stashed her behind the folding screen in a rage. There, nice and quiet. Time to go to sleep now. Her jet-black mantle with gold-thread details looked like a ghost hovering in the room. At least he couldn't see her eyes.

He held the stockings from the top and rolled the material down to the ankle. He inserted both hands into the cuff and pushed out, scrunching together one round at a time. First he did one leg, then the other. He raised his foot and held it up in the air like a bridge, like Odile in *Swan Lake* or one of Degas's little dancers. Toes together and pointed downward, sole curved. Such an elegant instep, perfect as a Gothic arch. He slowly pulled on the stockings, first one, then the other. The silk brushed his skin as it went up his legs, stopping mid-thigh. He wasn't wearing a suspender belt because he'd been too ashamed to buy one, so he had to hold up each stocking with one hand in order to admire himself in the mirror. He had a hunchback, but the stockings themselves were lovely. Once he was done, he carefully took them off and hung them over the back of the armchair in the bedroom. Every evening before bed, he strokes them in the dark, the only light in the room the faint glow of the streetlamp, which filters through the shutters, slat after slat, like the stripes on a zebra. He holds the stockings up to his cheek and thinks to himself that the glow from the streetlamp is actually the moon. It is in these moments that he feels he isn't so alone after all, that Judit, his Judit, is very close . . .

———

On Monday morning, Natàlia called Lluís's office. I need to see you, she said. Right now? Yes, it's urgent. Lluís suggested a bar on Plaça Núñez de Arce. Sure enough, the second Natàlia comes back, so the trouble begins. Someone had come clean. Was it Patrícia? No, his aunt had sworn not to tell, she'd promised to let Lluís handle all this business with his father. It's a family matter, he said. What can I do about it? Encarna? No, she had enough on her mind with the wedding. Besides, she was discreet. Mum's the word was her motto, she'd been saying that to him ever since he was a little boy. What about Sílvia? The woman could talk the hind legs off a donkey. Plus, she'd do anything to wind him up . . . Couldn't they have waited, damn it? It was his business. The man was his father, he was supposed to be the one to tell Natàlia. He should have written her a letter, but some things are hard to put in writing. The doctor had told him: Your father is incurably depressed and shows symptoms of chronic neuroses. To put it plainly, the man has senile dementia, and we believe he could become violent. Lluís had made sure his father would receive good care. He was in the private section of the hospital, the pensioners' wing, and had a nurse all to himself. Natàlia settled everything with "ideas": She vanished when things got hard— leaving her mother to be looked after by strangers, let's not forget—then came back to give *him* lessons on morality. Lluís finished a design that had to be taken to the copy center, then left his *sanctum sanctorum* to meet Natàlia.

What have you done with Dad? Natàlia spat out the minute they sat down. He ordered bitters and she a glass of dry white vermouth. What do you mean? What did you hear? I heard you had him committed to a mental asylum. There was a brief silence as the waiter served their drinks. After he left, Lluís asked, Who told you? It doesn't matter, I just need to know if it's true. Dad isn't in a mental asylum, Lluís answered, adding seltzer to his bitters. Then where is he? On the outside, Lluís appeared calm. He's at an institution. Of course, Natàlia said ironically, nowadays people refer to mental asylums as institutions. Listen, Dad got old and—Natàlia cut him off. Would you please just tell me where I can find him? Why are you so desperate to know all of a sudden? It's not as though you bothered to send him a single letter in the past twelve years. Tell me where Dad is, before I lose my temper. Dad is at—

—so my father is in a mental asylum, a mental asylum, a mental asy, a mental, a ment—According to the dictionary, mental asylums are institutions for the clinically insane, for people who harbor obsessions and fixed ideas. Modern science has made great strides, so great that psychiatrists get in as much of a muddle about the human psyche as the rest of us. Whatever happened to dear old Freud and his theories? Is madness a social ill? A brain lesion? Is it genetic? Natàlia had read a few articles on the subject in the UK, studying it in the same way she did human nature: as a spectator. All those theories and counter theories had twisted together in her head and took on a new weight. Her father is in trouble, that much is clear. The asylums of the nineteenth century—the era of de Sade, when patients were restrained to their beds, plunged into baths, and locked in cages—may very well be in the past, yet somehow her father is in one. Trapped, stripped of his agency to make decisions about his body and his mind. Cruel phrases, passed on to people of all walks of life, sprung up: What are you, from Sant Boi? You look like you live in Sant Boi . . . That guy is nuts. Insane, deranged, abnormal, demented, perturbed, unhinged, dippy, bats—and if you write literature—touched, away with the fairies, mad as a hatter, non compos mentis, out of his head, loco, up the pole, one sandwich short of a picnic, *s'ha begut l'enteniment, más loco que una cabra, il est fou*, meshuga, the man is stark raving mad . . . Don't act crazy.

Are you even listening? Lluís asked Natàlia, but her mind was far, far away. Lluís had just corroborated that their father was in a psychiatric institution and all she could do was come up with synonyms for *crazy*. Why didn't you write? Lluís said, I knew you'd ask for information, for details about the process, and we were in a hurry. Dad was getting more and more difficult to live with. He'd got old, her brother continued. After Mom died, he checked out. At first, he grieved her. He visited her grave every day for three months. He started obsessively leaving her a single red carnation. He got into arguments with florists when they tried to sell him other colors. Red was the only color he wanted. We asked Encarna to be patient with him. But he became increasingly erratic. He stopped working, although he'd already stepped back after the hotel fire in Lloret. He and Joan Claret were arrested, but as Claret is so well connected, he was released after only three days. Dad's reputation as an architect was destroyed. He'd rushed construction on the hotel so it'd be ready for the high season. He'd used cheap materials and hadn't checked to see what was left in the basement—flammable substances, paint, and a large canister of gas. That was Claret's fault, of course, and the fault of the site manager. But Dad hadn't bothered to give the basement proper ventilation. To make matters worse, they installed the door backward. Who does that? But never mind. The point is the hotel caught fire and several staff members burned to death. One of them—and we only found this out later—was a gay man. His co-workers didn't want him near them, so they made the guy sleep in a room off the wine cellar. You can imagine how he must have looked when he was found. Of course, Dad wasn't to blame for all of it. Which is why they released him so fast. The whole thing had a profound effect on him. Five people were dead, and he felt responsible. You know how sensitive Dad is, almost to a fault. He didn't know what to do with himself. Unlike Claret, who went on to build more hotels in Lloret and in Tosa—and nothing to see here . . . Claret is shrewd: He'll never go down with a sinking ship. Dad used to say to me, If only I could explain it all to your mother. Sitting in the conservatory with Mom and stroking her hand was an enormous comfort to him. When she died, that was it. Soon we noticed he'd developed certain quirks. He'd lock the door to his bedroom. We could hear him talking to himself. He refused to let us in. And when he did come out, he'd give us this mysterious, enigmatic smile. He barely made eye contact with us . . .

One time, Lluís continued, he was kicked out of Cafè de l'Òpera for kissing a fourteen-year-old girl. Imagine our embarrassment. He refused to let Encarna clean his room. She telephoned every day, and it was clear to Lluís she felt uneasy. It got to the point where she was scared of Dad. We begged her to be patient—he was just old and eccentric. One day he walked out and locked himself in the bathroom for a while. Encarna decided to tackle his bedroom. She found a doll on Mom's side of the bed. A doll? Natàlia asked. A porcelain doll with no eyes or hands. A massive doll Mom kept until the end, the one she used to have on her lap and hug to her chest when she sat in the conservatory. Dad had dressed the doll up in silk underwear— Encarna told us it was Mom's old underwear. Dad had propped the doll up on some cushions, right where she used to sleep. Did he talk to it? Natàlia asked. We assume so. He kept all of Mom's dolls, you know. Stored them in the mahogany wardrobe. But we thought that was the extent of it, so we gave Encarna a raise and asked her to stay on. He's just a doddery old man, we said. Have some patience. But less than a month goes by, and Dad starts throwing tantrums, ordering Encarna to bring him supper for

two in his bedroom. Going out for a couple of hours and coming
back laden with shopping bags. He was being wasteful: The psychiatrist explained that splurging like that was a symptom of a
major depressive disorder. One day Encarna calls us in a panic
and says our father just spent a huge amount of cash on women's
undergarments, silk stockings, straw Pamela hats, Italian scarves,
leather gloves, bras . . . He dumped all his purchases in the glass
display cases where Mom kept her trinkets, in the fan room, or-
ganized by brand: Warner's bras, Belcor, Christian Dior stockings, Panty . . . He became a recluse, stopped talking to us.
Encarna came to see us one day, said she'd had enough of Dad's
eccentricities, that he wasn't just a quirky old man anymore—
he'd lost his mind . . . We let go of the place on Carrer del Bruc,
sent Encarna over to Patrícia's, and brought Dad home to live
with us. But things only got worse. He thought we were trying to
poison him and refused to eat. He cranked up the volume on the
TV, then claimed the presenter was yelling because he knew
Dad was hard of hearing. He took a dislike to Felisa, the housekeeper, accused her of stalking him and stealing a hat he'd bought
at Can Prats. He was dirty and dressed in shabby clothing. But
one constant remained: He never went out without his hat. Or
his gloves or walking stick, for that matter. He'd wear a handkerchief in his jacket pocket in the shape of a triangle, and his
pocket-watch chain hanging outside his waistcoat. Sílvia tried to
get him to wear a sweater, but he refused: He'd die in that waistcoat. It was ridiculous. At night he yelled Judit! Judit! A red carnation! then let out a chilling laugh, like a raven or one of those
big eagles that flies high up in the mountains . . . He must have
been so lonely, Natàlia said. Maybe, Lluís conceded. But that
doesn't change how difficult he was to live with, you know. There
was no peace at home anymore—and when I get back from
work, I like calm and quiet. He used to run away. He'd go downstairs to chat with the doorman, looking like a vagrant, and it was
a real pain for us to get the man to understand Dad wasn't all

there. Dad accused us of stalking him, spying on him, said the neighbors cursed at him through the walls. We did our best, until one day . . .

———

. . . I touched myself because that's what I wanted to do. My sex belonged to me and only me. To me and Judit. It was the same sex Judit had kissed. It still got hard. I was young and my sex told me so: red carnation, you're still young, who is going to kiss you? Don't worry, little carnation, Judit will come, and she'll be like the morning dew . . . It's yours, Judit, kiss it . . . Don't laugh, little carnation, or I'll squeeze you inside me. I promise it won't hurt. Isn't it true it didn't hurt? Your petals will open like the moon spilling over my body, little carnation, then you'll touch my sex and, maybe you'll kiss me, here, very slowly, and I'll be the sea and you the sand, my hands the waves lapping at you in a gentle swell. I'll kiss your feet, one wave after another and will become a tired sea. The storm will sweep in and you will be the gloomy wind that calms the water. How to quiet the storm? Don't you hear the waves crashing? My sex will be a pebble kissed by the wind . . . and you'll be the bee on the carnation, stinging me and drinking me up—but what will be left of me? You'll be Gorg Negre and I'll plunge inside you and be no more, sucked down your whirlpool, living in your belly. And I will sleep . . .

———

. . . I found Dad masturbating next to the doll. It's awful, seeing an old man in that state! Even your father. There was something else too. Dad had money in the bank, a lot of it, even though he and Claret had to pay for damages and a lawyer after the hotel in Lloret. And I needed it. I wanted to expand the studio. I got a loan from Claret, but it drove me crazy to see Dad throwing money away on trifles while the rest of it rotted in the bank. On top of that, he refused to sell the estate in Gualba, even though it was in ruins and someone had offered him a fortune to develop the land . . . He wanted to keep all the cash for himself and his debaucheries. But when we saw the state he was in, we had him committed to a mental asylum and declared unfit... You could've led with that, Lluís. Natàlia's eyes were ablaze. You were after Dad's money. Here we go! Lluís responded. Always simplifying everything. It wasn't about the money ... Do you really think I don't have any principles? I lost as well, in the grand scheme of things. I don't mean lose in the sense of what I could've done if Dad had given me money when I needed it. I lost a lot, watching Mom become a vegetable and Dad withdraw into himself. I spent my whole life trying to get them to see me, to value my work. Our parents built a world just for themselves, and nobody else was allowed in. Is that my fault? Are you all the only good people out there? I'm curious what you mean by "you all," Natàlia replied. You clearly haven't changed, Lluís—still drawing lines between people, putting them in boxes. You're the same as ever: attacking in self-defense. The thing is, I still don't know what you're defending yourself against. My life isn't all glory, Natàlia. Lluís's voice was quieter now, more uncertain. I've always had to pay for things that come easily to you. Before Sílvia and I got married, I paid for my ration of love from a hooker. Sílvia wouldn't let me touch her. You're not laying a finger on me, she used to joke, though it was partly true. I pay for friendship. Ramon follows me around like a dog but the only reason we're friends is that he needs me. Sílvia's only married to me because she needs me too, because she knows she wouldn't get anywhere without me ... And Màrius? Natàlia asked. Màrius is all Sílvia, thin-skinned. I can tell he looks down on me. I didn't know as much at his age as he does now—I hadn't even left the country. He's incredibly knowledgeable, he has everything. Yet, somehow, he doesn't realize it. You know something? He's the only person in the world I really love. But his affection isn't free either: Last year I bought him a motorcycle for close to two hundred thousand pesetas—a gift for finishing high school with good grades. I'm still waiting for him to thank me. I think he wants to leave home for a bit, Natàlia said. Great, let him. I'd like to see him try to make a living for himself. Do you realize how hard I have to work to make money without bending rules like our father? I wish Mom could see me—nothing I ever did was good enough for her. I bring home a lot of money, you know. And what do I get in return? Dirty looks from my family.

—

...Joan Miralpeix was at Cafè de l'Òpera. They used to go there a lot when Judit was still alive, and watch the afternoon fade into evening. Judit treated him like a little boy, never letting him have a single hair out of place. Now that he doesn't work anymore, he's bored senseless. Encarna's always glowering at him and never lets him do anything. Don't touch it or you'll ruin it ... If you don't listen, I'm going to call Mr. Lluís and they'll give you that injection again. Encarna's a hag; she won't let him line up the dolls on the mahogany wardrobe, even though they make such a pretty picture. The second he looks away, she shoves them back inside. Encarna is wicked. He knows she goes through the display cases in the fan room because he keeps finding the little boxes and hunting horns turned over. At home, Encarna rules the roost. The other day he'd bought small, juicy strawberries from the Boqueria. Strawberries so tender they melted on your tongue and stained your lips red ... Then Encarna said, Oh, Mr. Miralpeix! Why, oh why do you insist on wasting money? Don't you know strawberries are expensive? I'm going to have to call Mr. Lluís ... But he wanted strawberries—strawberries, strawberries, strawberries! The doll with empty eye sockets had told him she wanted strawberries and so he gave her one, then used it to paint her cheeks pink. Joan cradled the doll and thought about Judit, then burst into tears. The hag came into his bedroom. Mr. Miralpeix! What are you doing? Come on, you're too old for that. I want Judit! She promised to come, but she isn't here yet. Don't be such a child. Can't you see Judit is dead? Liar! She's coming ... A girl in blue jeans just took a seat beside Joan Miralpeix, she looks around fourteen years old. The girl is licking a scoop of orange ice cream. She is a little chubby and has curly hair. A lone dark ringlet dangles on her forehead. The girl in blue jeans sits on the chair with her legs open. She brings the ice cream up to her mouth and licks it, wetting her lips. Her lips are like frosted strawberries. She loves sweets, licks the ice cream and giggles. Whoops! she says. Another girl cries out, Désirée! It seems the name of the girl in blue jeans with curly hair and frosted-strawberry lips is Désirée, Joan Miralpeix observes, then thinks: I'd love nothing more than to run my tongue over her orange ice cream and frosted-strawberry lips. The waiter comes up to him. What will it be today? A sherry, and whole Seville olives. He likes olives with pits, likes the feeling of his teeth bumping something hard. That way he can be sure he still has some, that he's still young . . . The girl in blue jeans is leafing through a fashion magazine while eating ice cream, her lips becoming moister, strawberry-bright . . . Another girl joins them. Désirée and her friend shout, Hey, Mabi! The three notice the old man staring and whisper among themselves. They giggle. A button near the top of Mabi's blouse comes undone as Désirée eats the orange ice cream. Mabi and the other girl head to the bathroom and the strange old man with a hat and walking stick goes over to Désirée and kisses her on the lips. Frosted strawberry lips, he says. After the old man has been removed from the bar, Mabi asks Désirée, What did you feel when he kissed you? I don't know, Désirée says. A little disgusted, maybe.

First there is the ward for the poor patients. Three rows of men sit on benches below a twenty-five-watt lightbulb, gleaming with sweat and sadness. Quiet, they stare into the middle distance. Every now and then there is the sound of whinnying or a gruff laugh. Someone flaps their arms as if holding a burning flag. A man with desolate eyes and rounded shoulders asks the doorman, Are they not coming today either? Across the bleak, dim reception is a door to a gravel garden edged with poplar trees. Through the garden is the pensioners' area, or private wing.

In this section, the patients are all mixed together. Natàlia had been to see Emilio's friend, the one who used to be a medical student. All those years later, he still recognized her. The medical student was now a doctor specializing in diabetes, and he knew a psychiatrist from the same graduating class. This was the person currently showing Natàlia around the psychiatric institution. It was a vast building with gray, crusty walls, several wings arranged around a park in the middle. Before she saw her father, Natàlia had wanted a tour of where he was living. The psychiatrist said, They throw people with learning disabilities in with the schizophrenics, cerebral palsy patients in with alcoholics and the people with Down syndrome . . . And there's nothing we can do about it. We hold psychotherapy sessions for the patients assigned to us. After that, the institution takes over: the nuns, the priests, and the nurses. They're the ones who decide who lives and dies. Some weeks I might see close to two hundred patients. Of course, your father is a different case entirely. He's a paying customer. I'm not in contact with his doctor, nor do I want to be. The man's a behaviorist. According to his way of thinking, there's nothing drugs and electroshock therapy can't fix. If, like you said, your father has neurotic depression, I doubt the drugs will do much. They just dull his senses. Two patients walked past them with a cart loaded with bricks. Do the patients work? Natàlia asked. Yes, at least the ones without resources. The priests who run the institution have their own brick and tile factory—they make millions. The patients complain about the low wages. The doctors say they should be charging double. So far it's come to nothing. They also make television and radio sets for a broadcasting school. The patients' labor is referred to as "work therapy."

As they passed a newsstand, Natàlia asked, Can the patients read whatever they want? The selection is carefully curated. The more educated patients like your father use the library, but it's mostly religious texts. All you'll find at the newsstand is magazines. No newspapers. Some patients have been here over twenty years and know virtually nothing about the world outside these walls. Some could leave if they wanted, but either don't have family or don't want to take responsibility for themselves. That's how it is for your father, isn't it? It doesn't matter, Natàlia said. I'm here now, and I'm going to take him home. You're doing the right thing, the psychiatrist observed. Your father will be a lot happier out there than in here. Some of the long-term patients get what we call "hospitalization disease" and never adapt to the outside. Do any try to run away? Natàlia asked. I know of one patient who managed to escape ten times—he's only twenty-nine years old. Eventually he comes back, and they give him a turpentine injection in his leg. It's extraordinarily painful.

The patients can find anything they need right here, the psychiatrist explained. It's like a prison, a world unto itself. There's a black market for everything. They walked into the bar. A young man in overalls stood at the door asking for money. An older man begged them to get him a coffee. There isn't a lot of cash in here, the psychiatrist said. But we can't exactly give them endless free coffee and tobacco. Natàlia and the psychiatrist sat beside the door. Next to them, a man with addled eyes was drooling. He drew a key up and down his face, tirelessly repeating the action. In a corner of the room, a fat man was shaving an imaginary customer while three men watched, mouths agape. I saw a tennis court in the park. Do they play? It's not for them, the psychiatrist said. It's for the folks in town. Once a year, on the eve of Sant Joan, they bring over the women from the psychiatric institution next door to celebrate together. The patients throw themselves at each other. The security guards run around trying to keep them apart. They look for them in the overgrowth near the walls, follow them with flashlights . . . The institution would far rather their patients were asexual, especially as sex is how many of their conditions started. A tall, youngish man with dark features and full shoulders walked toward them, a wool scarf wrapped around his neck. This, the psychiatrist said, is the guy who escaped ten times. The man with dark features greeted the psychiatrist, who observed him for a while. He's one of the smartest patients I've ever met. He's a poet, says he's writing a novel. He looks like Miguel Hernández, Natàlia said. You're right, he does. The man's had every job under the sun and can quote you Kant, Schopenhauer, and Nietzsche, all in the same breath. He's interested in existentialism and loves Antonio Machado. But as far as standards of "normalcy" go, he'll never adapt to the outside. He sleeps in the general ward alongside people with learning disabilities. His father, a manual laborer who died in a work accident, taught him to read and write. The patient never fully absorbed his death. He's been in here most of his life. He's what traditional psychiatry would refer to as someone with an "incurable mental disorder." All right, it's visiting hours. The psychiatrist looked at Natàlia. I need you to understand something, he said. Especially given your father is in here. The mentally ill have a very rich reality, and it's our duty to try to understand it. Trust me, he continued. There is always some logic to their worldview.

The psychiatrist walked Natàlia to the private wing. I'll say goodbye here. I gather you want to be alone with him. As Natàlia made her way down the hall—its walls white and clean—and toward her father's room, her body felt empty. Twelve years had passed, and she'd lived through enough to know now that there were shades of gray to every story. How would her father look when she saw him? What had become of the man who half threw her out of the house, the man ready to hand her over to the police when she had an abortion, even though he was responsible for the deaths of five people? Today, Natàlia felt she had it in her heart to love him. Her father wasn't just her father anymore; he was a poor old man that people deemed insane, an old man who was unfit and alone. The nurse pointed at a room. Over there, she said. Natàlia opened the door to a well-lit room with a window looking out on a poplar tree. There was birdsong. The window was barred. A smiling old man with childlike eyes sat in a chair.

Natàlia, sweetheart. The old man stood and gave her a hug. He'd recognized her. It was his daughter; his daughter was there. Disheveled, as ever. Earlier that day, when the nurse told him someone was coming to visit, his first thought had been: It's my daughter, she's home. And there she was, standing right in front of him. Tall, with Miralpeix Sr.'s energetic face and Judit's eyes, which always peered into the distance. They sat in silence, holding hands. Natàlia thought her father looked a little heavier. He was completely bald, the skin on his head as pink and shiny as a newborn's. The bags under his eyes weren't as deep or black as they used to be, maybe on account of the extra weight. He stared at her and smiled. I'm going to get you out of here, Natàlia said.

Joan Miralpeix started chatting away like a little boy. I didn't do anything wrong, Natàlia. I promise. They told me I did bad things, but all I did was sin, like Adam and Eve. I'm better now. And he repeated: I promise. If this is my punishment, then I swear I've made amends. I'm going to get you out of here, Natàlia said again. But the old man wasn't listening. Life is a circle, and we all wind up back at the beginning. I'm sleeping with Judit now, you know. The poplar trees stroke my body and hers . . . Natàlia gripped her father's hands. You're coming to live with me, Dad. But he didn't hear her. My father shouts at me to stop my daydreaming, he hits me. It hurts a lot, but Judit is going to protect me, you know. She and I are so happy we get to live together again. Natàlia walked out, crying.

. . . when he woke up, he didn't dare open his eyes. At the first signs of movement—the seven-o'clock church bell, the patient shuffling to the bathroom next door, a window clanging, the birds chittering, a door creaking in the wind—he'd clamp his eyes shut. Even when he could distinguish the sounds, which ushered in the monotony of yet another day, he refused to open them—not before his hands, drenched with sweat from a night of fitful dreams, were done gripping the warm bedsheets and rough creases in the blanket crumpled from all his twisting and turning. Only then did he relax his eyelids and let in a faint, pale yellow light. His eyelids were like butterfly wings—rosy, soft, somewhere between the night shadows and the new day. He opened his eyes one sliver at a time, then turned to face the wall on his left. He studied the nightstand: The photograph was still there. As his eyes registered its presence, they widened into a pair of circles in a sea of fine wrinkles. His face was transformed. He smiled, and his smile was full, refreshed. Seeing Judit there in the faded photograph, all dressed in gauze, with her curly hair, red carnation, snow-white skin, and distant gaze—seeing her and breathing in the essence of hollyhock could only mean that she was still alive.

Before the lights went out at night, he would hold the photograph at an oblique angle, polish it with his pajama sleeve, and blow away any stray specks of dust. He stared at the photograph for a long while—a string of intense, scattered recollections of everything that was done to him throughout the course of the day. Then he put the photograph back on the nightstand between his bed and the left wall of his room, where it belonged. The portrait said to him: You're still alive. He was scared of dying at night when the quiet was deep and dark like the waters of Gorg Negre. Quiet was his enemy, the lord of shadows. He was scared of closing his eyes and falling asleep, now that he could sleep. But he would never die because he had Judit.

Moià, October 1976
(Revised in Barcelona, 1990)

ABOUT THE AUTHOR

MONTSERRAT ROIG (1946–1991) was an award-winning writer and journalist based in Barcelona, and the recipient of numerous prestigious prizes including the Premi Víctor Català and the Premi Sant Jordi. Her journalistic work focused on forging a creative feminist tradition, and on recovering the country's political history. Her novels take similar stances, reflecting on the need to liberate women who were silenced by history.

ABOUT THE TRANSLATOR

JULIA SANCHES translates literature from Spanish, Portuguese, and Catalan into English. She is a founding member of Cedilla & Co., a collective of translators committed to making international voices heard in English, and chair of the Translators Group of the Authors Guild. Sanches's translation of *Migratory Birds* by Mariana Oliver won the PEN Translation Prize and her translation of *Undiscovered* by Gabriela Wiener was longlisted for the International Booker Prize. Born in São Paulo, Brazil, Sanches currently resides in Providence, Rhode Island.

ABOUT THE TYPE

The principal text of this Modern Library edition was set in a digitized version of Janson, a typeface that dates from about 1690 and was cut by Nicholas Kis (1650–1702), a Hungarian working in Amsterdam. The original matrices have survived and are held by the Stempel foundry in Germany. Hermann Zapf (1918–2015) redesigned some of the weights and sizes for Stempel, basing his revisions on the original design.